ABOUT THE AUTHOR

DAVID A. KYLE's experience in Science Fiction dates back to the "Golden Age" of the early 1930s when E. E. "Doc" Smith's works were setting the style for epic "space opera." An active force in both the earliest and present-day worlds of Science Fiction fandom, he began publishing fanzines as a teenager, and he participated in the first science fiction convention in Philadelphia in 1936. He attended the first World Science Fiction Convention in New York in 1939, and went on to chair the 14th Worldcon in 1956.

His professional career in the field spans six decades; beginning as a writer and illustrator for pulp magazines, then as publisher, anthologist, illustrator, book designer, editor, and literary agent. In 1947 he co-founded Gnome Press, the imprint that pioneered the first hardcover editions of works by such authors as Isaac Asimov, Sir Arthur C. Clarke, and Robert Howard.

He has collected an array of honors, among them First Fandom's Science Fiction Hall of Fame; a special award from the British Science Fiction Association; and an award for Outstanding Achievement from The International Society of Science Fiction, Horror and Fantasy. He has been chosen by *Starlog* as one of The 100 Most Important People in Science Fiction and Fantasy.

His works include the award-winning *A Pictorial History of Science Fiction* and *The Illustrated Book of Science Fiction Ideas and Dreams*. Kyle was a close friend of "Doc" Smith, and he was honored to continue to chronicle the future history of the Galactic Patrol in *The Dragon Lensman, Lensman from Rigel,* and *Z-Lensman*.

D1132462

Z-LENSMAN

BASED ON THE CHARACTERS
CREATED BY
E. E. "DOC" SMITH

By
DAVID A. KYLE

Illustrated by
RON MILLER

RED JACKET PRESS
MOHEGAN LAKE, NEW YORK 2004

Published by RED JACKET PRESS, 3099 Maqua Place, Mohegan Lake, New York 10547.
WWW.REDJACKETPRESS.COM

Hardcover: ISBN 0-9748895-4-7
Paperback: ISBN 0-9748895-7-1

Printed in China. First Printing.

First Red Jacket Press Edition published simultaneously in a limited edition hardcover and paperback in 2004.

CONTENTS

Introduction to the New Edition *by David A. Kyle* 6

Foreword 9

Prologue 13

1. Space Pirates Attack 17

2. Nadreck Accepts an Offer 31

3. The Wedding Gifts 47

4. Cadets Show Their Mettle 63

5. Reunion at The Circus 77

6. Raiders from Nowhere 93

7. Lensmen Get Their Orders 107

8. The Dregs of Onlo 123

9. Death Answers the Prayer 137

10. The Forbidden Galaxy 153

11. The Stolen Star 169

12. Hunting the Mech-Planet 185

13. The Battle of the Rim 205

14. The Call of the Lens 219

15. The Dance of Death 227

Epilogue 247

INTRODUCTION
TO THE NEW EDITION

IT WAS HUGO GERNSBACK WHO INTRODUCED AN UNPUB-
lished writer by the name of Edward Elmer Smith, Ph.D. to
the very selective readership of his unique *Amazing Stories*
magazine; any enthusiastic connoisseur of "Doc" knows this
history. It was in the printed pages of one of entrepreneur
Gernsback's pulps that I first encountered Doc and his
Galactic Patrol. He became a enormous influence on his
readers, other writers, the genre itself, and most assuredly
upon me. It was years later when I was twenty-one that
I met the legendary man himself at the second World
Science Fiction Convention in Chicago in 1940, and years
later I became his personal friend.

Doc was an extraordinary man. His radically different
first novel was written in the post-World War One era, but
found no publisher until Gernsback offered an expanded
market which was short of original material. Doc's "Skylark"
adventures, mind-boggling plunges into deep space, were an
instant success. Doc was not a professional writer; he was an
industrial scientist (a specialist in food processing, credited
with an important formula for a doughnut manufacturer)
whose creative thoughts roamed across the stars. He found
fiction offered him unlimited and unfettered opportunities

to express original ideas about Mankind's past, present and future among other worlds and alien cultures.

Doc was a moral, virtuous and ethical human being. His works reflect the best qualities of Earth's culture, his optimism for interplanetary civilization and sentient life. He was also a romantic, telling exciting stories about the triumph of Good over Evil. In every-day living he was a honorable, considerate father and husband. His wife, Jeannie, was as sweet in her disposition as her husband was warm-hearted. They were truly beloved by all.

Doc was a genuine, original fan of the imaginative literature he wrote. He enjoyed talking about ideas and the genre we all found so special. There was no barrier of age; he was comfortable with young and older readers alike. He was a celebrity in his field, but he never considered himself above our younger generation (of which he considered himself to be no less a part). So, too, was Jeannie one of us, always considered inseparable from her loving husband. They were unpretentious, truly genuine fans. He deserved to be the very first person to be chosen to be in the First Fandom Hall of Fame.

His daughter, Verna Smith Trestrail, adored her "Daddy" and was fiercely partisan about him and about his works. She enjoyed many discussions and convention panel appearances in his memory. I was fortunate to have her deep friendship and complete confidence.

She knew that the assignment to continue her Father's unique work would be difficult, because she demanded perfection. I was one of two writers suggested by editor Fred Pohl to follow Doc's pathway; Verna was fervid in her rejection of the other writer's Galactic Patrol novel and enthusiastic about my completed attempt. She knew I was working from no memos or notes, nor from any unpublished material from her father. She trusted me, but she read every word I wrote about hero Kimball Kinnison (thre personification of her Daddy) and the Patrol. She was not hesitant about correcting me ("Daddy wouldn't say that! Daddy wouldn't do that!"— fortunately rarely expressed), but never criticized my plotting nor offered creative opinions about the development of my characters and action.

My wife Ruth was, and is, a genuine fan, having attended innumerable conventions, regional and world. She, too, knew both the Smiths and felt close to them. In their later years, when they had a mobile home and moved around America, Ruth and I stopped by for a visit while we were traveling. He had just finished reading a serialization of his final "Skylark" novel in a magazine and had carefully annotated every typo, misspelling or editorial error for his own pleasure. He showed us this marked-up copy and then presented it to Ruth as a gift which gave her much pleasure and made her feel specially honored. Another time, at a world convention, knowing of Ruth's affection for the Smith family and her delight in his work, he told her in detail and in confidence what his next project would be. He never got around to writing it. She would not breach that promise to keep it secret. Many years later when I began my work on *The Dragon Lensman* I asked her to tell me what she had been told. Sadly, she could recall nothing except for the fact that the conversation took place. Perhaps, it's all for the best.

I am hopeful that this series of three "Lensmen" novels, newly reprinted by Red Jacket Press, will be found to be completely in keeping with the originals. Understandably, I want the Doc Smith fans and book collectors to feel the new editions belong with the fifty year old originals, and that Doc and Jeannie and Verna and all will be thrilled and well pleased.

DAVID A. KYLE
2004

FOREWORD

THE GENUS *homo sapiens* BELONGS TO THE FAMILY OF ARISIA. Human beings, together with all their related humanoid races, were the fruit of Arisian seed, and they lived, along with their bizarre cousins and exotic kindred, among the millions of planets throughout the island universe known as our Milky Way galaxy.

Within our space and time, the ancient Arisians were the genesis of all intelligent life. Where or how they began at the dawn of the Cosmos not even their records could tell for certain. Their home was the planet that must have been the very first upon which life formed. For eons, as the Arisians progressed beyond the stages of mechanics and technology and evolved from entities of flesh into entities of energy, they prospered alone and unthreatened. When their first mother sun grew old and died, they moved their planet to a bright, new star, until, as the eons rolled on, they had to move again. All that time, in the vastness of interstellar matter, they were alone.

Then came the time of the Coalescence, when the Milky Way and Lundmark's Nebula passed through each other, edge to edge, and billions of new planets were born. With this marvelous explosion of new opportunities came a sinister shadow of the ultimate terror, Eddore. This was another planet with another race from another existence. As good and Godlike as were the Arisians, so evil and Devilish were the Eddorians. Thus began the ages-old conflict that led to the formation of the mighty Arisian weapon, the Galactic Patrol.

On the countless new planets flourished galactic multitudes, a thousand million years younger than their ancestors. Slowly but relentlessly they climbed out of the primordial elements into Civilization and toward perfectionism. Serving as Guardians, secretly encouraging them, were the mental forces of the Arisians. In opposition, seeking absolute power over all minds and bodies through crime and corruption, were the Eddorians, with their infamous chief henchmen, the Eich, masterminding their conspiracy of a diabolic counterculture. Civilization was tested with the task of discovering the real enemy, not being told of the existence of the Eddorians, while the Eddorians, in turn, were brainwashed into ignorance of the existence of the Arisians.

So the Arisians, stressing self-reliance among the maturing races, let them fight their own battles. However, Mentor, the supremely wise entity of the Arisians, gave the elite officers of the Patrol a quasi-living instrument of telepathy, the Lens. The only other help offered by the Guardians was limited to counseling.

Mentor was the unit name of the fusion of the mentalities of four of the greatest Arisians, also known as the Molders of Civilization. Each one was concerned with the development of one of four extremely different races from four widely separated planets: Tellus (Earth), Velantia III, Rigel IV, and Palain VII. Each planet had eventually produced one exceptional Lensman, specially trained by Mentor as a Second Stage Lensman. Nadreck, the most illustrious Z-Lensman, although not the first Palainian Lensman, was the genuine genius who did reach the L2 or Second Stage.

The Molder in whose charge the destiny of Palain VII

was placed was called Brolenteen. Brolenteen had two tasks to perform simultaneously. Offensively, he had to encourage the growth and effectiveness of a meager number of Palainian Lensmen; defensively, he had to block the direct intervention of a top Master of the Innermost Circle of the All-Highest of Eddore and its vicious Boskonian conspiracy.

When Virgil Samms, the first wearer of the Lens, went to Palain VII to seek recruits from the New-Thought Club, Brolenteen was, secretly, already there. Samms's minimal success in that encounter would have seemed more heartening had he known that Brolenteen was subtly helping him. Within a year, five Palainians had visited the mysterious planet of Arisia and had been given their Lenses. Among them was Bovreck.

Bovreck was the ancestor of Nadreck.

Nadreck, later to become the only Second Stage Lensman in the history of Palain, has always seemed a baffling and inexplicable creature. Very little has heretofore been told of his background and personal life, primarily because he is overwhelmingly a Z-type in the Historian Smith twelve digit classification system.

This historical adventure, out of the files of the Galactic Patrol, is not a biography of Nadreck, the Z-Lensman from Palain VII, but the reporting of these events does cast a great deal of light upon who Nadreck really was — and why he was that way.

DAVID A. KYLE
Tellus

PROLOGUE

EUKONIDOR, THE YOUTHFUL WATCHER FROM ARISIA, HAD turned back the brazen attempt to invade Arisia by the mighty First and Eighth councilors of the Eich. He had changed the course of their mammoth torpedo so that, in a sweeping circle, it had returned to slam directly into the great cruiser of those foremost Eich leaders.

The worst was yet to come.

Far, far away, in the Second Galaxy, was Jarnevon, the home planet of the Eich, and it was soon to be the scene of one of the most titanic space battles in the history of Civilization, personally directed by the Tellurian Lensman Kimball Kinnison. The victory that was to come — an absolutely crucial one for the Galactic Patrol — would bring about the utter destruction of the Eich planet, crushed between the nutcracker of two guided worlds colliding.

But, as a Watcher, Eukonidor had discovered another plot, one in which the Eich could have a victory that would be nearly as great for Boskonia as the battle of Jarnevon would be for Arisian Civilization. This plot was developing in the Palainian system, the system least integrated into the plans of the Galactic Council and the most vulnerable — as Palain was a Z-type planet — the designs of blackguard

Z-type relations in other parts of the universe. Of those scheming monstrosities, the worst by far, of course, were the servile followers of the Eich high in the councils of Boskonia.

The plot had evolved out of the defeat of the notorious villain, Gray Roger, who had been defied by the Triplanetary Patrol, forerunner of the Galactic Patrol.

Gray Roger, a manifestation of the mighty Gharlane of Eddore, had then turned his attention to other systems and other planets, and Palain seemed the most likely victim.

Eukonidor was encouraged to find that two Palainian Lensmen already intuitively suspected the gathering onslaught against them. These two were the most outstanding members of a cadre of Patrolmen and Lensmen, which, though excellent in quality, was vexingly small in numbers. They did not know that it was the supermind of Gharlane that they were preparing to confront, but independently they were investigating and preparing to defend their world against anything on any plane. To encourage them, Eukonidor informed Brolenteen, the Mentorian Guardian overseeing that area. This resulted in the convening of a special Court of Gray Lensmen to promote the two Palainians into this elite corps of Unattached Lensmen who wore the distinctive gray leather harnesses of the Gray Legion.

That was how Angzex and Nadreck became Gray Lensmen. As such, they were free agents, no longer tied to a regular unit of the Patrol, able to formulate their own plans to protect the Palainian system, authorized to draw upon any asset of the Patrol without accountability.

Angzex concerned the personal self, that which could not be properly described as either "his" or "her" self, with defensive plans. This self gathered intelligence, monitored the First and Second Galaxy, and stood guard between them, for it was from the Second, the site of the mother world of the Eich, that the strength of the Boskonian conspiracy was drawn. Angzex enlisted an ancestor, old-Ymkzex, into sentinel duty, making Bovreck's deep-space laboratory the key picket-post.

Nadreck concentrated himself, in this case "himself" was a relatively accurate term, on the offensive side, looking for ways to attack the enemy before it could attack them, upsetting plans before they could be executed. This took Nadreck out among the stars and into direct involvement with the far-flung activities of the Patrol. As Angzex was to old-Ymkzex, so Nadreck was to old-Bovreck. Nadreck found that his relationship with old-Bovreck fitted perfectly into the elaboration of his plans. Bovreck's space lab became not only the early-warning station for Angzex, it also became the communications base for Nadreck's extensive operations. Just as the two *zex*-line family members harmonized perfectly in the intricacies of their thought processes, so did the *reck*-line family members. Nadreck had the decided advantage of Bovreck's Lens for increasing his ability for rapid and precise informational interchanges across the light-years.

It was inevitable, therefore, that the existence of the Palainian Research Laboratory Five should have precipitated what happened.

Not since the days of the Triplanetary League, with its Triplanetary Patrol, the predecessor of the Galactic Patrol, had Civilization's once audacious and dreadful foe attempted to fight back from his humiliating defeat. That once mighty entity, who singlehandedly had brought Tellus close to unsalvageable ruin, was Gharlane.

Gharlane, Master Number Two of the Innermost Circle of the All-Highest of the Eddorians, had never ceased planning for the day when he would again personally challenge the Patrol. Finally, he had decided to initiate his personal battle against Civilization by choosing Palain VII as his target.

Space Pirates Attack

T HE ATTACK OF THE SPACE
pirates on the intergalactic space station was sudden and unop-
posed. Brolenteen, his attention fixed tenaciously on his own plans,
arrived too late to stop it. He was not perturbed however. His
prodigious power as Arisian Guardian of Palain was reserved
for the true peril, which came not from the guns of the Boskonian
outlaws but from the menace that traveled with them.

Brolenteen was himself most particularly involved in the
lives of the two Palainians who were in danger of being killed.
Bovreck had been one of the first of the strange frigid beings to
have received the Lens of Arisia from Brolenteen's superentity,
Mentor. As for Bovreck's coresearcher, Ymkzex — although not
measuring up to being a Lensman — had nevertheless joined
the Galactic Patrol as a technician assigned permanently to
Bovreck. Their deaths were not the worst of what could happen
to them: they could be made into traitors, instruments to destroy
the Galactic Patrol and thereby all Civilized progress in that
sector of the galaxy.

The seriousness of the situation could he judged by the fact
that Mentor allowed Brolenteen to he here and not in the other
galaxy where Armageddon, it appeared, was about to happen at
the place called Jarnevon.

*Here, almost within the First Galaxy, a different, though
nonetheless momentous, conflict was about to happen, unnoticed
by all but a handful of participants. A small Palainian space
station, manned by old-Bovreck and old-Ymkzex, was to be the
focal point for an equally important defeat of an insidious plan
of the ultimate enemy, the Innermost Circle of Eddore.*

The pirate spaceship, motionless, now hung in deep
space with all its instruments targeted ahead on an invisible speck. Although no light illuminated the distant object,
it registered as a faint dot on the vitascope; it was a small,
inhabited space station. On the front screen, the lifeform
radiation pulsed against the electromagnetic net of distant
stars sprinkled across the jet-velvet blanket of the universe.
On the rear screen, a trillion miles behind the rear of the
fifteen-hundred-ton, cylindrical black raider, was spread the
glorious edge of the Milky Way galaxy, a hundred thousand
light-years from end to end. Ahead, on the forward screen,
a glowing smear above the calibrated bull's-eye, millions of
light-years beyond the space station, was the barely discernible disc of the Second Galaxy, Lundmark's Nebula.

The pirate captain, a half-caste with slick dark hair and
bluish skin, nervously cast his eyes back and forth from his
instruments to his charts. His arms were stiff, hands spread
wide, pressing back his curious mates who kept crowding
against him on either side.

"Humpf!" he said aloud. "Damn if you're not right, Val-
d'or. It's the Palainian Research Laboratory Five. The chart
coordinates are wrong, like you said. No doubt deliberate."

"No doubt," said Val-d'or, the navigator. "No doubt,
Captain Balltis. It's their wealth they're afraid for."

"Humpf. You're damned good as a navigator, Val-d'or. I
admit it. We're lucky to have you. Finding you when Joey got
himself killed was the only good thing that's happened to us
in the last three months. You got us out of the galaxy right
past the Patrol. And then to find this place is practically a

miracle. Now we hope you're right about the treasure."

"I'm right. My source is infallible. There will be practically no resistance. And no Patrolmen."

"No defenses, no Patrol." said the second-in-command, undisguised suspicion in his voice. "How do you know that?"

"Stands to reason. A small Palainian lab," Val-d'or said. "Strictly oddball, elderly Palainians, in a toxic atmosphere. Two or three of them, at most. You afraid?"

"I'm cautious, smart guy. We all are. That's how we keep alive. There are such things as Palainian Patrolmen."

"Palainian Patrolmen? Not many of them around. Very few. And very unlikely out here. You got no worries.

Captain Balltis was keenly glancing from one to the other, in his fidgety way, out of the corners of his putty black eyes. When the exchange of remarks was over, he examined the faces of the rest of his crew crowded into the tiny pilothouse. He intimately knew eight of the nine of them, all tough, experienced rogues. He saw that he would have to make the decision. They were all on edge, ready to crack from frustration, desperate for some action and some profit, and concerned about being in uncharted deep-space, where they had been driven by a Patrol ship that their clever navigator, a stranger, had managed to outwit.

"I say we attack," Captain Balltis said. "We'll make it quick. Quick success or quick retreat. Palainians are cowards, but we'll take no chances."

"Palainians are also known to he poor," one spaceburned pirate said, pink scarred flesh permanently drawn back from his big, yellow teeth. "Talk of treasure still seems foolish to me. But I don't really care. I've never seen a Palainian, let alone killed one. That chance makes it interesting."

"You can't really see Palainians," the captain said, "They distort your vision. They're always moving, so even pictures are worthless. They can't be depicted. I've seen a few and even I can't describe them."

"Well, I can describe them," one of the crew said, "They're repulsive, poisonous monsters, unless there's money to steal, or we can sell their bones or skin, I say let's forget 'em and find a safe port and bust loose from this tin can."

"Well, that's the point," the captain said, scratching his whiskers and obviously becoming impatient. "I don't believe they're poor, I think Val-d'or's right. The way they're forever furtively poking around the weirdest corners of the galaxy, always loners, acting like misers, my guess is they got unlimited funds. I'll bet they have hoards of valuable things waiting for some enterprising freebooters like us to lift 'em, Val-d'or got us here, I say we attack. How say you?"

There were two mild dissents, but after the briefest of arguments, there was an unanimous agreement.

Captain Balltis wasted no time. He accelerated toward the station, barking orders. The crew scrambled into frantic action, five of them suiting up in armor and arming themselves as a boarding party, although seven wanted to go and only two or three should have been going.

"Gimme a reading," the captain said. "What're we up against?"

"Nothing. Absolutely. No defense screen. No weapons. A lead-pipe cinch."

With the speed and skill developed over their years as an outlaw team, the pirates, their ship firmly pressed against the docking port of the station, assaulted the space station. Three of the five penetrated the station's inner hull in a shower of sparks and swirling smoke, while the other two covered them. Brownish-green gas, the station's deadly atmosphere, boiled out under pressure and crystallized in space.

The trio in the vanguard died first, inexplicably. At one moment they were charging forward, irresistible; in the next moment, for no apparent reason, they were sprawled out in the passageway, dead. They had made no outcry, showed no reaction.

Then the other two, weapons weightlessly spinning

free, collapsed in silence, equally unmarred and equally dead.

In the pilothouse there was panic among the remaining pirates. The captain attempted to disengage and flee, even with plates extended, the side of his ship open. His hands froze over the control buttons, quivering, and his face rippled under his whiskers as though from a continuous series of electric shocks, He fell forward on the console. Then the second-in-command and the helmsman collapsed, falling upon the back of the dead captain.

Only Val-d'or, with a queer, incomprehensible expression around his wide, brilliant eyes, remained alive, his body fixed in a grotesque pose against the room's main stanchion.

Brolenteen, although en route and still light-years away, knew instantaneously what had happened. He was not surprised, for he long ago had visualized the event. When he reached the station within hours after the deadly attack, he found exactly what the newly arrived Lensman Armstrong had found earlier.

Tellurian Lensman Dick Armstrong was thoroughly puzzled. The station was without life. There was no Bovreck, no Ymkzex, nor any trace of them, He stood in the passageway of windowless, unlighted Laboratory Five, staring down at the three human bodies disclosed by his headlamp, talking to himself.

"Three bodies in the pilothouse, two more inside the open air lock. Eight corpses with no signs of wounds, but certainly death by some kind of violence . . ."

He set the time of death at from ninety to a hundred minutes before he had sped to the scene under full emergency power, He had been in a globular cluster, picking up supplies at the outpost GP base, when the urgent Lensed message had arrived from Research Laboratory Five.

The message had been directed to "Ang, Dingwall outpost" and stated: "Boskone imminent. Category 23x4y blackpatch. B plus Y." For some inexplicable reason, Armstrong was the sole recipient of the Lensed signal. When he attempted to acknowledge it, however, he made no contact. Instead, a third mind impressed itself upon his own with an explanation: "Armstrong, you are to act in the absence of Ang. Laboratory Five is shortly to suffer a pirate attack, categorized as a minor menace but possibly a forerunner of a different disaster, as judged by both Bovreck and Ymkzex, Leave Dingwall at once, go to their aid, Keep a tight thought-screen, no Lens."

Armstrong, his ship already fueled and packed with the priority freight, left Dingwall outpost in less than eight GP minutes, He had traveled thousands of light-years already without incident; he was close to his destination; as an armchair Lensman he had expected anything to happen out there on the frontier. So, although he was extremely excited, he wasn't as bothered as he should have been about the unorthodox and illogical situation. That was, as he was to learn, why he had been chosen to be involved.

His trip across the light-years to the station in less than two hours had been as swift as possible, He had, however, been too late. He wished he could have Lensed Bovreck on his way, but he had obeyed his commanding instructions. Instead, he reviewed his assignment, something that had come about overnight, completely without warning, He was to go to Palainian Research Laboratory Five. Sealed orders would await him there, That was it, plain and simple, He had the right, because of his age and disability, to decline to go, but, naturally, he didn't, His swift courier-freighter, empty until his stop at Dingwall, was sufficiently automated to have made the trip without him. He was no mere truck driver. Why had he been chosen to come all the way from Tellus? Why was a racial-psychologist needed? Why him? He had never met a Palainian in all his thirty-nine years of duty in the Galactic Patrol, despite his specialization, He had never left the Solar System in all that time. The reason for his insular service had been explained as his being "too brilliant" to be taken away from Prime Base, the gigantic Patrol base on Tellus, headquarters for the Grand Fleet. Unspoken was the fact that he was "too disabled"— something more technically true than actually true. His shorter, stiff left arm was unimportant; it was the missing twenty-five percent of his brain, a fluid-filled section covered by a plastic skull-plate, that put him on limited duty. The zwilnik bullet that had done that to him, however, had turned him into a sentient encyclopedia of "racial sensibilities" and a GP "resource" to be given special treatment, Anyhow, the few Palainians that he had almost seen had always been encased in heavily refrigerated atmosuits. and eyen these glimpses had occurred a mere half-dozen times, Usually each Palainian "visit" to Prime Base was made in synchronous orbit overhead in a personal speedster, obviously only a person of great importance to rate such a vehicle.

Dick Armstrong, he told himself. was the most unlikely Lensman to have been sent on this most bewildering mission. He had asked for an explanation on Tellus and again at Dingwall, but he had received none. As for his retirement, he was assured that "a few weeks temporary duty" would make no difference.

Armstrong was a slim and handsome man. with strands of white in his thick black hair, which he combed over his plate, a true Tellurian with the blood of all the human races of Earth flowing in his aging veins. He had risen, in his two working lifetimes, to high administrative responsibility within the elite GP officer corps. He had had opportunities to be sent off Tellus; one offer had been excellent, hut he had refused, and his decision had been exactly right, for he had then been given the disciplined life of a special GP assignment at Prime Base. He had become "racial psychology analyst," an important but sedentary task far removed from the popular idea of an adventurous Lensman, and he thoroughly enjoyed this regimented life. He had planned to end the second of his working lifetimes shortly by taking his third full Life-Restoration and retiring into some research center.

How could it be that he was here, on the border of nowhere, between two galaxies, on a deserted alien space station, standing amid the corpses of pirates, and faced with a weird riddle?

At the heart of the puzzle was the disappearance of Bovreck and Ymkzex. They had presumably both been on the station less than two hours ago, at the time of the attack. Now there was no physical trace of them, of that Armstrong was certain, having searched all monitors and records. The only clue was the recording, on nonelectronic, telepathic broadwave, filed on the message board, He had played it three times to be certain he had registered it properly.

"This is Bovreck. If I die and Ymkzex lives, neutralize Ymkzex as untrustworthy. Do not destroy this order, Ymkzex, if you hear it; instead, destroy yourself. If, however, Ymkzex dies and I live, I must be purged. I order myself not to destroy this message, but to act on it. In any case, Angzex must be informed of all this, and he is to determine who else must be informed."

To Armstrong the message was perfectly clear, although the reasoning behind it was not.

Who was Angzex?

Could it be that Bovreck and Ymkzex were already dead, perhaps even as a consequence of this order by Bovreck?

Armstrong could have used at that moment a Palainian sense of perception, that mental ability to perceive the innermost structure of physical objects, that incredibly effective substitute for sight. He did have, though never adequately tested, the use of an extremely sensitive rapport with all lifeforms, but this talent now was producing nothing but chaotic feelings within him. Any hope of understanding was dependent upon his ability as a Lensman. It was time to use his Lens.

He raised his left wrist and stared at the thing strapped there, on the palladium-iridium bracelet was a convex disc, like silver-pink nacre or a tinted piece of sunset cloud, suggesting fires burning deep within it. Under the waves of thought in which he was now bathing it, the disc, his own unique Lens of Arisia, swirled to life, A thousand thousand tiny gems seemed to travel across its surface in straight lines and curves, palpitating to the rhythm of his own life forces. The beauty of its speckled mass of polychromatic colors was awesome, His thoughts were being gathered by its crystalline structure, amplified, and disseminated at infinite speed.

"Bovreck. Ymkzex. Where are you?"

At first, he swept the ether with his mind, probing for a sense of life, then he drew back to push out meticulously yard by yard and mile after mile. Back he came and out again. At every moment his mental search was being steadily subjected to a blanketing or a constriction, like nothing he had ever experienced. He did not know if such a screen was ordinary, but from its firm and unyielding quality he suspected it was not.

He had no doubt that the resistance was the product of life forces; the screen was alive; he sensed it was being generated by an extraordinary superpower. At the same time, he felt something else, a cyclonic hole of emptiness into which his mental probing sank and was annihilated.

He attempted to reach out, back to the galaxy, beyond Dingwall, for contact with another wearer of the Lens, It was, however, as if he were in a prison, surrounded by movable yet impenetrable, invisible walls.

"Bovreck. Ymkzex. Bovreck. Ymkzex."

He sensed the mind screen more strongly now. There was a lifeform, overpoweringly strong, nauseatingly evil, undeniably Boskonian, He had never met the worst of the villains, an Eich, and only once had he felt its devilish mind, but intuitively he knew that this mind was far, far worse.

Armstrong tried to connect and unify every cellular particle of his central nervous system through the instrument of his Lens to discover the source of the mind screen through that whirling hole. Instead, he felt the presence of a different life form. It was coming through the maelstrom.

It was then that he began to see his first Palainian.

The figure materialized as a barely perceptible luminosity out in the void, a mile or more away. It was rushing rapidly at him, emitting a mental humming that grew louder as the form increased in size. It was on a line between the bows of his freighter and the silent pirate ship. At first he believed it to be a projection, but it wasn't. It was solid. It was real.

From a faint wraith, it solidified into pieces of a creature, fifty feet away from the open port in which Armstrong stood. The Lensman, never before having drawn a gun for self-defense, but nonetheless perfectly trained, unholstered his hand weapon and leveled it at the floating jumble of organic parts. That the precaution might be futile did not discourage him. The slender fingers on his thinner and longer right arm were firmly wrapped around the gun butt; his hand was steady, and with a flick of his thumb. he released the safety catch.

Armstrong had seen many aliens and nonhumanoids in his half-century at Prime Base, but all entities, although many had been very strange, had either mingled freely as equals or moved restrictedly encased in functional life-support dress. He had seen holographic motion pictures of many exotic lifeforms. He had only heard about Palainians. For him to encounter one personally, however, was a unique and ghastly occasion.

At first the Palainian appeared as a sort of gelatinous mass squirming into a spidery form — a dozen spiky limbs mingled together with many shapes and sizes of ugly, glistening sacks of plasmic flesh. It quivered all over. Then the appendages fused together into a wet, hairy covering like a sea anemone, hands of tentacles thrusting from a bloated, pulsating body. The underside twisted upward, turning inside out, and with a rim of innumerably faceted gems as eyes, or teeth, ringing a membrane-grilled mouth or gill, the creature stared back at him.

As he looked through the view plate of his space helmet, which seemed to have become as distorting as two feet of flowing water, he was no less startled because he expected something like this from a Palainian: a metamorphosis, the thing changing into a rainbow-hued, scaly worm whose eyes crawled like bugs across its iridescent skin. The worm itself reshaped into a burst of cold fire, tiny blue and green tongues of flame outlining a new ovoid form. The flames solidified into feathers, and appendages grew into wings and fins. In turn they were formed into arms, claws turning into multi-fingered hands. The creature now was almost humanoid, with two, three, or four arms, the asymmetrically fingered hands more consistently attached to wrists instead of sprouting from elbows or shoulders. In amongst the limbs and tentacles there flared, from moment to moment, the face of a Lens.

Armstrong held a vision as nearly humanoid as his concentration could retain. To him, now, this was the appearance of the Palainian with minimal, though constant, variations.

"I am Bovreck," the thing projected, delicately and calmly, into the Tellurian's brain. "You are Lensman Richard Armstrong. Where is Angzex?"

"Hello, Colonel Bovreck," Armstrong said, so off balance he sounded inane. He automatically clicked the safety catch to neutral, where two squeezes would be needed for firing. "I'm reporting for duty. I don't know who Angzex is."

"Angzex was scheduled to come with you. You are worthless at this moment to me, worse than worthless. It is my blame to have requested a weak, but intelligent Tellurian — an earthman, that is, not a colonist — for my experiment. Ymkzex's offspring on Palain, Angzex, tried to have your orders canceled. Failing that in time — a sickening fault of GP bureaucracy — he said he would come with you. You look like what I ordered, but Angzex has visualized such trouble that my work has been suspended. It is a shame, for I am near the end of my life. You must be nearly at that point, too, for you must be as old as I am, comparatively speaking, of course. Tellurians, I am told, become senile with age, unlike Palainians. I trust that you are not. Don't gray strands in your hair mean you are worn out?"

"I should hope not," Armstrong said. The image of Colonel Bovreck he was holding through the function of his interpretive Lens was shifting far less wildly; the Palainian was now an imitation of a badly assembled human figure composed of misshapen parts, sometimes with wrinkled skin and sometimes of raw flesh. The two eyes were black, bottomless holes appearing and disappearing by expansion and contraction.

"Your Lens reveals that you are disgusted by my appearance. No matter you recognize that my body is an illusion because of my multidimensional aspect. Your Lens also reveals that you cannot trust me to react like a true Lensman because of my despicable Palainian behavioral patterns. Your doubt is stupid, of course. You must know of the infallibility in the bestowal of a Lens. You cannot fear me — I will do what is expected of one who wears a Lens."

"Sir . . ." Armstrong began. He was chastened and embarrassed. He hadn't realized his prejudices had shown through. It was common knowledge that Palainians tended to be somewhat ignoble and weak in human ethics and moral fiber — relative to the standards of Tellurians, that is, Armstrong quickly thought. concerned that he might be read as impolite.

"Correct," Bovreck said immediately. "We are different. Palainians are always practical and realistic. You humans are often impractical and too idealistic. Right now I need a clear thinking, ruthless assistant. Perhaps you will do, if Angzex has been selfish enough to stay away and avoid the present danger as any intelligent entity should. Perhaps the naiveté of your life, your unwordliness, your instinctive revulsion for Z-type aliens will substitute for ruthlessness, should I ask you to kill me or Ymkzex when and if we confront each other. If a misplaced conscience doesn't get in your way, I expect you to be brave. Expediency makes cowards of all Palainians."

]"A cowardly Lensman?" Armstrong had heard about this, but never believed it.

"A Palainian Patrolman is a contradiction in terms, seemingly, a paradox. I note that you have never met a Palainian before this moment. Not one of us at Prime Base, with so many opportunities — not even on Dingwall, where Ymkzex's grandson Angzex, our security-watcher, is. How insular some Tellurians are. But then you are a Lensman for personal gain, like me."

"Personal gain!" Armstrong objected. "Nothing of the kind." He was injured enough to show some anger. "You are insulting."

"Insulting? I am truthful. Probably the truth insults you. I am a Lensman because it brings me personal satisfaction. Every Palainian demands that. You are a Lensman for the same reason, are you not? We are both old men; I never had any illusions — you should have outgrown yours. Did you not become a Lensman for personal gain?"

"Well," Armstrong said, "I cannot argue with you. By personal gain, we mean different things. I say I reject material gain, meaning wealth."

"Then you must realize we are the same. With our — how should I say it? — within our souls. I know of no Palainian who is interested in wealth. We are interested in knowledge."

"I apologize, sir," Armstrong said. "Aren't we wasting time? Aren't we in some immediate and terrible danger? I have felt a malevolent presence . . ."

"Danger, yes. Wasting time, no. An apology, a quaint and irrational custom, is not needed by me, for I do not take offense. However, you do need such an expression, and I beg your pardon for taking up your valuable and limited time, when my own time is virtually unlimited. Do you wish for danger to come more quickly? It is almost upon us. There is no need to hurry it."

Brolenteen saw the danger coming, too, even more clearly than Bovreck. Bovreck was destined to die.

As for the villainous Tellurian half-breed pirate, Val-d'or; who floated undetected in the cooling pool containing the station's nuclear reactor; he also would die.

Brolenteen wondered briefly if ingenuous Armstrong would be able to survive his inevitable gunfight with his half of the enemy. The destiny of the multiracial human was not yet defined.

Ymkzex was as good as dead.

Angzex, great-offspring of Ymkzex was, of course, already dead.

There remained the crux of this situation. The deadly duel was about to be fought. The salvation of a quarter of the galaxy was at stake.

Brolenteen, representing Mentor himself, could not stop the Master Eddorian who had come for the showdown.

It was now all up to Brolenteen's champion, the gunfighter whose bullet was fourth dimensional.

The gunfighter was Bovreck's great-offspring: Nadreck, Lensman from Palain VII.

Nadreck Accepts an Offer

W HEN THE HULL OF THE SPACE
station had been breeched and the pirates had burst in, waving their guns and ready to kill, Bovreck and Ymkzex had been nonchalant. They were old scientists, never warriors, alone and without any means of defense, but they had a plan. The odds against their ever being discovered, let alone attacked, were astronomical. However, typically cautious and apprehensive in their Palainian ways, they were primed for any emergency.

Palainians could he killed, although with great difficulty. The fluid, amorphous parts of them constantly in flux in the third dimension were as vulnerable as any normal organic material. Projectile guns, space-axes, and knives were generally ineffective against them. Energy weapons — that is, most beams and rays — and mental thunderbolts were their concern. Their natural environment was very protective under extraordinary conditions, enveloped as they were by poisonous air in an extremely frigid climate. Other races, far from the category of Z, were fortunate that Palainians were not warlike but were instead proudly humble and aggressively passive and arrogantly introverted, qualities human beings had great difficulty understanding and dealing with.

Bovreck and Ymkzex, therefore, treated the attack of the pirates with contempt. Their plan of defense was to quickly retreat into individual square vaults of shielded dureum, almost impervious to common thieves, and patiently to wait, months if necessary, until the danger was over. Should that tactic be unsatisfactory, perhaps with the prospect of being permanently entrapped. they could flee directly into space without spacesuits, a theoretical possibility yet to be tested. Existing in space with only their metabolic extension in another dimension to sustain them was one of their new experimental developments. A dozen years of study had gone into this activity of dexitroboping — such a length of time to them was insignificant, irrelevant, and unmeasured. The idea that this experimenting might be based on cowardice was a meaningless concept to them.

When the pirates broke into their station with an ease no ordinary pirates should have displayed, they had been prepared to go into hiding in their strong boxes. But what happened sent them, instead, hurrying directly into space.

They had immediately sensed the presence of a high-level Boskonian force planning to capture, not their bodies, but their minds. The *dynamikos* struck all the life forces in and around the station, killing all the humanoids by burning out their brains. Bovreck had been too quick to be harmed, slipping his mind into the other dimension for as long as he could hold it there. Ymkzex, zooming away from the station, had been pursued by the evil spirit, probably because of his greater vulnerability, not being a Lensman as Bovreck was.

Bovreck worried that Ymkzex might be caught and thus cause the great harm about which Angzex had vaguely forewarned. Bovreck, therefore, recognizing the danger not as "23x 4y pirates," as sent to Angzex — who did not acknowledge it — but as "1x 1y Eich-plus," went in pursuit of Ymkzex. Before going, he left the message on the board for any Patrolman or good citizen. If Ymkzex were caught and remained alive, he would have to be rescued and rehabilitated, or killed. Killing was the more secure way. And that certainly applied to Bovreck as well.

Bovreck went on his search, blinded by incoherent mental images jamming his Lens-enhanced telepathic powers and unable to reach any other Lens. His sustaining hope was that Angzex, young and vital and talented and as far above an ordinary Lensman as an ordinary Lensman was above an ordinary Palainian, would soon arrive at the laboratory and come to his assistance and join in rescuing Ymkzex.

At last a Lensing mind touched him, just strong enough to reach him and not beyond. To his disappointment, it was not Angzex. It was that Tellurian Lensman, Armstrong, who was coming in from distant Tellus on the specific suggestion of Angzex for research on lungless, nonbreathing, deep-space intelligent races. An A-Lensman could be more harmful than helpful in the current situation. Why hadn't his orders been canceled? Did Angzex actually want a human at the lab for another reason? Bovreck considered this new idea and decided it was the truth. Angzex wanted an A-Lensman for some unrevealed reason; it had to do with the ripening menace that Bovreck now sensed — could the enemy be a renegade Tellurian? The Boskonian leaders were always described as devils in monstrous shapes, emotionally unbalanced, lustful, and greedy — did that not describe the fiery blooded, tox-oxygenated ugly beasts that were human?

Bovreck sped back to the station, on his guard.

A quick glimpse into Armstrong's mind, done within the bounds of Lensman probity, calmed his fears. The Tellurian was an academic innocent. stuffed with knowledge but bereft of experience with violence. With part of his Palainian mind, Bovreck began poking away at the earthman, learning about him, looking for something that might help, seeking some clue to young-Angzex's intentions. With the other part of his mind, he stood guard, waiting for old-Ymkzex and waiting for some further move by the Boskonian presence.

Armstrong did not know that it was he who was being interviewed and examined. To him, it seemed that it was the Palainian who provided all the self-revealing talk. The expert racial psychologist would have been very disconcerted and self-conscious if he had known the truth.

"Danger is almost upon us — do you wish it to come more quickly," Colonel Bovreck had said. How could such an appalling being remain so calm with danger close by? What had he meant by "unlimited time" when time was obviously running out?

Armstrong recognized the paradoxical complexity of Bovreck's thinking. Time, though relative, was still being wasted by this creature who talked endlessly. "No, sir," Armstrong said flatly, "I don't want danger to come more quickly."

"In your terminology," Bovreck said, "I am not a 'sir.' You are a male, I can call you 'sir,' but I am not like you."

"Sorry," Armstrong said, taken aback. "Ma'am — or miss?"

"Neither, really. For an expert, you are an ignoramus." Armstrong felt foolish and unaccustomedly resentful.

This inhuman monster's character was a frustrating mixture of order and chaos. The blunt truthfulness but propensity for indirection was quite irritating to experience. Armstrong was a proficient psychologist who, in this real-life situation, was making ridiculous blunders. The explanation was inescapable: this Palainian, or, for that matter, any Palainian, had a physical semblance and bizarre personality such as to disorient any humanoid, even one who was supposed to repress all subjective reactions.

"I will call you Colonel, unless you prefer Professor."

"Call me Bovreck."

"Yes, Bovreck."

"I do note that you have a problem. You are wondering how to refer to me. Do you say, 'He is certainly far more clever than I?' Or do you say, 'She is certainly more intelligent than I?' Or perhaps you should use 'it?' I am a Palainian 'two,' the defensive or protective sex, like a 'mother.' Use the female term for me, if you must. Ymkzex, in contrast is a 'three,' like the offensive or aggressive sex, a 'father,' as is Nadreck, my offspring once removed. Angzex, the absent one, who so wisely chooses not to aid me, to ignore me, is a 'one,' like a prenuptial catalyst as opposed to a postnuptial catalyst such as 'four.' Emmfozing — breeding, that is — is a complicated process."

"This Angzex, is he a Patrolman?"

"Angzex is a Lensman."

"A Lensman?" Armstrong said, scandalized. "And he refuses to help you?"

"The prime tenet of a Palainian is to ignore and be ignored. Altruism is usually not worthwhile. What Angzex has done, or will do, will nevertheless be right, proper, and consistent with being a Lensman — and a Palainian. I am humbly sorry that our ways could cost you your life. My life is unimportant. I apologize for endangering yours.

Armstrong stared at the figure of Bovreck, accepting without agitation the shifting of the pieces in and out of focus. Bovreck apologizes? Bovreck's life is unimportant? These were absurd inconsistencies. Could any Palainian be truly understood? Could any Palainian ever be loved, even if only by one individual from a single race among the tens of thousands of humanoid races? It seemed unlikely. No wonder few humanoids knew or associated with Palainians. No wonder he, Armstrong, had never done so.

(No wonder, too, that in the near future a Palainian by the name of Nadreck would become one of the four greatest Lensman of the Civilized universe and yet remain for many, many years unknown and mysterious to Kimball Kinnison, the greatest of the great.)

"Colonel — I mean, Bovreck — I am here to help you. I ask again: Aren't we wasting time?"

"Time? We have exchanged these thoughts, since we

met, in a microsecond. You have been drawn in, as it were, under the influence of my metabolic extension into the hyperdimension. Time is subjective when one awaits, as we are awaiting. Observe. When you first spoke to me, you latched your gun. Listen —"

Within his space suit, transmitted by vibrations through the fabric, Armstrong head a sharp, low-pitched note. What was that? The recognition formed in his mind. Bovreck was giving him the power to understand — to understand that this continuous sound was the click of his safety catch! The past and the future remained locked in the present! Time was standing still! Or seemed to be, so fast were they thinking, passing thoughts between themselves! Incredible!

Armstrong now knew the extraordinary power of a Palainian mind. What must a truly great Palainian Lensman be capable of? Could a youthful Angzex possibly be greater than an elderly Bovreck?

"You wish to know what we are awaiting? We wait for Ymkzex. He is out there, somewhere. I chased him, but he eluded me. Neither of us have been out in deep space before without a three-dimensional space suit of this space-time continuum. At least, not for the 4,980 GP seconds that have now elapsed."

"In space without armor?" Armstrong was astounded.

"You seem to disbelieve. I assure you that we Palainians do need an atmosphere to breathe. Poisonous to you, of course, and so cold that it seems a thick syrup. Nonetheless, we do breathe and cannot live in temperatures of absolute zero. That is the nature of my research. And of Ymkzex's, too. We are preparing for the day when Palain VII will have lost the envelope of gas that supports our life. Have you ever been to Palain? No, of course not. It is a barren planet. It is mostly rocky, metallic soil, so frigid that it would burn your feet off, even through your insulated soles. The surface of Palain is a wilderness. Only the junkyards of our abandoned cities, the deserted buildings of every size and shape tumbled together, would indicate that intelligent life had lived there. That plus the pitted landing fields, with their scars and puddled pools of metallic, unnatural lava. This is all there is to see on our bleak plains, which stand shrouded in an intense darkness where nights are indistinguishable from days, where our sun seems only another feeble star in the sky."

Armstrong shuddered at the grim and desolate picture Bovreck so vividly painted in his mind with words and images.

"You, Armstrong, were to help me test my theories. It would hardly be startling for me or Ymkzex to survive in space without space suits. But if a Tellurian were to do so, a ground-gripping Tellurian, at that, then such a demonstration would be remarkable and prove the theories."

"Use me? *Me?* In space without a suit?"

"Without any clothes whatsoever. Which would be a stiff test indeed, as Palainians don't wear clothes."

"I would be mad to let you use me in such a way!"

"I would expect to be able to convince you to do it voluntarily. Think of the pleasure of such a success for you. I would make every effort to see that you didn't die."

"Thank you very much," Armstrong said, hoping that his sarcasm would not be lost on Bovreck "I am not particularly brave, nor am I particularly foolhardy. I would not have volunteered. Nor could I have accepted any orders to do so."

"I knew this from the very beginning," Bovreck said, "but I thought I would try such a request anyhow. No, you would not have gone out in space, but your assistance would still have been most valuable. I stress this. Most essential. Angzex the Young One insisted that a human being is needed. He has a special role for you, I am certain."

"I was promised sealed orders."

"There are no sealed orders. Angzex commands."

Armstrong suddenly was scorched by a torrent of intense emotion that poured through him. He was startled. half frightened. In the course of the conversation between

him and Bovreck, they had drifted farther down the passageway and into the interior of the ship. The blackness was
absolute beyond the circle of light from his headlamp. The
shadows accentuated the distorted image of the Palainian
and showed only the dull gray shapes of the ship's skeletal
structure. The limits of the room could not be accurately
gauged, but it felt oppressively small. The absence of gravity
left him uncertain as to where the floor and doorways were.
As for the shifting reflections of Bovreck, they showed eerie
deformations in which top could not be distinguished from
bottom.

What was that horrible feeling?

"Prepare!" Bovreck said. "He's coming!"

"Who?" Armstrong was really afraid of this unknown.
"Prepare for what?"

"Ymkzex." Bovreck seemed to be pointing with tentacles. "Ymkzex? Are you hurt? The creature with me is the
Lensman Armstrong. Ymkzex! What is wrong?"

Armstrong twisted his head in all directions, casting
his light around, looking for old-Ymkzex. Optically he saw
nothing, while Bovreck, with his eyeless senses, seemed to
perceive something nearby — in another room? Outside?
Armstrong attempted to compensate for his handicap by
using his Lens to pick up mental images or auras of living matter. In part he succeeded. There was a lifeform in
the center of the ship. Human! And now another, stronger
force, growing around the human, "bright" enough and "loud"
enough to create the falsehood of seeing and hearing —
Ymkzex, his intuition told him. This was Ymkzex, the other
old Palainian.

"Fight it, Ymkzex! Resist! Draw on me for strength!"
Old-Bovreck sounded frenzied — and hopeless.

To Armstrong, the human mental and physical radiation
seemed suddenly to he submerged by the Ymkzex domi-
nation and become something exceedingly more powerful,
and distinctively and strangely alien. Even the background

clicking of the nuclear pile was obliterated. How could a human be there?

"Get back to the freighter!" This a loud mental command in his head. Was this from Bovreck? Or from someone else? "Get back to the freighter immediately!" It most definitely was another mentality giving orders!

"Is that you, Angzex?" Bovreck blasted out. "Where are you? Is Ymkzex all right?"

"Ymkzex is lost to us. I almost brought him back safely to you, but he's slipped into . . ." The crackling interference, Armstrong instantly knew, was deliberate censorship. "Slipped into" what? He was also conscious now of the two different screening sensations he had first experienced at the moment he had attempted to Lens Bovreck and Ymkzex. Armstrong could read the sources now. The blanketing was coming from Ymkzex. As for the square hole of emptiness into which his Lensed thoughts had sunk to be annihilated— it was one of the crates he had carried from Dingwall!

His body passed through the freighter's cargo door quicker than he could believe, even with all maneuverjets blowing from his suit, Bovreck was right behind him.

Armstrong looked back and his lamplight showed the familiar out-of-focus figure of the Palainian just coming through the door — and instantaneously, faster than his light beam moved, the figure was now on the other side of him, standing in front of an open crate. Bovreck? No!

There were two figures! Two Palainians? Ymkzex had jumped through space? Or was it another? Angzex?

"Angzex?" Bovreck seemed to be echoing Armstrong's puzzlement. "Angzex? But no . . . You're not Angzex!" Bovreck was confused and distressed. "And yet, you seem to be, you really are Angzex, aren't you?"

"I am the . . . *c-r-a-c-k-l-e*. . . Stand ready! Ymkzex is . . . *c-r-a-c-k-l-e*. . . Armstrong! Defend yourself! The doorway!"

All at once the cargo room, the doorway. and the passageway into the space laboratory were brightly lighted, as if by magnesium flares. Coming out of passageway and into the cargo hold was a wild-eyed humanoid, teeth bared in a snarl, face flushed, sputa flecking his mouth and nostrils. It was the navigator Val-d'or, a baleful puppet appearing to Armstrong as a maniac. Val-d'or had a knife in his left hand and an atomizing automatic pistol in his right.

Handguns seemed to appear in profusion among the many appendages of Angzex and Bovreck. Streaks of fire passed around Armstrong and into — and through — the chest of Val-d'or, but the pirate did not fall. Val-d'or's own shots had the remarkable accuracy of a superlative marksman. Two or three in succession struck the Lens of Bovreck in the brief moments that the disc appeared. Expanding rings of stinging colors flew from Bovreck's Lens, and the ether was filled with a screeching cry, "Die, Lensman!" followed by a soul-shaking mental thunderbolt that burst within Bovreck's mind and killed him.

Bovreck's protection had been neutralized by the bullets from Val-d'or, but Armstrong knew from the wisdom that flooded around him that the cry and the thunderbolt had come from a furtive someone else who was greater than an Eich.

Within Armstrong's brain a voice was saying, "Lensman! Only you can strike down the other human with your mind. You have the racial insight to destroy him. Do so! Destroy him!"

Armstrong's DeLameter had been in his hand, scoring on Val-d'or's body without effect. Now Armstrong brought up his right hand and pressed his Lens to his forehead, concentrating. Val-d'or was intent on shooting Angzex's Lens and, being no Lensman himself. with no support from his invisible ally, was not prepared for the massive mental blow from Armstrong. He fell to the deck, his gun still firing, erratically now, as his fingers kept working the buttons even in death. But the last careful shot from the pirate had hit Armstrong in the center of his forehead, passing completely through his brain.

The Tellurian Lensman tumbled over backward, stretching out on the deck that was now slippery with fluids from the living, the dead, and the machinery. He faced his death with complete satisfaction and heard, more clearly than ever, the mental turmoil that bubbled around him. As he died he had, temporarily, a sense of perception. He saw the third Palainian come into the room. This was Ymkzex.

Ymkzex looked no different from his offspring Angzex. His warped persona, however, was radically unlike Bovreck's, in no way cowardly or retiring. He, too, was bristling with weapons, firing rapidly and accurately. The fissile, nuclide bullets struck Angzex's exposed Lens as Ymkzex screamed, "I have you now, Angzex!" and hurled his mental thunderbolt. The bullets, however, simply plunged through the Lens without effect and the thunderbolt was halted in midflight by Angzex's unyielding screen.

"You face more than Angzex," said the other mind, as calm and blunt as Bovreck had been. "Angzex is dead. This is merely Angzex's body. A stronger mind fights you now.

"I thought so!" Ymkzex did not slacken his futile assaults. "But you are just another Lensman from a different world. I will destroy you, too!"

In the far side of the cargo room, which was no longer lighted, not even by Armstrong's inoperative lamp, the position of one Palainian was marked by a glowing Lens that appeared and disappeared with the pulsing of the simulation of Angzex's metabolism. On the other side, dimly outlined by the distant galaxy beyond the open port, floated the other Palainian, Ymkzex. To them, however, the absence of light meant nothing, for to them there was no such thing as darkness.

"I am more than what you think I am. Give up Ymkzex's body and go back to Eddore."

"You mention Eddore! Who are you to mention Eddore?"

"Does that worry you, Eddorian?"

"I am not worried because I possess a body with which to strike at you. You are only a phantom. Also, I possess an the knowledge from the *zex*-line and I know the family psychic secrets. You have the weaker position. Success for you is impossible. I tell you, instead, that unless you run away from me, you will be snuffed out like a flame."

"Who am I to mention Eddore? That is the question whose answer you dare not face."

"Whom do you claim to be?" Ymkzex said.

"Don't pretend such guilelessness. I know you as well as you know me."

"I only know that you are a foolish Lensman."

To the Angzex-manifestation this had the ring of an honest belief. Perhaps a mental blockade, that zone of compulsion that Arisians had from time to time and from one occasion to another imposed on Eddorians, had erased the memory. Angzex-the-imposter decided to permit a glimpse of the truth.

As Brolenteen, he said, "Think! Admit that you are the Eddorian who once uncovered the forbidden truth — that the ultimate nemesis of Eddore is Arisia!"

"Eddorian? Of course, I am Eddorian!"

"Such admission betrays two facts. You are an arrogant Eddorian Master, for only such would so flagrantly disregard your age-old rules of secrecy. And, secondly, you recognize me as an Arisian!"

The Eddorian was nearly thrown off balance. Brolenteen, who was Angzex, slammed into the Eddorian's mind, if not strong enough to destroy, at least strong enough to throw him out of the system.

"My pride betrays me," the Eddorian boasted. "Does it matter, since you will be destroyed? The insanity of the human mind that I threw against you failed. You were clever to anticipate my attack from two extremes of intelligent life. You are a worthy opponent — and thus I will have greater pleasure in smashing you. Why should I believe you are an Arisian?" He tried a trick, without expecting it to work. "Come out of your shell and *show me* yourself."

"I will not expose myself. But I will remind you of a painful memory. You were the Eddorian who was once driven from the Tellurian sector by someone like me."

"I remember! But I remember it with pleasure, not with pain." The Eddorian's thoughts were tempestuous. "Yes, as I recall, I shot him seven times, as fast as I could pull the trigger, through the brain and through the spine, with bullets that volatilized the flesh. Speak my name and tremble!"

"GHARLANE."

"Yes, I am Gharlane! Eddorian Master Number Two, second only to the All-Highest in power and ruthlessness! Now you know it is futile to oppose me!" For the very first time, the possessed body of Ymkzex began to shiver with repressed excitement. "You! We meet at last!" A weird mixture of fear and pleasure was in the thoughts. "You are — the Director of all Lensmen. You are — STAR A STAR!"

The image of Angzex flickered as Brolenteen's steady concentration faltered. Gharlane's incredible notion confounded him. Gharlane's response was so intense, so overwrought with emotion, so ridiculously wrong about the imaginary Star A Star, that Brolenteen for an infinitesimal part of a fraction of time allowed the tiniest of flaws, the merest microscopic crack to exist in his perfect shield against the Eddorian.

In a sudden, savage, maddened, frenzied assault, Gharlane struck into Brolenteen's psyche.

The real essence of the *zex*-line of the living Ymkzex dissolved the imitation *zex*-line of Angzex. The specter of Angzex vanished.

Brolenteen, the energizer of the Angzex manifestation, was stripped bare of all shielding. He reached for some spirit or lifeform on which to steady himself. If he did not recover his equilibrium immediately, the equally startled Eddorian would recover first and strip away every secret. He reached out and grabbed — Armstrong! The human was not quite dead — unconscious and dying, but not yet dead. Brolenteen desperately tried to anchor himself to the human mind, unable, however, to draw enough power there to keep himself from possibly being swept away by Gharlane and hurled ignominiously back toward Arisia in a terrible, perhaps fatal, psychological defeat.

Gharlane snorted and whined and squealed with glee, hesitating so he could gloat before his decisive blow.

Nadreck perceived his chance and acted.

From the other crated dureum vault in which he had hidden, Nadreck extruded, uncoiled, and precipitated himself into the room.

Brolenteen promptly and adroitly strengthened his hold on his mode of existence by switching from Armstrong to Nadreck.

Nadreck launched his optimal blow against the foe.

Gharlane, overconfident and overextended, was sent reeling back, shaken off Ymkzex's body, which instantly collapsed lifelessly to the deck.

Nadreck was streaming mental pulses against the disembodied mind of Gharlane. It was a direct channel between the two, which invited a counterstroke by Gharlane that could destroy Nadreck. Gharlane opened the barriers to his mind to make his fatal thrust.

"Now!" said Nadreck to the Arisian, who had stabilized his condition. "Now!"

Brolenteen needed no special clue, no urging. He knew what to do. Before Gharlane could fling his spear of energy, Brolenteen threw his. It plunged deep into the mental web of Gharlane, disappearing on some long and instantaneous journey to wherever it was that Gharlane's body really rested.

Gharlane, Eddorian Master Number Two, was gone.

Nadreck was alone in the cargo room with the dying Armstrong. Bovreck's Lens was already cold and inanimate and fast decaying, but the Tellurian's was strong and vital. Proper attention would save his life, so Nadreck gave it. The human's eyes were open, but until Nadreck snapped on Armstrong's headlamp, the man had assumed he was blind. Nadreck sat Armstrong up, touching his mind to evaluate the damage. The bullets had not exploded in his head; he would live and, with a Restoration, recover. The swelling of the organ of the brain was the most serious problem and was quickly reversed.

Nadreck next pulled some cargo tarpaulins over the bodies of Bovreck, Ymkzex, and Val-d'or, as Armstrong quietly watched him. The Palainian caught the Tellurian's wonderment: "Why, Bovreck looks positively *human!*" Nadreck, without any preliminaries, said, "She's completely three-dimensional now, and your logic presents you with a more logical gestalt effect. I am Nadreck. I am glad you are alive. You have completed your mission, I think, and can return to Tellus as soon as you are well enough. That will be sensible. I know you are strangely thrilled by this adventure and feel that it is over too quickly for you. Don't be as imbecilic as the rest of your race seems to be. Go home where it is safe."

"I congratulate you, Nadreck," said the voice of Brolenteen. "I understand why you are ashamed, but that is even more reason for me to congratulate you. I commend you for saving the Palainian system from enslavement and for saving me from humiliation."

"I was foolhardy," Nadreck said. "After Angzex's death, I hid in the cargo of this ship, perfectly hidden and secure in the vault, telling myself I would be available if needed. Actually I believe I did it out of cowardice. That I should have appeared in time to help was more luck than anything. I don't deserve praise for being naturally selfish, deceitful, furtive, and sly. Yes, I am, in fact, simply a fool."

Brolenteen regretted the loss of Angzex, a Palainian Lensman who should have been destined to climb high in the

Patrol. Now, however, he had a greater appreciation for this even more complex fellow, Nadreck, the Gray Lensman. The time had come to make him the offer, and Nadreck would say, "It might only make my life more dangerous, but on the other hand, I will have greater ability to defend myself and to develop a possible invincibility. I am much too feeble, as driving away that Eddorian showed me by bringing me much too close to the limits of my power. Yes, I think I may accept your offer. Besides, I have a certain project that I would be reluctant to undertake as I know the possibility is good that I may suffer some personal harm and this will help me.

"Yes, I will accept."

And so Brolenteen took Nadreck to Arisia, where he received his advanced training and became a Second Stage Lensman.

That elevation in rank and power was pleasing to the vanity of Nadreck.

What he didn't like, however, was the revelation that Gharlane had not died.

Worse yet, Mentor had allowed, actually allowed, Gharlane to escape.

The Wedding Gifts

NADRECK OF PALAIN VII, UN-
attached 1.2, curled an amorphous tentacle caressingly around
the shimmering jewel and absorbed its beauty with his mind.
It sparkled in many frequencies, tickling his many senses,
stimulating the sensuous pleasures of his biomentalis or
intrinsic mind.

As the oscillating waves blended in lights and sounds
and freezing radiations, much as a warm-blooded human
monster might enjoy his high fidelity and three-dimensional
pleasures in the comfort of his fiery home, Nadreck relaxed
and pondered.

So, at last: Gharlane was dead.

There are moments that are important turning points
in history. Such a time was the downfall of the Eich and the
obliteration of Jarnevon. Billions of dwellers in the two galaxies remembered it as the salvation of the First Galaxy when
the leadership of Boskone had collapsed. To the thousands
of Patrolmen who manned the Grand Fleet of the Galactic
Patrol, it was a moment in their lives when three worlds were
fused together by their heroism for a cataclysmic triumph.
As they sped homeward through intergalactic space they all
could see the incredible pyre they were leaving behind them.

Where Jarnevon had been was a new star, the gravestone of the enemy that would have conquered them.

For Kimball Kinnison, the victorious commander of the Grand Fleet, that moment was later climaxed by his betrothal to his red-haired head nurse, the incomparable Clarrissa, destined to be the first female Lensman.

To Nadreck of Palain VII, the reluctant hero of the incident at Research Laboratory Five, this historical moment had marked the completion of his special training as a Second Stage Lensman. The psychological effect of that upon him had been profound, reshaping him from an inwardly selfish entity to one who only outwardly appeared to be that way. No Lensman was more dedicated to the greater principles of the Galactic Patrol and the Galactic Council and Civilization itself than he was now. He had the wit and intelligence to realize that he had not been changed by his education by Mentor — he had been induced to find his real self.

The fall of Jarnevon and the Eich has been recorded in the official history of the Patrol as the climax to the volume of *The Time of the Gray Lensman*. It did not, however, mark the beginning of the expected universal peace or the marriage of Kim Kinnison to the red-haired beauty. Instead, it was really the prologue to what followed, as was recorded in the *Days of the Second Stage Lensmen* by "Doc" Smith, chief of the historical section. Halfway through that account of the Second Stage Lensmen is recorded Nadreck's first meeting with Kinnison and his becoming involved extensively in the activities of the higher headquarters of the gigantic Patrol. Nadreck had distinguished himself in the "debacles" at Shingvors and Antigan, closely monitoring the infrequent traces of the unrepentant Gharlane, and then had narrowed his attention to Kandron, who was on the planet Onlo, forcing that cold creature to abandon his high position and to flee. Kinnison, on the neighboring planet of Thrale working to destroy the Thrale-Onlonian Empire, uncovered a remarkable situation--the sinister adviser to the Tyrant of the Empire was actually Gharlane. And Kinnison defeated him.

Gharlane was dead.

To Nadreck, this was a distinct, personal disappointment. He had wanted to track down Gharlane and avenge the death of the *reck*-paternal Bovreck, not for sentimental reasons, but in keeping with the traditional Palainian obsession with self-preservation through tribal inviolability. At the time of Gharlane's escape from the space station struggle, Nadreck had believed that the outcome had been the result of Brolenteen being too weak and Gharlane being too strong. In his training, however, he had learned the truth. In fact, for reasons of strategy, Brolenteen had allowed Gharlane to escape and had deliberately cultivated the deception that Arisians were weaker, not stronger, than Eddorians, thus encouraging an arrogant overconfidence about a vincible foe.

The pursuit and final disposal of Gharlane was a challenge that Nadreck missed, although he was mollified by the knowledge that it had taken a supreme effort by the great Kinnison to accomplish the task. Fortunately, Nadreck had another villain to chase. This was the Onlonian, Kandron, who, although not as despicable nor as prestigious as Gharlane, was much more devious and delectably more interesting as a similar frigid-blooded, poison-breathing entity. In a way, Nadreck rationalized, he had had his victory over Gharlane, which Brolenteen had chosen to nullify. And that was what had bothered him, and still bothered him. Nadreck did not understand Brolenteen's reasoning and judgment.

Why didn't Nadreck understand? He was an intelligent entity, a Palainian Second Stage Lensman. He was one of the smartest entities in two galaxies — maybe even the smartest, smarter even than Worsel — so why didn't he understand Arisian thinking? Arisians were his ancestors. They were billions of years more ancient than his own race, but they were not any brainier than he was, just more experienced and psionically developed. Nadreck couldn't help but feel slightly ashamed of himself. Worsel and Tregonsee and Kinnison seemed to understand the Arisian point of view. Yet these other three Second Stage Lensmen, to Nadreck, were seriously flawed by personal uncertainty and an incomprehensible unselfishness. Perhaps these weaknesses were some kind of strength? Possibly, but not probably. He was encouraged to know that he did think about these things, unlike most Palainians. Maybe one day he would understand the Cosmic All more nearly as the Arisians did.

Gharlane dead. And Kinnison killed him. Nadreck would have to have Brolenteen confirm this, before Nadreck would finally be convinced it was true.

So, for the first time in what seemed years, Nadreck was relaxed. His special project, retribution on Gharlane — for which he had, in part, become an L2 — was gone.

Nadreck's attention came back to the jewel he was examining. His preferred appendage, at the moment still looking like a tentacle, shaped its tip into a sort of hand, picked up the red gem, and placed it back in its crystal box on a cushion of ammonia snowflakes.

The precious gem, perfectly and intricately faceted, was unsuitable as a gift to the bride. On her hot planet, the stone, would evaporate in seconds.

What was needed was the fire of a Manarkan stardrop, the brilliance of a diamond, and the psychedelic properties of an Ordovik crystal. It had to be capable of being handled and worn in the intolerable temperatures of Klovia or Tellus. Nothing in Nadreck's collection would be exactly right.

And then there was the, problem of a gift for the groom.

The marriage of Kimball Kinnison to Clarrissa MacDougall would probably be the greatest social occasion that Civilization, in all of its billions of planets, would witness. In fact, Nadreck suspected with good cause, it would probably be the most important event in the Arisians' plans for Civilization, based on their Visualization of the Cosmic All, the causal view of all history and the future in all of time and space.

Yes, a very special gem for Mrs. Clarrissa Kinnison, the Red Lensman.

And for Kinnison? What was he interested in? Did he have any hobby besides hunting Boskonians?

Nadreck had an inspiration.

Now he knew exactly how to solve his problem of the wedding gifts. His would be the equal of the best of the billions of presents that would be pouring in for the happy pair.

Nadreck didn't have to ponder long over his plan to get the gifts. He had a workable plan left over from his various traps prepared for Gharlane. The only major difference was that the reward Nadreck had planned for himself would go to Clarrissa.

The first thing that Nadreck did was to make certain that Perbat, the Palainian zwilnik, and Chak, the Onlonian dealer in thionite, and every other illegal substance, object, or crime, were still in business at the same old disreputable hangouts. They were.

The second thing that Nadreck did was to take his Lens from around a forearm and place it in a small jewel case, among the priceless items that were his finest treasures.

Then, without his Lens, Nadreck went to Palain VI, directly to the simple home of Perbat, which was buried a thousand feet straight down into the frozen ground. Nadreck knew Perbat's personality well enough to have no qualms about allowing himself to be cornered in the enemy's lair. Perbat felt utterly secure in his own personal fortress. Aside from the expense of maintaining his network of criminals, he spent most of his money on security devices and body-guards. Being a Palainian, however, he had no fear of the mysterious fourth dimensional properties of his race that humanoid zwilniks had difficulty in handling.

To Nadreck, whose body needed no disguise but whose mind was impersonating an entirely different and carefully constructed individual from his repertoire, Perbat was an oaf who was easy to deceive. Nadreck considered the danger to himself to be absolutely nil.

"I know you have never met me," Nadreck said, ostentatiously staring around the expensively furnished room and allowing thoughts of greed and envy to seep through to Perbat. "But you no doubt have heard of me. I am, as I say, the notorious Betical." Nadreck's "Betical" wasn't notorious, but the character was a documented felon with a well-contrived record counterfeited by both local and Patrol law enforcement agencies.

"Yes, Betical, I know of you," Perbat said, flashing rings and bracelets on his arms and legs. "I looked you up. I know everything about you. I know everything about everyone."

"Well, sir," Nadreck said. "You also know your guards have taken my samples."

"Yes, I know. They seem good samples. But they will have to be tested."

Nadreck knew what was coming. Perbat's method of doing business was considered practical if not amusing. Nevertheless, Nadreck pretended ignorance and said, "How long will that take?"

"No time at all," Perbat said. He waved his hand and one of the dozen bodyguards handed Nadreck a tiny, transparent capsule. It looked like it contained Nadreck's special bentlam derivation, but he couldn't be sure until he tasted it.

"Take it, chew it, swallow it," Perbat said. Nadreck let the manservant put it in his mouth, noted that it was not poisoned, and did as he was told.

Many, many minutes passed before Perbat spoke. "You have passed the test." Of course, Nadreck knew that Perbat had already had one of his attendants eat some.

"It is a very good grade of benweed," Nadreck said. "Have some. Have it all."

"Yeah," Perbat said, taking just enough to have an ecstatic fantasy. Nadreck felt nothing; he had saturated himself with anti-bentlam medication before he had arrived on Palain VI.

"Now take the thionite," Perbat said, beginning a different procedure. He took a generous pinch of the purple powder and pushed it into the side compartment of an aerosol dispenser. A squeeze of the trigger would send the powder, suspended in an icy stream of oxygen crystals, into the soft tissues of a being. Without oxygen, the thionite would be inactive; with too much oxygen, the dose would be fatal.

"Please, sir," Nadreck protested, "That is too treacherous to take when I am here to discuss business with you. I am a dealer, not a user. It is dangerous for me. I must have a clear head to tell you my request." Nadreck was not really fearful, although he recognized that the chance of a bad reaction was one in several million. If he could avoid taking it, that would be prudent.

"All right," Perbat said. "Don't take it. Tell me what you want."

Nadreck outlined his scheme. He had, he said, tons of raw bentlam stored away in a secret place. He also had hundreds of pounds of thionite, the drug that was the most difficult to obtain and the one that was the most in demand by oxygen-breathers. Operation Zwilnik — the Galactic Patrol's constant fight against the drugs that Boskonia and the "zwilniks" continually pushed for profit and for the destruction of Civilization — had impounded much of the illicit narcotics. Nadreck explained that Betical had highjacked large quantities.

"It's not the first time that's been done," Perbat said. "But it's also a trick used by narco agents to destroy my business and capture me."

Nadreck said nothing.

"So you want me to buy your stuff," Perbat finally said.

"No," Nadreck said. "I want you to introduce me to

Chak the Onlonian so I can make a deal with him."

"What?" Perbat bellowed. "You are crazy! I am no inter-mediary!"

Nadreck finally calmed him down by making him understand. Nadreck didn't want money. Nadreck, that is, Betical, wanted to swap his almost priceless cache of drugs for some of Chak's almost priceless gems. Chak didn't deal with the small fry, so Perbat was necessary. Perbat would get a commission, maybe even some of the goods, if he would simply set up the meeting.

Perbat finally agreed. They exchanged contracts, more for Perbat's protection than for Nadreck's. As a gesture of partnership, Nadreck told Perbat that the samples could be kept at no charge. Nadreck turned to go.

"One moment," Perbat said. He held out the aerosol container of thionite in one of his hands and waved it in front of Nadreck's twisting head.

"Now, Betical," Perbat commanded, "now do as I say. Take the thionite!"

Nadreck did.

By the time he was back on a commercial liner leaving Palain VI for Palain VII he was feeling the effects, despite all his preconditioning. He felt as if all of himself were slipping entirely into the fourth dimension. And then he had a "thionite dream." It was so pleasant, while leaving him with an overpowering craving for more, that Nadreck knew he had never been in more danger. He told himself he would never take it again, even at Chak's demand.

The call for a rendezvous came sooner than Nadreck had thought possible, within days.

Nadreck was told to board a liner out of Palain VII for a long voyage into another solar system, ultimate destination unrevealed. The ship was designed for deep space, capable of traveling at nearly a hundred parsecs per hour. He was told to go to the cabin that had been booked for him and to remain there until he was contacted. The only piece of baggage Nadreck had was a large case with preserved foods, toilet articles, and his small box of jewels.

Aboard, Nadreck saw Perbat and six of his most sinister musclemen. Under the suspicious eyes of the omnipresent Patrolmen, they studiously ignored each other.

After a seven-hour flight, the space liner, having covered 1500 light-years, stopped at a transfer station. "Get out of here!" came a telepathic order to him.

Nadreck, taking his bag, left the liner, checked into a transient room, where he left the bag, and waited in the lounge.

Perbat soon came to him. "Follow me," he said, and they walked along several corridors in the completely dark and cold section of the station where the Palainians, the Onlonians, and other such types passed their time. In front of a door Perbat's bodyguards searched him thoroughly. They entered a large, exorbitantly expensive, high-security stateroom, where another evil-looking party of six was gathered. Nadreck was searched again, even more thoroughly.

Chak was lounging in a fluid-chair and did not get up when he was introduced to Nadreck.

Chak was one of the most obnoxious, vile persons Nadreck had ever encountered. Considering that Nadreck had just spent a great deal of time on Onlo, the most heavily fortified planet in the universe, secretly learning the identifying patterns of every Onlonian of any importance, to think this of Chak was extremely deferential.

Chak was almost completely three-dimensional. The unpleasant details of his grotesque figure, therefore, were not softened by extradimensional extensions. His color was distinctively silvery green, with a mantle of hoarfrost, which was rather attractive. The revolting aspects of his appearance were the streamers of green that hung like rubbery sputum from his mouth, the thick drippings of icy mucus around his eyes and ears. His mouths boiled out bilious, greenish vapors, which were deadly to humanoids, but merely stunk to the poison-breathers. Drops of phlegm squeezed from the edges of his bug eyes and formed into little pellets that rolled off his face and fell to the ground, sometimes shattering. Everywhere he walked, his huge, acidic footsteps coldly burned patches on the ground and the toughest floor-coverings alike.

To a humanoid, Chak made Nadreck appear handsome in contrast.

Nadreck stuck out a tentacle in greeting, offering to exchange touches knowing that such an offer would be spurned. Chak had a reputation for being one hundred percent antisocial and so completely selfish that he would do absolutely any despicable thing for a profit. He was, therefore, the most infamous butcher of all the henchmen of the Eich. He was precisely the sort of creature that Gharlane would have used if he had decided to go toward this end of the First Galaxy instead of to the star Thrallis in the Second.

The telepathic interchange with Chak was very guarded. Nadreck presented his proposition, suggesting a neutral meeting place where their bartered goods could be transferred. Nadreck was somewhat apprehensive to be dealing with Chak without his Lens, for Chak was as shrewd, sly, and sharp as Perbat was stupid. For one brief moment Nadreck considered equivocating, retreating, and giving up his plan; instead, he calculated the chances of his discovery at a thousand to one odds against, and he judged that the risk to his life was negligible. This was a bit of a surprise to himself. Heretofore he had never acted unless the odds were a million to one in his favor. Anyhow, he would take the plunge into testing the wily Chak's intuition and understanding.

"This ugly old fellow," Nadreck said to himself, "is not going to creep into my mind. If he knows where I have my stuff hidden, he'll simply kill me and take it all. I will not let down the double mental screen around the information in my mind. I will not let down the screens." Nadreck was satisfied that "the ugly old fellow" had picked up those thoughts.

They would serve to misdirect and prepare.

"You know what I want," Nadreck said. "Show me what you have to offer."

Chak opened a travel case and took out an ornamented, round, platinum container.

The gems inside were not many, but they were an odd assortment. Perhaps a dozen were ordinary or a bit above average, and three were exceptionally good. One, however, was extraordinarily exciting. This gem Nadreck tentatively identified as a Zelcon-28 — or higher.

Nadreck pretended moderate interest, although the Zelcon would have made the whole box of jewels a reasonable offer for the goods he claimed to have.

"This is not what I had in mind," Nadreck said. "I am thinking of a Heartbeat."

The phlegmatic mind of Chak burst into a torrent of activity. He babbled angrily. Finally he settled down and said, suspiciously, "Only a dozen entities know of its existence. And whosoever speaks of it to anyone but me will die. Who told you of it? I will kill him."

"I heard it from a Lensman," Nadreck lied solemnly. "He was an agent impersonating a smuggler and died of an overdose of my good stuff." Such things sometimes happened; this was a good story, and Nadreck knew that villains like Chak and Perbat would believe most anything about Lensmen. To have Betical dare to mention a Lensman was almost proof that what he said was true.

Chak's conceit had been tickled.

From under frost-covered green material that could have been either Chak's own natural growth or a piece of clothing, he drew out an icy-beaded pouch. From it he took the only Heartbeat gem Nadreck had ever seen. It was an ebony-black pea, so black that not a single wave of visible or invisible light was reflected by it.

"It is cold, now," Chak said. "But when I feed it warm meat, it comes alive. I have seen it come to life a score of times. And the memory is pleasant."

Nadreck read the pictures flashing from Chak and was horrified.

The bloody body of a Tellurian.

The mangled corpse of a Chickladorian.

The dismembered parts of a Vegian.

The maimed carcass of a Klovian.

The mutilated cadaver of a Radeligian.

. . . And more, more, more.

All Galactic Patrolmen.

The Heartbeat was a crystalline gemstone whose optimum temperature was 15 to 35 degrees Celsius. The Heartbeat, black and inert in the cold, would slowly transform itself in the warmth of a humanoid atmosphere: from rose-pink to blood-red, it was round outside but intricately faceted within, and it pulsed. It beat in rhythm with the beating heart of the wearer. Yet, if no living creature with pounding heart was near, it would still click irregularly, as though measuring the irregular passage of the cosmic rays. Its essence was impeccably harmonious, and the measured logic of its existence unaccountably stirred the dispassionate Nadreck. What was horrifying was how, in the past, Chak had made it blossom into beauty.

He would place it on the tortured or dying body of a captured Patrolman, whether soldier or Lensman.

Chak lived to see the Heartbeat gemstone come to life — marking the approaching death, and death, and after death of his hated enemies.

Only a superior being such as Nadreck was capable of masking the blazing intensity of his feelings. Palainians were stern and tough and shockingly insensitive in contrast to the warm-blooded men, but they were not cruel, nor, beneath their icy skin, uncompassionate. So Nadreck was emotionally distressed, as he had never been before. His anguish was so soul-searing that he vowed at that moment never to be so susceptible to such empathic pain again; for as long as he lived, he would present the face of a brusque, somewhat dour and surly, archetypal Palainian.

The images of the ghastly, heinous crimes that this barbarian was so proudly permitting to be read in his mind were shrewdly calculated to serve a purpose. Nadreck immediately understood that. Chak used them as a rude shock to lure an undercover Patrolman or Lensman into revealing himself. That it was a successful ploy was sickeningly evident.

Nadreck's composure never waivered. It was as if he had not glimpsed a thing.

"It is an unimpressive looking bit of stone," Nadreck said flatly. "I expected more." He sounded convincingly disappointed. "However, throw it in with the rest of the jewels and it's a deal."

"Yeah, sure," Chak said. "Now, Betical, it's time for you to show us your stuff. We'll take my ship to wherever you say." Chak put away his pouch. As he started to close the lid to the container, Nadreck said, "I'll just hold one of those stones now, that Zelcon, if you don't mind," and pocketed it in his belt.

Chak did not object. Chak, Nadreck knew, was planning to take it back, and everything else, too, including Nadreck's life.

"Yes, Betical," Perbat blustered, feeling left out of the negotiations, "show us your stuff."

Nadreck proceeded to do just that, but not in the manner that was expected.

While they were waiting for the Patrol to complete their search of Chak's private vessel, making the inspection much more thorough than a routine one, Nadreck made as if to excuse himself to pick up his bag but was obliged to let Chak and Perbat and a handful of Chak's guards crowd into his transient room.

Nadreck's bag was opened, as he watched, and the few items examined, after which the locked jewel box was placed before Chak for his consideration.

"These are some of my own precious jewels," Nadreck explained. "Like you, I carry my favorites with me. Open the case and perhaps we may have future business with them."

Chak was constantly alert for trouble.

"Give Perbat the key, Betical," he said. "Now, Perbat, open the case."

When the lid swung back, Perbat gasped with pleasure. "Look, Great Chak! Jewels that glow with their own fires!"

Indeed, in that square, dark cubicle of a room, they radiated frequencies that these dim-sighted or blind inhuman creatures could sense and even partly see.

Perbat plunged his hands into the collection.

The scream that came from his many lips was abruptly ended with his death rattle. His fingers had touched the Palainian's lethal trap — Nadreck's Lens, whose contact was deadly when not worn by him, the Lensman for whom it had been created.

Nadreck was prepared for what followed. As the Lens flew up into the air under the convulsive jerk of Perbat's hand, Nadreck grabbed it. Using the Lens, which in his own knotted fist had become the supercharger of his already extraordinary mental powers, Nadreck struck down Chak in a paralyzing mental blow. Simultaneously, a telepsychic grenade smashed the dazed guards into senselessness. Under their bodies sprawled the permanently crippled Chak — temporarily in a coma, but forever shattered.

At Nadreck's Lensed call, Patrolmen swarmed all around the area. The doltish guards of Perbat were arrested, the private vessel seized, and the unconscious body of Chak sealed in a dureum vault for transporting.

In a pocket in one of Nadreck's belts rested the pouch with the Heartbeat jewel. The wedding gift for Clarrissa was secure, and though she would never be told of its grisly history, someday, no doubt, she would learn to appreciate it even more as a semiliving memorial for all the brave Patrolmen who had died in the Service.

"About Chak," Nadreck said, explaining to the assembled Patrolmen the importance of the criminal, "I want him shipped unharmed to Prime Base on Tellus. I will personally inform the Port Admiral." And, he mused to himself, I will personally inform Kinnison by a note in a gift-wrapped package.

Chak was Nadreck's special wedding present for Kinnison.

Nadreck knew that for such a dedicated man nothing would be more auspicious for the happy occasion of his marriage.

As for Nadreck, he had the magnificent Zelcon to add to his collection.

Nadreck didn't for one moment consider that he was stealing property rightfully belonging to the Patrol. He considered it, as any normal Palainian would, fair payment for his trouble.

Cadets Show Their Mettle

THE FAT FACE OF THE FIRST
Minister of Noyyon turned a foul shade of orange from his
fierce emotion. His humanoid figure sprang to its feet, one
fist pounding the wooden table, the diaphanous folds of his
chain-mail regal robes swirling.

"I say it's war!" The First Minister glared at the rest of
his Council of Twelve. The other faces were various hues
of yellow, ochre, and orange, depending on the intensity
of their feelings. Their little black eyes shifted back and
forth from one to the other. "I say, no more talk! It is time
to act! Vote!"

The eyes of the war cabinet were fixed on him as they
turned their bicolored cubes beneath their outspread right
hands. One half was white, the other half was black. White
end up was a yes vote; black end up was a no vote; sidewise
was for abstention. One by one they turned and twisted the
rectangles and put them down.

A black, a white. Two whites, a black. Around the table
went the display of votes. Twelve votes. Six white, six black —
a tie. The fate of the Northern Hemisphere, whether or not
they were to be bombed by air and sea and thereafter invaded
by the amphibious forces of Noyyon, now depended on the

First Minister himself. There was no doubt about the way he felt; he had been tenaciously in favor of conflict from the start. He turned his cube so that the white side was up.

"War it is!" The First Minister was jubilant. His resolution had passed by seven to six. They had begun the morning discussion with only two council members on the minister's side, six undecided, and five adamantly opposed. He had swung four to his side and had cast the deciding vote. The Council had made the fateful decision, carefully weighing the arguments for and against. At least, that is what the minister believed.

Actually, the vote had been unduly influenced, not by the native Noyyonese leader, but by the alien Lensman from Palain, Nadreck.

Nadreck and his half-dozen Palainian cadets had nudged the undecided ones into the minister's corner.

The Boskonian planet of Togra, home of the Noyyonese and other humanoid races, was now about to tear itself apart and become a hindrance, rather than a help, to the revival of Boskonia through the new organizing force of the Spawn. The supplies for the economy of the Spawn confederacy and the rebuilding of the pirate ships and the privateers would be disrupted. The degeneration of the Boskonian menace after the recent fall of the Second Galaxy to the Galactic Patrol would be accelerated by this one small action of Nadreck and his trainees.

Nadreck and his young cohorts had been fifty miles removed from the Noyyonese House of Ministries when they had silently exerted their influence on the council members. The Palainians had been assembled in the central room of their special GP training ship, *Sapphire*, which had been parked in the wooded mountain clearing where it had quietly landed a week before. Nadreck had sent out his mental probes earlier, as they had circled the planet, and had chosen this point for their Palainian Academy exercise. There had been many opportunities for them to sow their insidious seeds of dissension on the planet Togra, but Nadreck had picked the most propitious one.

"I congratulate Cadets One, Two, Three, and Five for your successes. I commend Cadets Four and Six for your excellent attempts and note your humiliation and despair. This has been a very successful exercise, and you all have passing grades, although in the future Four and Six will have extra field training and additional chances to practice."

Nadreck was nestled in his soft cushion in the center of the group, the six Palainian cadets from the Z-Academy of Palain VII in various attitudes around him. Nadreck's special training party numbered three Palainians, one apo-Onlonian, one apo-Eich'on, and one Kinchook. They were all more or less males except for the Kinchook, who was female — all Kinchookian males died at mating time. To each other they looked solid and distinct, appearing in their true form, which certainly no humanoid had ever comprehended, nor ever would, because of that peculiar metabolic extension into the hyperdimension.

All of them were Z-types, naturally — a requirement for any cadet for admittance to the Z-Academy, which Nadreck had helped found — but the Kinchook was somewhat different chemically and physically. Whereas the others had the usual cartilaginous vertibral column passing through the center of the horizontal torso off which, like branches of a tree, came the many appendages, the Kinchook was more like a Rigellian. The Kinchook had a leathery, chitinous exoskeleton with tentacles anchored to her shell. Unlike the Kinchook, the others' upper limbs were "arms," many jointed and so flexible as to appear like tentacles, the lower ones being stiffer and thicker. All had their heads, or brain cases, sitting on top of the torso with orifices for eating and breathing. The vestigial eyes now were the centers of their perceptual senses. None of the cadets had a distinctive visual color, but the Palainian aura was characteristic for types from different environments and helped Palainians easily recognize each other as individuals. Their body sizes ranged from four feet tall to eight feet tall, depending on the mood of the entity or its mode of movement. If a humanoid could have seen more clearly, he would have been startled to find the Palainian shape, not utterly amorphous, but vaguely anthropoidal, with a triplicated torso having three double-joined arms topped by a trilocular head with compartmented brain, and quadruplicated from the hips down with four double-joined, many jointed legs.

"We have concluded our training on this planet," Nadreck said. "I am both pleased and disappointed. I am disappointed because we have not discovered the Boskonian mastermind controlling this world of Togra. I am still convinced that the Dregs of Onlo are its corrupters. Perhaps another time and another place will lead me to the Dregs."

Nadreck's ability to turn frustration into a renewed dogged persistence was clearly felt by the cadets. They knew that, with the infinite patience of a Palainian, he would simply try and try again until he reached his goal. Of the six, those who most appreciated and understood Nadreck's disappointment in not uncovering the puppet-masters of Togra were the dissenter Eich and the maverick Onlonian, known as Two and Three. The apo-Eich'on and the apo-Onlonian were two of Nadreck's special recruits, whom he had picked out as potential candidates after diligent mind-searching around the Krish-kree system. As kin to two of the most evil races that acted for the as yet undiscovered Eddorians, this pair of cadets was Nadreck's particular interest. Developing them into Lensmen who would be distinctly different living weapons fighting for the Patrol would enormously gratify the Second Stage Lensman from Palain. But above all, Nadreck had plans to use them in his pursuit of his "personal" enemies — the fugitive Onlonians and those even more sinister ones, Eichwoor and the Eich, who bothered his friends, the Second Stage Lensman Worsel and the robotic Lensman Kallatra.

"However," Nadreck said, "as far as you would-be Lensmen are concerned, we have achieved a total triumph. Togra will deteriorate into a dark age, and, when it has purged itself, its people will be ready to rise to the standards of Civilization. We have upset three governments, sabotaged the Boskonian research station of advanced sciences, and have now started a war that should become worldwide. What is the most important lesson you have learned from all this?"

"That the fire people or Tellurian types," One replied, "can be made to arrange their own destruction."

Two then spoke up quickly: "That we have the power to sit safely in our own environment and send our minds out to do the damage."

"I agree with Two," Three said. "But the emphasis is one of mental power versus material power, in which the Lens of Arisia and higher stage training may eventually completely replace all technologically based weaponry."

"It is interesting that both of you, Two and Three," Nadreck said, "should be thinking of mental power and its superiority over material power as the most important points. As you are apo-types, one from the strain of Eich and the other from the strain of Onlo, you have the queer reliance on technology in opposition to mental powers. I have long sensed that the Eich, for instance, have been unduly influenced by perhaps some higher authority into reliance on technology. I say this is in contrast to the echelons of Civilization that have been tending, in the course of evolution, to replace technology with paraphysics and psionics. Someday we will have to apply our Z-techniques of study, dissection, and analysis to the racial lines of the Onlonians and the Eich."

"I think the most significant thing I've learned in this exercise," said Four, "is the vulnerability of the humans and the humanoids to their own self-destructive thoughts. They are strange creatures who are overwhelmingly concerned with others, mistakenly believing that a profitable selfishness grows out of envy and jealousy, when, in fact, they should treat their rivals unemotionally."

"That is very true, Four," Nadreck said. "They think we are cowardly, lazy, egocentric, or conceited and often all these things, when we are simply logical and pragmatic. They are, I'm afraid, often mentally unbalanced. You have found a truly important understanding. I am pleased."

"What has surprised me, Nadreck," Five said, "is the self-deception of human beings who are supposedly intelligent. Are Tograns untypical of humanoids?"

"No, Five," Nadreck said. "Even Tellurians are this way. Tellurians have greater self-control, but they still have very strong similar feelings. This planet of Togra is very much like Tellus used to be before space flight was invented, and it's been kept isolated and planet-bound by Boskonians for reasons of slavery. This section of the Second Galaxy has a thousand Togra types for our experimentation and their eventual edification. We are thus fortunate to be able to study barbaric humanoids without embarrassing our friends."

"Surely Kimball Kinnison does not think this way?" Five asked, incredulously, glimpsing the truth. He was looking forward to becoming a Lensman and then meeting with, perhaps even working with, the legendary Galactic Coordinator.

"Oh, but he does," Nadreck said. "Kinnison is most remarkable in being logical, like a Palainian, but uncomfortably flustered about our truths. He always seems to be emotionally fighting his savage self. You will certainly find him fascinating, almost unbelievable, when someday you meet and work with him."

"The others have said what I would have said," Number Six, the Kinchook, commented. "However, the idea I have found most profitable is that all lifeforms have free-thinking minds and honestly believe themselves to be the clearest thinkers who are closest to the absolute truths of life. I hadn't realized humanoids were capable of such complex and profound thought, even if muddled and erroneous."

"Oh, human beings are not to be underestimated," Nadreck said. "Even the barbarians have strange moral codes. You may not be able to follow their rules, but you must understand their ways."

"Yes, Nadreck," the Kinchook said, "that seems to be a problem for me. That is why I did not sway my Noyyonese enough to make him vote for war. He believed it was wrong. He seems to be anti-Boskonian, and his principles are strong. Therefore I am bothered that he will suffer with those who deserve to suffer. I think Four found a similar situation. Shouldn't we try to help such humanoids? I mean help them instead of abandoning them?"

"That is an interesting philosophical point, Six," Nadreck admitted, "but not a Palainian one. To us, everyone on the wrong side is equally wrong. He will go along with what is wrong, and therefore he, too, is wrong. We do not attempt to save such entities, we simply eliminate them."

"I am uneasy about your argument, Nadreck. Can it be that I am not worthy to be graduated and receive my Lens of Arisia?"

"Not at all, Six. Not at all," Nadreck was unmoved. "You have an affinity for the warm-blooded, human sense of compassion, and, of course, your religion is far different from mine. You will make a good Lensman, able to work closely with the fireheads."

The Kinchook then proposed a startling idea: offer her council member the choice of leaving Togra or staying to face the devastating wars. The proposal, she said, should be simple: join the "aliens" for a trip to another world and be a pampered "guest" in laboratory confinement for as long as he was happy. Back on Palain VII the Academy could profit immensely from having a live humanoid barbarian to study.

"That is a provocative idea, Six," Nadreck said. "That

council member is the cleric of highest rank for their official church. If he were to come to the Academy, the entire Galactic Patrol, as well as our Chaplain General, could be the beneficiary. Yes, we will put the question to him."

"Why not just take him?" the apo-Eich'on asked.

"Perhaps we will do just that," Nadreck said, "but we would be best served by having him volunteer and thus encourage his cooperation."

Nadreck, now thoroughly familiar with the Noyyonese culture, swiftly contrived a plan to tempt the Noyyonese high official, called Gronitskog. As the six cadets observed, the Lensman's mind sought out Archbishop Gronitskog within the government offices and then firmly yet softly shaped a thought and sent it into the Noyyonese's head.

"I must get out of here, " Nadreck whispered. "I must find a lonely place to think. I will go into the park and think what I should do." These thoughts caressed the humanoid's mind, insinuating themselves down into his unconsciousness. "I must go into the park and pray."

And while the six cadets watched through their senses of perception, assisted by their master, Nadreck, they saw Gronitskog make his way through the corridors and the exits and the gates into the adjoining park lawn.

Then Nadreck threw over the area a zone of compulsion, masking from all but Gronitskog the event that followed. From the sky came a whirling aircraft. It was the Palainian ship, *Sapphire*, appearing in a form — as suggested by Nadreck in the humanoid's mind — from contemporary Noyyonese lore. The real, though distorted, image was immediately recognized.

"The disk from the sky!" the man said, recognizing and naming in his own tongue the legendary flying saucer of humanoid cultures. The man wanted to turn and run, but Nadreck encouraged his paralysis of wonderment.

"Gronitskog!" Nadreck placed a call in the excited brain. "We come from another world and we give you a choice." The choice, Nadreck explained, was that the man could either keep his present, uncertain life or embark on a new adventure in the stars. Nadreck had no fear of disclosing forbidden information, so he told the truth of the Z-Academy and what it would mean to the humanoid. Nadreck did not speak of gods, nor did he mention the actual place or the Galactic Patrol or the Lensman; any future monitoring Boskonians would come to their own bewildering conclusions.

Nadreck was already planning for Gronitskog — the Togran humanoid, archbishop of Noyyon, uncommitted Boskonian dupe — to be assigned, on alternating halfyears, as a resident alien at both the Palainian and Tellurian GP academies. Yet, in his heart, Nadreck had a sense of impending doom. He had no suspicion, however, that it would lead to the exposure of an extraordinary spy within the ranks and at the very heart of the Galactic Patrol.

Because of Gronitskog, Nadreck altered his plan to return directly to Palain VII. He and his band of Z-cadets went to Tellus so that humans at the Academy might examine, indoctrinate, and certify as psychologically fit for duty the volunteer Gronitskog. It was there, in the towering skyscraper, Wentworth Hall, heart of the humanoid Academy of the Galactic Patrol, that by chance they met Kimball Kinnison. The informal conference that followed this meeting of old friends was the beginning of what was to become the death struggle of two galaxies against the pernicious, diametrically-opposed double assault of two preposterous enemies.

A score of variously colored spheres whirled crazily around in the air. They wove themselves into a hemisphere surrounding the small band of Patrolmen, zooming in close for an attack and scooting away. They varied in size from a foot in diameter to nearly three feet, and each one, brilliant in their primary coloring, was studded with gun barrels poking out an inch above their crisscrossed shells. Wisps of smoke from burning oil and powder puffed from each muzzle as it fired.

Lieutenant Benson Cloudd, sweat streaking his face, turned and dodged and fired again and again. Sometimes he was in front of his charges, six young men in the spotless silvery gray uniforms of Academy cadets, and sometimes behind them.

The young men were equally busy fighting off the spheres. In their right hands were compact DeLameters sending out short but continuous bursts of energy beams. Half of the beams were tuned for high intensity — thin, flaming rods of enormous power. The other half were set at large aperture, one making a cone-shaped pattern and two forming fans of energy. The cones, with minimal penetration capacity, slowed all approaching projectiles to a walking pace so that they could be picked off by expert marksmanship. The fans were another defensive tactic, exploding the bullets that passed through them. The rods, although used to pick off the shells individually, spent most of their force on offense, raking the sides of the spheres, leaving black marks and slashes with each hit. One energy rod would score on a bright blue ball, another blast would strike a green globe squarely. In each case, there would be a shower of sparks and the attacker would bounce away unharmed. Blue, green, red, yellow, orange — they crowded in.

"Great! Great!" Cloudd was shouting. "Cover each other! Keep moving!"

Like some extraordinarily violent dance, the seven of them were hopping madly up and down and back and forth on the brown-carpeted floor. Most of the time they seemed to be synchronized in an exceedingly well choreographed routine, two or three of them hitting, or nearly hitting, a sphere as it drove in, on them, forcing the attacker to be inaccurate in its fire.

"Keep going!" Cloudd urged, gasping for breath.

"Don't slacken! They'll soon — suffer — power drain!"

One of the cadets was knocked to his knees by a direct hit. The spotless fabric over his left shoulder blade had turned into an ugly brown-and-purple splotch. Two of the others managed to pull him erect with their left arms, never losing their concentration on the flying objects and firing steadily.

Three quick hits were scored by the spheres, on the thighs of two cadets and on Cloudd's right calf. He felt the sting, but no pain. In return, five or six of the globes spit a shower of sparks and spun downward, half out of control, thinning out the strength of the hemisphere.

Every human being was marked with wounds now, except for one red-haired youth. Suddenly, in the middle of his chest, the nasty brownish purple splattering appeared.

"You're dead!" Cloudd shouted. "Stay down!" Although with no visible cue, the remaining six simultaneously moved a few paces to the side, away from the prone body, to clear their footing for the continuing fight. The brown carpet was splashed with dark brown-and-purple stains soaking into the fabric.

The rapid fire from the spheres was intermittent now, growing noticeably weaker. The beams from the Patrolmen's guns were intercepting the projectiles from the spheres almost without fail.

"They're out — of ammunition," Cloudd said. "Ready for — the axe!"

With a prodigious series of bounds, acting as one, the group of six moved several yards to some stacked space-axes.

"Now!" Cloudd commanded.

Their pistols went back into their holsters as each one's left hand reached for an axe.

Cloudd wrapped his huge fists around a tacky handle and hefted his axe, his eyes on the circling spheres. From second to second he and the others dodged the occasional pellet fired at them. They were all in a ring now, axes at the

ready, fending off the spheres, but not seriously striking at
them.

A space-axe in the two hands of a skilled, strong man
is an awesomely deadly weapon. Few, if any, force screens
could deflect the cutting edge of an axe that worked, not
from energetic frequencies, but from sheer physical power.
Its pure dureum mass, thirty pounds perfectly balanced, slid
almost unimpeded through force fields designed to strength-
en with every increase of the megavelocity of a projectile or
the megavolt of a projector. Its molecular-sharp edge would
cut through the strongest personal armor and lightly plated
defenses. No wonder that the most renowned fighting men,
vanBuskirk's crew of Valerian Patrolmen, preferred the space-
axe to any other weapon.

"Now!" Cloudd barked out, and one by one, as the
opportunity presented itself, their blades bit into the shell
of a globe that came too close.

Within a minute the ranks of the balls had been deci-
mated. The remainder whirled about in a spiral and disappeared.

A happy Cloudd threw his axe to the ground and
attempted to embrace the five jubilant cadets who surrounded him. Then, quickly, he moved over to the fallen figure
and helped him to his feet. "Sorry, Djereth," Cloudd said,
"Someone was bound to die. You were it. But you were just
as outstanding in this fight as all the others." He gave the
red-haired young man a playful tap on his chin. "For your
sacrifice, you'll lead the victory parade tonight."

"And you, Lieutenant Benson Cloudd — " came a powerful thought, which they all clearly heard, " — you were
truly magnificent. Foolhardy, but magnificent. Not that my
own young students agree — to them your performance was
rather absurd, if not downright silly for being so contrary
to reason and commonsense. But then, I tell them you are
human."

Cloudd looked up in amazement.

Standing on the platform that encircled the gymnasium, were seven large figures in atmosuits, and one of them had the distinctive markings of a Palainian Second Stage Lensman. Cloudd recognized the suit, confirming his identification of the telepathic thought. He knew who this was, but found it hard to believe that the Palainian was really there.

"Nadreck!" Cloudd burst out, with genuine pleasure.

Reunion at The Circus

"N ADRECK!" CLOUDD REPEATED —
and smiled.

From wherever it was that the Palainian had come, and for whatever reason, he had come in good spirits, playing his little joke. Nadreck was wearing his frivolous Gray Suit. There were six other large figures in atmosuits standing next to him, in their plain metal mummy cases with movable feet, all obviously Z-types, and they made Nadreck's outrageous parody of a Tellurian's Gray Uniform stand out like the proverbial sore thumb. Nadreck didn't wear clothes at home and couldn't wear clothes while associating with the humans, but he expressed his peculiar sense of humor by dressing his light armor or atmosuit with impractical garments and buttons and belts and badges on occasion. He found it particularly effective in making himself seem much less of a monster, and sort of fun, when meeting humans who weren't used to him. After he had created his effect and made his point, much like a heavy nudge in the ribs of his human friends, he would strip off his costume, and with the exception of his Patrolman's rank and the transparent panel, about where a normal heart would be-to display his Lens when necessary — he would be as plain and unadorned as his cadets. Actually

it was all the fault of the dragon Lensman, that mischievous
Worsel of Velantia. Nadreck was noted for his lack of sense
of humor — a condition that was the target for the teasing
banter of Worsel — and this was Nadreck's logical, if heavy-
handed, manner of disarming Worsel and indicating that
humor was not entirely unknown to him.

"Nadreck!" Cloudd repeated, dismissing his cadets with
a wave of his hand. "Where did you come from?"

"I came from my own training exercise. Against a real
foe. With my own six cadets, like yours. I taught mine to
stay out of trouble, not like you. Hand-to-hand combat is
barbaric when one has a good mind — and you do, Cloudd,
even if you aren't a Lensman. With Lenses, why should your
human young ones get into such trouble?"

"Yes, Nadreck," Cloudd sighed, brushing away some of
the brown and purple powder that had dried on his calf. He
had spent a long time in Nadreck's company while they had
been chasing first the Dregs of Onlo through the Kresh-kree
system and then the datadrones at the Pinwheel DW433
nebula with no success. He had been lectured to frequently —
when Nadreck hadn't been completely incommunicado.
Nadreck was a "funny duck" to Cloudd, but he was always
frank, logical, and single-minded. Even with the physical
barrier between them, always forcing one or the other to be
suited up in the other's presence, a masking curtain keeping
them apart, it was difficult for the Tellurian to overcome
his visceral repugnance for the strange entity. The humanoid
races had an instinctive revulsion for the Z-races, worse than
the Homo sapiens had for reptiles. This was reinforced by
the fact that most of the worst of the Boskonian villains
were Z-types or their kin. This sense of rejection was in part
responsible for Nadreck and his ilk being secretive, introspec-
tive, and egocentric. Cloudd ultimately had had a marvelous
time being uninhibited and mentally free, relaxing his iron
composure, because Nadreck was absolutely uninterested in
the man's personal affairs once Cloudd had been classified

and his life-pattern filed away in Nadreck's cavernous mind.

"Please join me in the visitor's lounge tonight, Cloudd," Nadreck said. "We have some talking to do." He turned away and led his cadets back through a door off the balcony.

The visitor's lounge in Wentworth Hall was known discreetly as The Circus because it was round with glassed-in segmented sections like a spoked wheel. The hub of the amphitheater could be utilized alternately by any of the aliens whose segment had been environmentally adjusted. Depending on the number of races or types of aliens in conference, the description was, within the Academy, modified appropriately, such as, "It's a two ring circus today," or "Five rings tonight at The Circus."

When Benson Cloudd arrived that evening, Nadreck was already there, talking mentally through the walls with the Academy Commandant, while the archbishop Gronitskog was in a section by himself. Nadreck was half out of his flexible pressure suit, which he usually wore under his armor. The empty armor, looking like a sarcophagus from which a monster had emerged, was grotesquely resting at an angle in a corner. Through the eddying, frosty soup of Nadreck's atmosphere, Cloudd could see his shifting shape, like a dimly seen deep-sea man-creature. The commandant was in the center and nodded to Cloudd when he came to his front window.

"I've been discussing with the commandant the future of that barbarian over there," Nadreck said, giving Cloudd a mental picture of the dignified humanoid sitting stilly on a chair, a white Academy gown draping him. To Cloudd the alien looked like a Tellurian-Martian with features that suggested a cultured man rather than a barbarian. Nadreck's thoughts quickly filled Cloudd in with the details.

"I have agreed to leave Gronitskog here on Tellus for a few days of examination. I hope he will be sent on to Palain VII to show to our graduating class before they depart in about ten days. I have also requested the commandant to release you as soon as possible in order for you to come to Palain to lecture the upper classes on datadrones. Can you follow me in a few days?"

Cloudd, although accustomed to Nadreck's precipitous decisions, found this one too quick and unexpected even for his own impetuous lifestyle. "Why, ah, that's nice, I guess, Nadreck, but my work — "

"Your work here is completed, Cloudd," Nadreck said imperiously. "You've been here weeks and have lectured on the datadrones, and you've taught everything there is for you to teach. The Z-cadets need to hear of your experiences first-hand. What's to interfere with these plans?"

"Nothing, really, I suppose," Cloudd said. He cocked his head at the commandant. "Perhaps the commandant has some more definite plans for me?"

"No, Lieutenant," the commandant said. "I have no plans for you to be on permanent staff. And there's no appointment being considered for you as an officer trainee for the Lens — you have stated, I believe, that you wouldn't be interested."

"Well . . ." Cloudd said, unsure of what he wanted.

"Then it's settled," Nadreck said. "I'm leaving at midnight. You can follow in two or three days on the monthly shuttle run. Agreed?"

"Why don't you stay for a few days, Nadreck?" Cloudd said, avoiding the question, stalling for time to compose himself, and finding his idea worthwhile even as he broached it. "Stay and see our graduation. This is the third class this year and it numbers over a hundred and twenty. You'll have plenty of time to get back to your own graduation ceremonies, which, I understand, aren't held for another week or ten days."

"No, Cloudd," Nadreck said. "Thank you, but I must return. Before I do, however, I want to know the latest about the datadrones. Sit down, Cloudd. I'll be with you in a moment."

Cloudd idly watched Nadreck conclude the conversation with the commandant and considered what he had to say. Over a year had passed since the phenomenon of the datadrones had brought him into contact with the highest echelon of the Galactic Council and its Patrol. His independent studies of the plague of probes that had flooded through the First Galaxy had led to his commissioning in the Special Missions Forces, changing him from the independent space rover known as D. D. "Double-dee" Cloudd into Patrol Technician Class Triple-A, then into Lieutenant Benson Cloud. He had tracked them, caught them, and dissected them, but he had not solved their mystery. Where did they come from and where did they go to? He and Nadreck had scoured the Pinwheel sector for a trace of them and had failed. They had simply evaporated.

That they had headed out of the galaxy toward Andromeda had never been confirmed. Cloudd had wanted to check out a Patrol ship and press on toward Andromeda, too, but going out of the vicinity of the "neighborhood," meaning the two galaxies of Civilization and their satellite galactic clusters, was absolutely forbidden by all the highest authorities. That in itself was a mystery that bothered Cloudd. So, he had spent the past half year establishing a Department of Datadrones for Kinnison and the Galactic Council, sometimes prospecting by himself for the elusive datadrones, but most of the time overseeing the compilation of all reports and statistics concerning these information-collecting machines that had appeared, seemingly from nowhere, for a year or so and then vanished as inexplicably as they had come. He knew nothing more now than he had when he had last met with Nadreck. The only thing that had changed was his attitude. He was fed up with the paperwork, he was bored stiff with the lecturing, and he was dying to get out on the trail once more, cold and dead as the trail was.

When the commandant had gone, taking Gronitskog with him, Nadreck turned back to Cloudd and found the

Tellurian worked up into a consuming desire for a change of scene and action.

"Perhaps," Nadreck said, "after you do your briefing next week at Palain, I will arrange for some of my cadets, my new Lensmen, to make one more search. Perhaps, I say, Cloudd. It will be up to you to inflame them with the desire to pursue this course of action."

"I will!" Cloudd vowed. "I damn well will!"

"Good," Nadreck said. "I must confess that the Z's and the Z-oid's are not easily inspired. They do not have the burning enthusiasm that you and other Tellurians, especially Kinnison, can develop. If you can inspire them, I will be much pleased and I will help you in every way to make your work meaningful, too."

"What shall I prepare for?" Cloudd asked, He had heard rumors of what the Z-Academy was like from the Tellurian cadets, but he knew he could not believe any of the stories.

"Let me show you," Nadreck said. "Relax and follow my thoughts."

Cloudd was suddenly in an utterly dark place. "You are underground in Palain VII," Nadreck explained. "Look with your eyes and feel with your senses so you can understand, but I will have to help you a bit." In Cloudd's mind's eye, the scene grew bright with lights. "We have no lights, of course, but for you it will seem we have." The classrooms were inter-locking, randomly joined boxes, like a mass of square-shaped soap bubbles. "They are solid on three sides, but for you they will seem transparent," In the cells, sitting, moving, some-times upside down or spread out on walls, were the cadets. Occasionally one would flow down from one half-open side into another cell or would attenuate itself upward into a cell above. Everywhere there was equipment in strange designs, all transparent, and seeming to be as multidimensional as the Z-cadets themselves. "The machinery is not that way, really, but I have made it easier for you to see."

Cloudd could recognize the instructors by the silvery harnesses that passed around and in and out of their bodies. Most of the entities looked alike, varying only slightly in size, much like Nadreck, obviously Palainians, But there were other monstrosities there, too. They were more strange and more grotesque than any entity Cloudd had ever encountered. The variety of Z-life impressed him. "They are only a few of the billions from thousands of Z-types, I must humbly confess," Nadreck said. "We are lucky to get even a minimum for our recruiting purposes for our standards are high and the personal motivation is not at all as natural as it is with you Tellurians."

Through Nadreck's mind, Cloudd moved rapidly around the warren of rooms and came, for the first time, to a corridor that had separate doors. Behind the walls were a half dozen or so other lifeforms in their own environments, a couple of A's, Q's, T's, and a VWZY and other mixed types. "Yes, they are 'cages,' as you immediately think, but they do get out in pressure suits, and they do have recreational leaves when needed, and, please note, there are already two Tellurians temporarily on the staff, so you will have companionship. One is of the female sex, so you may find a mate, who knows?"

"Fascinating," Cloudd said. "I'm not interested in a wife." He thought of the bride he had almost had who had died because of the zwilnik pirates. "Besides, she's probably interested in the other Tellurian considering the circumstances," Cloudd added, drily.

"That is true," Nadreck said. "I was only suggesting that a new combination might make new possibilities. Do you really find this picture I have shown you so depressing?"

"Well, let's say, it's an acceptable starting point. It will be new, it will be different, and it will lead to our renewed chase of the datadrones, won't it, Nadreck?"

Cloudd, now brightening at the prospect of adventure, took less than a day to wrap up all his loose ends.

When evening had come, just after the final supper hour when the graduating class had sung their traditional songs in the mess hall, Cloudd went to his quarters for his last minute preparations and an early bedtime. The following day would be a full one for him. There would be the graduation ceremonies in the morning and in the afternoon he would be boarding the shuttle run to Palain VII, the last one for a month.

He was relaxed, his feet up on a cushion, listening to the life of the Academy, when he got the call to go to The Circus. His door had been open and the off-duty sounds from The Shaft came sharply to his ears. Five hundred feet up, from a wing of the topmost, ninetieth floor, came the jubilant sounds of the noble Five-Year Men, those who would be graduating on the morrow. The Shaft was twenty feet square, with ninety balconies without railings, the hollow core of the magnificent, dazzling chromium and glass tower of Wentworth Hall. The Shaft was filled with floating students in jump belts going and coming along its passageway, but there was no noise from them, for the graduating cadets were ruling this week. Only they were allowed to be heard, and the joyous laughter and shouts and occasional, spontaneous renderings of "Our Patrol" were as thrilling to the underclassmen, who anticipated the day when they would be up in the Eyrie.

Cloudd felt the moment keenly. He hadn't been in the Hall for even one, short semester, but he had been caught up in its traditions. There was gnawing within him the desire to come here and earn the Lens, but he knew that he could never, space-bitten veteran as he was, ever share in the youthful enthusiasm of these exceptional young men. He would never "drop free" on commencement day. He would never, no never, as much as he dreamed it, step from the top floor for that glorious free-fall to the ground, The dizzying, breathtaking plunge like a human stone was a thousand feet straight down, Only a graduating classman could take it — timed to an exquisite finish with heels a fraction of an inch above the marble floor as inertia was snapped back on by the steady hand at the uniform belt.

"Lieutenant Cloudd," the message had come. "Your presence is wanted in the visitor's lounge."

When Cloudd walked down the steps of the amphitheater, through the staff section, he found the two glass doors leading into the Hub were wide open. Inside the Hub there were two dozen people, all Tellurians, but when he raised his head and glanced at the enclosed sections, he saw that one was occupied. Through the reddish-blue, frozen haze of Ring-One he saw Nadreck.

Nadreck! The Palainian should have been gone two days ago!

"I've been waiting for you, Cloudd. You are not going to get much sleep tonight. You will be meeting with your friends now, but shortly we will be having a conference."

Cloudd pressed courteously through the outer line of people in service uniforms milling around and caught sight of the aging form of the most powerful man in Civilization, Port Admiral Hayes, the president of the Galactic Council!

Next to him was the chaplain general of the Patrol, Chon, in a black civilian suit! Who was that he was talking to? It was! The slim figure with the silver face was the robotoid woman Lensman, Lalla Kallatra! A flush of mixed irritation and pleasure burned through him. That bizarre and disturbing Lalla Kallatra!

A greater shock, however, came from the recognition of the sturdy, broad-shouldered figure behind her. Impeccably dressed and groomed, his dark hair sweeping across his broad forehead and his jutting chin thrusting from a stiff collar that glittered with braid and badges, it had to be . . . The ruggedly handsome face, stern and humorous at the same time, turned toward him. Their eyes met. The man raised his hand in casual greeting. This was the person Cloudd most admired, the hero of the galaxies, Kimball Kinnison! Kimball Kinnison, himself!

Cloudd opened his mouth to speak a welcome, but the Galactic Coordinator had turned away to talk to someone else.

What in the devil was Kinnison doing here? Why was Nadreck still here? Wasn't that —? Yes! That was LaForge, admiral of the Grand Fleet! Why all the notables?

"Hello, Lieutenant Cloudd," said a soft, but powerful voice.

Cloudd turned. The small, iron-gray beard and the florid face belonged to Chaplain General Chon, and Cloudd stammered out a greeting. The first thing Cloudd said, impulsively and to his embarrassment, was, "What is Kimball Kinnison doing here?"

"He's come to see his son, Christopher. You know about the baby's training, of course?"

"Yes . . . That is, I believe . . . *infans vitae* . . ."

"That's how it's formally known, through most human cultures, that is. More popularly, it's the Better Baby Course — that's what we call it. You ever had any experience with children, sons or daughters, I mean, nieces or nephews, perhaps?"

"No," Cloudd said. All the pain of his past life with Lucille surged up to choke him. He had had his dreams with her — marriage and children. Almost on the eve of their marriage the pirates had killed her. Nearly three thousand entities had died when the space liner had been cut to pieces by the Spawn raider. There had been one survivor; ironically it was the owner, the man whom the vindictive outlaws had really wanted to destroy — D. D. Cloudd. The wonder of it came to him again, and the torture — why was it that he lived and that such a pretty, sweet, innocent girl as Lucille had died? His subsequent wild career as an adventurer along the spaceways, in and out of the Patrol, had healed the wound, but left a tender scar. "Lucille and I would have followed the Better Baby practice, of course."

"I am sorry, Benson," Chon said, his cheeks even more flushed with distress. "I phrased that awkwardly. Forgive me. I know how much you loved her."

"No, no," Cloudd said, "I'm the culprit. It was all the recent excitement over Christopher Kinnison's birth that raised the old ghosts. I'm known as the perennial bachelor, so what you said, knowing what you know about me, released those deep down feelings I've built up. Actually, I appreciate your understanding. Anyhow, about the Better Baby Course, I'm not a hundred percent sold on the idea that all geniuses are made, not born. But I'm highly in favor of planned stimulation right from birth. Lucille felt no effort should be spared during the first few months. In fact, she felt that planning before and during her pregnant period was also vital. We had things well thought out, as you can guess. Anyhow, heredity is important, too."

"Certainly. That's still a hot controversy. I take the middle view, of course. Naturally I feel that God still gives us our potential and it's up to us to make the best of it. I go along with the computer analogy up to a point, but someone has to build the computer, for good or for bad, and there are certain preprogrammed things put in the organism — instincts, animating essences, or, if you will, the soul."

Cloudd's mind was drifting off the subject. His thoughts were on Lalla Kallatra. What had she been doing for the past six months since he had briefly seen her when Nadreck and he had skipped through Ultra Prime, the Patrol base on Kinnison's planet, Klovia, the center of the hustle and bustle prevalent now in the Second Galaxy?

"What's Lana Kallatra doing here, sir?" Cloudd said, feeling that Chon would not resent the prying of a lowly lieutenant. "Is she still doing psychical research? Have there been any developments about Eichwoor?"

"Lalla is here as Mrs. Kinnison's companion."

"Mrs. Kinnison? The Red Lensman is here?" Cloudd

swivelled his head back and forth, his dark eyes searching the room, anxious to catch a glimpse of Clarrissa May MacDougall Kinnison, the fabulous first woman Lensman. The expectation he now had of meeting her thrilled him. The fact that Lalla Kallatra was a woman Lensman, too — to his knowledge the only other one in two galaxies, and someone he had worked with — didn't diminish the allure of the Red Lensman one particle. Kallatra was a robotoid — yes, a freak, just a young kid with enormous talent and an unlucky life — but Clarrissa MacDougall was the undisputed beautiful heroine of two galaxies, the female of the legendary matched pair.

"Well, actually," said Chon, "she's at the Institute of Advanced Pediatrics. Visiting Christopher, you know. He's been here for a number of weeks and obviously she's missed him. He's been away from her longer than she'd had him. But now she'll begin her training along with him, and I dare say, knowing the abilities of Mrs. Kinnison and suspecting the abilities of her child, they'll both be returning to Klovia in a few months. I expect she'll come by to see us all before this little social gathering breaks up. You haven't met her yet? You've a real treat in store for you. And incidentally, Benson, I don't believe I've had a chance to say how glad I am to see you. You look fine. Do you like lecturing? Don't you wish you were back out there in deep space chasing those things you were after? I wish I were younger. I'd have chosen a few years of wild adventure. There's so much going on, so many things to do, and I'm afraid I'll never have the chance. You know, these high level visits get awfully dull sometimes."

Cloudd was a bit taken aback by Chon's frank self-revelation. Yet it wasn't so remarkable. Cloudd had a high degree of intuitiveness; he was very sensitive to the person-alities and reactions of people despite his strong attempts to tone down if not ignore this softness in his nature — and Chaplain General Chon had impressed him as being forthright from that very first day in Kinnison's office at

Ultra Prime on Klovia.

"In fact," Chon added, "she's here now."

Cloudd caught a glimpse of the famous red hair, but before he could move closer, there was a shifting of the group in her direction, she was swallowed up in the uniforms, and then she and her husband were moving out the far doorway.

Cloudd turned away, disappointed, and almost knocked down Lalla Kallatra,

Her reaction was swift. Instead of a stiff-legged movement away from him, she apparently activated the wheels under the soles of her knee-high boots and skated a few inches backward out of danger. Their faces had come close to touching and, for an interminably long split-second, her wide eyes had gazed into his. Were those electrifying, bluish-gray orbs of hers real? He had wondered that once before. Surely such deep eyes had to be living cells to affect him so?

"Hello, Cloudd." Her polished metal face, a Lens imbedded in the middle of her shining forehead, could give no expression. From under her cloth skullcap there peeked curls of brown hair. This was something different from how she appeared last time. Vanity, Cloudd thought. The android is typically female. That touch, however, made her seem more human and his feelings warmed toward her.

"Hello, Kallatra. Welcome to the Milky Way." He extended his hand. "How have you been? General Chon tells me you came with Mrs. Kinnison. Will you stay with her while she's here? It's good to see you." He really meant it.

"I'm fine. I hope you have been, too." She made no effort to take his hand in hers. He remembered the cool, hard feel of those metal fingers the last time. "Please excuse me, Cloudd," she said. "Cris has left and I must be with her, I expect to stay a few days, perhaps we'll find a chance to visit." She began to stalk around him.

Cloudd suddenly felt angry. She was snubbing him and no machine was going to do that to him.

He grasped her left shoulder, gently. It was the first time he had touched her, except for their hands, and he was shocked at his audacity. She stopped but didn't turn her head.

"Don't go away mad, Kallatra," he said. He tried to sound lighthearted.

"I'm sorry, Cloudd," she said. "I really do have a lot on my mind. please believe me. I do hope we meet again. Call the Institute tomorrow. Please excuse me. I must go."

And she left.

Cloudd watched her leaving the room, moving stilly in her standard tunic-and-pantaloon uniform.

"Well, I'll be damned," Cloudd said under his breath, his mind in confusion.

"Go along, Cloudd," a voice said within his head. It was Nadreck. "Go along with them."

Cloudd looked up at the compartment Nadreck was in. The monster seemed to be waving his tentacles or arms.

"I'm not invited, Nadreck," Cloudd said. "That's the entrance to the private reception hall. Nobody goes there without an invitation."

"You are invited. I invited you. You will be my representative," Nadreck said. "Don't waste time, Go!"

"You?" Cloudd said, startled, "You invited me? But they have to invite me — don't you understand?"

"I understand. It's been arranged. The conference is to take place now. I'll be there by my sense of perception. You must be there physically. There are documents to look at. What's the matter with you — don't I make myself clear?"

"Oh, yes, Nadreck. You do. I'm sorry." Cloudd shook his head as though to clear it, The whole past half hour had been bewildering. But Nadreck was a Second Stage Lensman, and Nadreck knew what he was doing.

Cloudd went into the room at the end of the long corridor. The reception hall was just large enough to hold the dozen people comfortably. It was luxuriously furnished in ancient earthly style, with thick carpets, upholstered furniture, pictures in gilt frames on the paneled walls. It was a room strictly for Tellurians and their kin, with one wall of full-length wooden folding doors suggesting it could be made larger,

Almost everyone was seated on the soft couches and in the easy chairs when Cloudd came in. Kallatra stood at the far right. Kinnison stood in the center, holding a sheaf of papers in his hand. When Kinnison saw Cloudd enter, he gave him a cheery wave of his hand and a big smile. Then he became serious again.

"We have received these reports since we've been in The Circus," Kinnison said, waving the sheaf of papers to emphasize his point, "and they are all garbled. We have done our social duties in the past hour, We have just the graduation ceremonies tomorrow. I think we can all attend. I believe there is no suspicion as to our real purpose for being here. You have all been convincing in your reasons for coming to Wentworth Hall. Let's keep it this way."

Kinnison leaned against the edge of the heavy table and rested informally in his favorite lecturing pose.

"The garbled reports are proof, if we needed any more. Our machines are playing funny tricks. Patrol communications are in a shambles. We've got interference and aberrations in all our equipment."

Kinnison tossed the papers down next to him and put his hands on his thighs, bending over in that between-you-and-me posture, massive head tilted up, dark eyes under his frowning eyebrows peering at each person individually.

"Friends, we've lost contact with ten percent of our forces on the other side of this galaxy. I concur with the majority of you. This galaxy is about to be invaded by some, as yet, undetectable enemy."

Raiders from Nowhere

HE ELECTRONIC NOISE BEGAN as an inaudible hum and rapidly rose in frequency and amplitude to a skullshattering scream. The entire spaceship quivered under the vibrations, with relays and cutoffs popping open as danger points were reached. One by one, the mixed crew of non-Oxos writhed to the decks and lost consciousness.

Lensman Dick Armstrong, the only one aboard who was A-Oxo, being a Tellurian oxygen breather, was in his pressure suit on his way to the navigation room when the trouble began. As the only one isolated from the environment, the rest of the crew breathing their, to Armstrong, poisonous air and working without clothes, he was among those least affected. By the time he reached the chart room, only the tough old Onlonian navigator, Noc, was still on his loose-jointed legs. Armstrong couldn't speak Onlonian, although he could read and write it, but his Lens sorted out the frantic messages passing between Noc and Finndha, the Palainian captain of the freighter *Palai-kai*.

"Bad trouble, Cap'n!" Noc was not only strongly projecting his concern, he was literally shouting his agitation above the piercing din, blasting messages through the communication pipes. "No collision reported. We ain't hit nothing. All outside readings are normal. The breakdown's inside. My monitors show disruption of the Bergenholm chips. What's Praast say?" Praast was the engineering officer.

"Praast went into the boxes at the first sign that we had a problem and he hasn't come out," the captain replied. "And none of his staff are answering either."

Noc had his upper appendages wrapped around his head and didn't see Armstrong, but he sensed his presence. "Do something for us, Lensman! Use your Lens!"

The situation didn't appear critical, although Noc obviously was in a panic, and there was nothing that Armstrong could do about it anyhow. He had no job as part of the crew. He was simply a Patrolman on rim patrol, autonomous and unfamiliar with the ship's routine, most especially this ship, which he had never been on before.

"It's the damned drive," Noc said. "I told ya and I told Praast the thing would give out one of these days when we're in top free flight. So it's finally happened. Even I can tell that."

"Don't overheat yourself, Noc," the captain said.

"We got two hundred passengers on board," Noc yelled. "And we got another hundred fifty raw, ignorant menials. This scow's a freighter, not a passenger ship — and I'm a navigator, not a pampering chief steward. Whattamuh gonna do when they run riot?"

That explains a lot, Armstrong thought to himself as he heard Noc's complaint. They had insisted on a human for the rim Patrolman to avoid "psychological intimidation of the pleasure-seeking passengers" when actually they were relying on his human ignorance to avoid criticism of their substandard accommodations for their living cargo. Noc was probably right; a serious panic was a distinct possibility.

"Shut up, Noc!" the captain ordered. "Watch your instruments. I've pulled the plug. We're going inert."

This "rim patrol" was supposed to be simple and utterly boring. It was a Galactic Patrol surveillance assignment established around the edge of the Milky Way, carried on most intently on the side toward the Second Galaxy, as an early warning system. With Boskonia so potent in the Second Galaxy, invasion from that direction had been a constant threat before the Patrol had launched its own invasion, fought the Battle of Klovia, and subdued the Second. Now that the level of danger had been substantially reduced, with only small fleets of pirates anticipated, a rim patrol assignment was certain to be dull. The duty was not made any more bearable by the use of nonscheduled, independent, tramp cargo ships to carry the Lensman.

The deep-space freighters, irregularly coming and going over obscure routes, were ideal observation posts for the occasional, unpredictable Patrol surveillance assignments. The vessels, usually small and unobtrusive, curved around the flattened side of the disk of the Milky Way en route from one side to the other, free of the complexities of intragalactic navigation.

Armstrong considered himself lucky to be given even this dull chore. He saw it as a unique opportunity for study and experience to further his forthcoming civilian ambitions to be a consultant in racial psychology for a big transportation company. Nadreck had arranged the special duty for him at his request, still appreciative of the help Armstrong had given him not so long ago on Palainian Research Laboratory Five. That taste of real adventure had made it possible for him to emotionally accept this task, so different and lonely, especially with Z-types.

"Nothing's happening!" Noc said. "My readings're still crazy!"

No sooner had Noc complained than the ship gave a lurch. Noc bounced against his chart table, while Armstrong banged into the wall. Armstrong was shaken but unhurt because of the cushioning of his suit.

"The ship's slipping out," Captain Finndha said. Armstrong rightly took that to mean that the freighter was losing its inertialess mode in an erratic manner, which could end in an atomic explosion. "By Klono, I'm switching back in!"

Buffeting started as the ship wavered between the two states. Under Bergenholm drive, theoretically only the tenuous matter in space prevented the ship from reaching infinite speed. Making top speed, so important for profitable tramp freighter operations, was why this ship and so many like it circled on the outside of the galaxy instead of going through it. Bergenholm "free" speed was in inverse ratio to the density of matter in space. Going around or over the galaxy produced the fastest speeds and the least chance for any surprises. Rim patrol was a quick trip through empty space, at the fastest practical speed, fit for only semiretired, retired, and reserve Patrolmen. Once in a long, long while, however, somebody never came back.

The buffeting stopped.

"We're back into free," the captain said, his voice coming out of all tubes and electric speakers throughout the entire ship. "Check for damage."

The response came back quickly from the regular crew. There were a few minor injuries, but nothing serious.

The report from the hospitality crew, on the other hand, was rather unsettling. "Chief Steward" Noc was told that a couple of crew members were dead or dying and that among the passengers "even worse" had taken place.

Noc pulled an assistant up from the table he had crumpled over, shoved him in front of his control board, and left in a great hurry to straighten out the mess below. The scene on the monitoring screen for the passengers' lounge was distressing even to Armstrong, who under ordinary circumstances had difficulty judging the health or condition of a Z-entity. This freighter had once been primarily a passenger carrier; later, the main lounge had been converted into cargo space; recently, because of the increase in personal travel after the reduction of the Boskonian piracy menace, the cargo hold had been reconverted back into a passengers' salon. The decorations were new but cheap, the furniture was chosen more for durability than beauty, and the floor plan was awkward and led to overcrowding. The result, even to Armstrong, was obvious chaos: grotesque passengers collapsed on chairs and floor, having pulled down the decorations trying to retain their balance, and the lightweight furniture shoved around in a hazardous fashion.

Armstrong was suddenly conscious of something far more remarkable on the exterior monitoring screens.

Space wasn't empty!

Spaceships seemed to be everywhere!

"Noc! Betzman! Riam! Get back to your posts!" The captain's face was on the command viewing screen, his face uglier than ever to Armstrong, undoubtedly distorted by strong emotion. An alarm began to whistle and clang. "Defensive positions! Unidentified mechware!"

Crewmen were crowding into the navigation room, including Noc. There was much excitement, with flashing lights and dozens of glowing visualizations on all the screens. Armstrong was roughly shoved into a corner and ignored while he kept probing the minds around him with his Lens, trying to find out what was happening. He had the clear and universal impression that whatever was happening was unexplainable and frighteningly mysterious. The Lensman projected his telepathic feelers out into space in search of any other sentient beings, but he felt no response. He checked his Ordovik crystal detector; the reading was negative — no hyperspatial tube nearby.

"Stand by!" Captain Finndha said. "Stand by for inert!" The captain was bringing the freighter out of free flight into inertia. Like everyone else, Armstrong braced for the expected jolt when the shift took place.

Again there was a shock that unpleasantly shook the

ship. Armstrong could imagine the additional pandemonium and injury among the terrified passengers.

"Curses of Klono!" the captain exclaimed. "The damned things have dropped down along with us! We're headed upstream into the thick of them! Deflector screens full on! Collision course! Prepare for deflections! Prepare for collisions!"

Noc had all the screens focused outside, from visible light frequencies on down to supraetheric. Moving swiftly past the freighter were objects of assorted sizes and various shades of silver. They vaguely resembled torpedo-shaped spaceships. No identification markings were visible.

"All gravity fields reverse! Check! All engines reverse!"

Armstrong had barely time to grab a handhold before the artificial gravitation began fighting the inertia of the deceleration process. He felt as if his arms were going to be dragged from their sockets. Captain Finndha was slamming on full emergency stop, trusting that the gravity field reversal would be working properly to prevent every loose object within the ship from being squashed flat against the forward bulkheads. Good God! Armstrong thought, if the fields weren't operating properly in the passengers' quarters, they would have their already shapeless masses mashed into puddles of jelly. The captain was shutting down to zero forward motion, jockeying from side to side to avoid the objects that seemed to be on a direct line with him, obviously afraid to make a sweeping turn, which would expose the ship broadside. The silvery projectiles now seemed to number in the hundreds.

Armstrong felt the deck turning under him. The captain was executing a pinwheel turn, rotating the ship on its own axis. This was a fancy maneuver expected from a warship, not from an ancient passenger-cargo vessel!

"Full ahead!" the captain shouted.

The Tellurian Lensman again felt the deck pressing up against him, his body straining to resist the compression.

A full pinwheel turn and a jumping acceleration on a one hundred eighty degree reversal! Some trick! Oh, the poor passengers and their staff!

"Prepare for inertialess drive!" The captain sounded calmer now, although Armstrong had to marvel that Finndha had never lost his self-composure under the assorted problems that a Patrol captain would have found trying. Armstrong swung around slightly, into a more comfortable position, wedged in between the squirming, leathery torso of one of the crew and the wall of the small room. He could still see the screens with their pictures of silvery cigars. The projectiles had slowed down relative to the freighter, which was now picking up inert speed.

Silvery projectiles. What was that? Farther away they were grayer, fading off into invisibility. Their numbers could be infinite, more unseen than those seen. There was an obvious correlation between their appearance and their distance from the ship. The closest ones were the brightest, almost mirrorlike in their sheen; slightly farther away they were silver; far away they were gray, and then almost black. There weren't just hundreds, there were thousands upon thousands!

"Betzman! Where are our rear deflector screens?"

"I put all the power into our front ones, sir."

"Y'damn fool! Our rear is uncovered now. Shunt some power into — "

Crash! The noise vibrated up from the bottom of the ship through air and metal and rattled everyone in the navigating room.

"This is Riam, Captain. The enemy just blew a hole into aft section R. The autoseals have isolated sections Q, R, and S."

"Classification now hostile," the captain informed his ship. "Prepare to repel boarders."

Armstrong, at the first identification of the location of the crash, immediately probed the area with his Lens. His powers were limited to registration of life forces and he could read none.

"This is Lensman Armstrong, Captain Finndha," the Tellurian telepathed. "I've scanned the damaged area. There are no lifeforms."

"Check, Lensman! Do what you can aboard. Also Lens out our position and status and get some help. Riam! Round up some of the purser's men and be ready to arm them to repel boarders. The Lensman says no pirates are aboard, but it may happen in the next stage."

Lensman Dick Armstrong sent out his messages, an official report and a low priority call for help. His calls went back into the galaxy to the chief of the Rim Surveillance Section, but there was added a special signal for Nadreck's attention, which fulfilled Armstrong's promise to "keep in touch." He reported the appearance of unknown craft and the possibility of destruction by chance or by choice. He stressed that there were possibly thousands of unidentified objects, varying in size, but he couldn't be sure what sizes. Having no fixed reference point, they could range from a small space torpedo up to a large freighter. They had not made a hostile move, although damage, by design or accident, to the rear of the undefended freighter had been reported. The unidentified swarms were heading in an angle that would take them into an outer arm of the Milky Way. The freighter might be in need of rescue momentarily. A score of Lensmen picked up his messages for relay on to Operations HQ.

". . . don't know where they came from," Noc was saying. "None of my charts and none of my records show a thing. My guess is that our path crossed theirs in free flight and that they had no instrumentation to notice us, to notify us, or to anticipate overlapping fields of influence that would disrupt both our tracks."

"A chance encounter, in other words," the captain said. "Could be. One of us knocked the other out of free flight and we're still entangled. That means we got bumped accidentally when I pulled back from ramming one of those things we were running down. D'ja hear that, Riam?"

"I heard, Captain. But I'm breaking out the weapons for my party of thirty."

"What?"

"I looked through the autoscal windows. There are things moving around on the other side." Riam was a cold-blooded Ylorian who couldn't raise his emotional level one degree if he were standing in front of an execution squad.

Armstrong immediately looked at the screens that Noc and Captain Finndha had redirected, but they were blank. The assumption was that they had been made inoperative by the collision, but now the situation was uncertain. Armstrong threw his mind into the penetrated area. He did not have the power of perception and there was no lifeform through which he could get any impressions, so he saw and felt nothing.

"Lensman," Finndha said. "Take a look . . ."

"Sorry, Captain," Armstrong said. "I'm unable to find any trace of organic life. There might be other forms or robots. I can't tell."

"Captain!" Noc's shout was painfully sharp. "Captain, look at starboard screens three and four! It's a mammoth spaceship!"

Armstrong glanced above Noc's head. There it was, a huge gray sphere! Ten or twenty miles in diameter, maybe larger, for judging the size was difficult, if not impossible. And beyond it? Beyond it?

"Captain!" This time it was Armstrong's turn to sound, agitated. "There are more than one. I see another beyond it. Darker. Maybe even bigger."

"Yes, Lensman," the captain said. "There are dozens of them."

"Dozens?"

"We can read the screens better than you," Noc said. "Look on the port screens. There are more." He flipped through the entire battery of screens.

"There must be hundreds, Noc," the captain said. "If there are black ones out there, the number could be unlimited."

"Captain," Riam broke in, quietly. "Those things — they're trying to break into the ship."

"Things? What things?" Captain Finndha asked, distracted by the situation outside.

"The invaders."

"The invaders?" Several screens in the navigating room flashed white or gray as he tried to picture something. "We're getting nothing on our screens. Whatta they look like? Whatta they doing?"

"They opened the bulkhead doors and are moving slowly down the main corridor toward the lounge. I can't see too well through the glassports. Looks to me like a hundred spheres about two feet in diameter. They could break in at any of the connecting passageways. I've issued weapons to my group and I've dispatched three maids to cover each doorway. They have no authority to fire until you issue instructions. I recommend I circle around into the lounge and issue weapons to all competent passengers."

"Klono!" the captain exclaimed. "If they start wrecking doors, . . . we'll lose our atmosphere, and we're a thousand personal life-support systems short . . . It'll be murder!"

"That may not be a problem, Captain. They've kept the corridor sealed. They open doors, they don't blast them."

"Boskonians!" the captain said. "Sure as the nine purple hells! Do what you have to, Riam. You have my complete authority . . . Lensman! Who're the enemy? Find out. Use your Lens . . . Noc! I want to know more about those ships outside."

Armstrong had anticipated the captain's request. He had taken the initiative to punch up screenings on the corridor and doorways, without any success. He had carefully sifted through all the mental waves filling the ether, finding the feelings of the inhuman passengers a turmoil of pain. Through all frequencies he found some kind of pervasive interference, going right down partway into thought and etheric wavelengths. The screenings did not hold firm against the Lens, but nevertheless he found nothing he could identify as intelligence. He combed the ship. Then he projected outside and mentally poked at random samplings of everything he could see. Nothing.

Dick Armstrong was a trained Lensman. He hadn't exercised a fraction of his inherent talents and latent abilities; now he summoned everything within his willpower and aimed it at the main deck corridor. He conjured up a two-foot spheroid, and he threw his full energies against it.

He felt something! His sense of power was incredible! The thrill of realizing he was so potent overwhelmed him for a moment. He was showing himself to be a true Lensman, a positive force, not a passive intellectual, and he was very greatly pleased.

The spheroid he visualized bounced away, glancing from one companion to another. Somehow his mental powers had made this happen.

"They're suddenly moving around faster," Riam reported without prompting. "The spheres are kind of excited, but they're pushing ahead at the same rate. I expect the lounge doors to slide open at any moment. I'm here with about a hundred passengers, passing out weapons. I'm using part of my force to police the rest of the passengers and even some of the crew. They're almost insane with fear. I'm going to try to drive them back to their quarters."

Armstrong, elated to be making some kind of positive contribution, was, however, realistically disappointed that nothing was being accomplished. He directed his rudimentary psionic powers outside. He visualized, with the help of the central starboard screen, the nearest silvery cylinder, and strove to penetrate its hull. The cylinder immediately vanished.

Armstrong tried the same procedure on another, larger spheroid. This one seemed to waver and become unstable, but it did not vanish. Could be, the Lensman guessed, they react to inimical thoughts, so the first had gone into free flight and the second one was on the edge of doing it.

The Tellurian shifted his attention to a big cylinder, big enough to be a destroyer-class spaceship. Again he tried to press his mind into the interior. He couldn't. This time he asked, "Who are you? We are friends. We are fellow Boskonians." Amazingly, the side of the ship materialized a huge black emblem, the traditional skull and crossbones! The ship was a pirate! There were other markings, too. This sleek cigar-shaped machine now showed other special numbers and markings in black letters. In red letters was A-ZZ. No doubt about it, this ship was part of an organized fleet. One and all, they were manifestly Boskonian probes, warships, or both.

The strain on Armstrong was too much. He had to drop his concentration. He had, however, found out something important. He reported it to Captain Finndha.

"It figures," the captain said. "The raiding parties are robots. In the past few minutes, while you've been in a trance, they've invaded the lounge and have a smaller party coming through the crew's stairwells toward our control room. They seem to open and close our doors at will. The lounge looks like something out of Dante's Delgonian Inferno. The robots are sucking the life out of our people."

To illustrate what he was saying, the captain put up several screens from the lounge. They weren't white or gray or blank anymore; they displayed incredible visions of a battle and a ghoulish feast going on simultaneously.

In a semicircle, backed against a wall near the doorway to the main corridor, a small party of uniformed and naked monstrosities was blasting away at a wall of globes churning two or three deep. Farther into the lounge were others of the passenger-monsters, as Armstrong now saw them in their primitive crawlings and posturings, in various stages of prostration. Over them hovered scores of the spheres. To Armstrong, they seemed to be *pumping* fluids out of the writhing bodies! The sight was nauseating.

The ray beams slipped off the sides of the globes like sprays of water off greased paper. The globes had many-jointed, sticklike appendages thrusting from sockets at their bases and waving about haphazardly. Some of them had standard GP-approved weapons in their grasp, stuck out at the end of their arm-rods, pointing in every direction and not firing. Some of the globes were dragging passengers off the tops of piles of passengers.

The scene was utter, horrible chaos.

"Lensman!" It was the captain, speaking sharply to get his attention, and shutting down the screens. "What have you heard from the Patrol? We can't raise them on our standard bands."

"I've sent out information and calls for help, Captain."

"Call Nadreck, can you, Lensman? You have the power, you have the authority, you know him — and he knows me. Call him, sir. I implore you. He's got a speedster that can get him here in hours, maybe even within minutes. It's bad enough that I'm going to lose many or all of my passengers, that I'm losing my ship — but I think I'm going to lose my own existence. My lifeboat doesn't stand a purple chance of breaking through all these Boskonians. I'll take you along with me, of course, Lensman, but I think we're doomed. Get that message across to Nadreck, will you? He's a superbody. He's my friend. For my sake — for Klono's sake — get him here now!"

Lensmen Get Their Orders

HE ALARM CLOCK WAS BUZZ-
ing, at first softly, and then more insistently. It was six A. M.

Cloudd groaned, rolled over, turned it off, and put his feet on the cool floor. He was extremely fatigued. His night had been terrible, filled with much tossing and turning and unpleasant dreams.

The evening had not lasted very long, but when refreshments were served, Cloudd had lingered awhile, hoping to talk to Kallatra. He was disappointed to learn that she had excused herself immediately in order to arrive early the next day at the Institute of Advanced Pediatrics, but he did talk to Kimball Kinnison, who always made a point of speaking personally with as many people as possible.

After some chitchat, Kinnison had said, "I understand that you're part of this conference, Cloudd, at Nadreck's request, which makes plenty of sense to me. We're working out assignments tonight to give out tomorrow morning, and you're included, teamed with Nadreck. In you he's got a Tellurian to be close to, one to identify with. Nadreck's always worked alone in the past — he just doesn't mingle well with humans, and no wonder. That goes for Z-types, too — their lethargic ways irritate him. Now, you're the exception.

Since you knocked about together out around Pinwheel, chasing the datadrones, he's got immense confidence in you. And so do I."

"Sir," Cloudd began. If anyone could give him advice, it should be Kinnison — who was concerned with everyone of his men — especially since Cloudd had chosen Kinnison as his standard of excellence. "Sir, I'm not a Lensman and I don't know if I can measure up. If I were on my own I'd be gung ho, but I'm not sure I should accept this duty. Don't get me wrong — I'm not looking to be a Lensman."

"Cloudd," Kinnison said with a laugh, "half the Lensmen I know felt that way. Don't worry about it, just do your job, that's all that's expected of you. Nadreck knows what he's doing, believe me. Trust him."

So Cloudd left feeling better about himself, but worried about the universe — what did it all mean?

Before going to bed, Cloudd softly called Nadreck's name, not wanting to awaken the Palainian if he was resting for the grueling morrow. He wondered what ideas Nadreck, who had monitored the meeting through Cloudd's mind, might have.

"Lieutenant Cloudd." Nadreck, awake, instantaneously entered his mind. "Do you doubt me? Have my past performances been so pathetic that you should question my wisdom? I was hurt by your expression of doubts to Kinnison concerning my choice of you."

Cloudd was surprised and genuinely contrite. "I apologize, Nadreck." He should have put his worries directly to Nadreck without showing disloyalty. "I didn't doubt you, I doubted myself. But you are right."

"We are both at fault, I more than you. You doubted because I failed to convince you of your worth. Remember, I know your capabilities, and you are neither worse nor better than what I know you to be. I reject your apology as unneeded."

Cloudd felt strong again, knowing Nadreck's evaluation.

His self-doubt was vicious and puzzling. Why? Lucille's death had driven him from conventional respectability to reckless space adventuring, facing everything and fearing nothing. Since joining the inner circle of Lensmen, though himself not a Lensman, for no discernible reason he had felt inferior. He was being changed and part of himself resented it. What did he really want to do, to be? Fortunately he was about to see action again. He could decide his future later. He said, "No apologies on either side, then, Nadreck. I'm QX and I'm with you."

"Good. You Tellurians are complex creatures, and we do not think alike. Tell me always when you have misgivings so that I may understand you. We do not have the same intuition, as you are Tellurian and are different, and that is why I chose you. I do not need nor want a Lensman.

"Now let me tell you how this has all come about. You Tellurians have a need to know things, and you are a fine specimen of a Tellurian, intelligent yet irrational, optimistic while pessimistic, stupid yet brilliant. But it is your intuition that I need, Tellurian intuition, and you do have it to a remarkable degree.

"This conference was brought to my attention by accident. I came to the Academy just as it was happening. This is a Tellurian conference, because the Tellurians and their humanoid relations seem to be most affected. I have not solved that riddle yet — although I believe it has something to do with you humans having the best technology and therefore are prime targets.

"This Tellurian conference is top secret, but having inadvertently become aware of the basis for it and because I am a Second Stage Lensman, and at hand, I was invited. I don't think I was really wanted there, even telepathically, for diplomatic reasons and as a matter of precedence. My presence is considered premature. That is why you are my representative, my Tellurian representative. President Haynes, and Kinnison, too, now consider my presence fortuitous — they did not invite me by slighting others — and the first rule of absolute secrecy concerning knowledge limited strictly to only those who need to know has been maintained."

Nadreck seemed to be through, so Cloudd thought; "I really don't know what this is all about. I have not been briefed. Should I know? Do I need to know?"

"I can tell you this. There have been a disconcerting series of events taking place, starting at the edge of our galaxy in the direction of Cassiopeia and moving inward. Communications become garbled and spacecraft go temporarily out of control. Our computer banks have started malfunctioning. Nothing disastrous has happened, but the symptoms are very serious. Because our defense systems were the first technology to be affected, the Galactic Council became concerned and turned the problem over to Tregonsee, as head of the Military Intelligence Service. The M.I.S. gave the opinion that this could be a prelude to an invasion from outside the galaxy."

"From outside?" Cloudd said. "But that's from the wrong direction if we assume it will be Boskonian. I would think any threat would come from the direction of Saggitarius."

"And so would I. That is what would indicate that the attacking vessels would have to be invisible and not register on any detectors. Otherwise, they wouldn't be able to circle around our galaxy and attack us, as it were, from the rear. But let us save the speculation. The meeting in seven hours may furnish us with more details."

And so Cloudd had retired and had his fitful rest.

The meeting was scheduled for nine o'clock back at the lounge, but Cloudd had determined to be at the Institute building before eight o'clock to look for Kallatra. She wouldn't be expecting him, but he hoped to have a bit of time with her before the official gathering.

When Cloudd found the right section, he had to talk his way through a security check. The Kinnison heir was thoroughly guarded, even in this two hundred square miles of highly restricted military property. He had the credentials to get up to the BB wing, and no sooner had he stepped out of the elevator than he saw Clarrissa Kinnison in the center of a huddle of mothers, presumably, and department personnel. Lalla Kallatra, however, was not one of them.

"Thank you, thank you very much," Clarrissa was saying. "I appreciate your kind wishes." She was nodding and smiling as she moved toward the doorway to the nursery.

Cloudd quickly stepped close to her, before she could slip through, drawing two guards toward him. The younger was a Lensman, with a broad white streak in his dark blond hair, wearing the lapel badge of an M.I.S. officer. Security furnished by Tregonsee's Military Intelligence seemed unusual to Cloudd, but considering the lady and her baby it made sense.

"Excuse me, ma'am," Cloudd said. "I'm Lieutenant Benson Cloudd and I'm looking for Lensman Kallatra."

She looked him squarely in the eyes. Her direct, forceful gaze was almost a physical shock. Her tawny brown, gold-flecked eyes showed him a truly remarkable woman. She shook her short bronze-red hair negatively. "I'm sorry, Lieutenant, she's not here this morning. She has an important meeting in an hour and she's resting. "

"Is she all right?" Cloudd asked, on an unexplainable impulse.

"She's a bit under the weather," the Red Lensman said. "Nothing serious." Her eyebrows arched quizzically and her attitude warmed. "Weren't you and she involved last year in working out some trouble with my husband?" When he nodded, she said, "I remember your name. You were spoken of highly. I'm very pleased to meet you." She held out a firm, young hand for him to take.

She had drawn him inside the room, and they were talking small talk, which he, in a daze to find her such a fine person, hardly heard or comprehended.

". . . and being here at the Academy, you're familiar with

the Better Baby Course," she was saying.

"Well, not really . . ."

"I'm learning myself. It's nothing new — the idea that the ability to take in facts, basic facts, is an inverse function of age. Genius is acquired by the earliest possible frequent, intense, and extended stimulation of the brain to develop a sophisticated cortex." Clarrissa was an enthusiast.

"The brain is an organ to be exercised, encouraging the myelin insulating sheaths surrounding the tails of the brain cells for proper interconnections. The more synapses, the more brain power. Christopher is being provided with an operating system, to use computer jargon, basic skills for performing future complex tasks." She stopped and laughed.

"I do go on, don't I? I must be keeping you from your work. You'll find Lalla with my husband in the Hall someplace. But before you go, wouldn't you like to take a peek at my young one?" She turned to the plate glass window and tapped on it with a ring to summon a nurse. Cloudd noticed that she wore no Lens on either of her slim arms. For the first time he noticed also that she was dressed simply in a softly feminine dress, a very attractive lady.

The nurse brought a baby in his arms, and the two in front of the glass looked down at it, one with great pride and love, the other with awe and respect.

The baby was beautiful, of course — nothing remarkable, being so incredibly tiny and barely weeks old, but somehow appearing strong and powerful. The little eyes opened, there was a flash, a glint, a sparkle, that seemed peculiarly striking, and the eyes closed and the vision was gone.

Christopher K. Kinnison, child of the Lens.

Cloudd left the hospital feeling uplifted and depressed at the same time. He didn't try to analyze his feelings, instead he simply allowed himself to recognize that he had had a unique, never to be forgotten experience. The baby was the ultimate, perfection. He was suddenly conscious of his own physical imperfection, and he jammed his left hand into his side pocket as though to hide the fact that half of the last two fingers of his left hand were missing. Someday. Someday something was going to happen to him and he would dare to seek to become a Lensman.

He was there at five minutes to nine and so was Lalla Kallatra, but there was no time to talk to her. He studied her under lowered eyelashes. She was a statue, a parody of a woman; to think that she was the other woman Lensman was to be aware of the almost inconceivable contrast. Was there something wrong with her? What did Clarrissa Kinnison mean by saying the robotoid was "under the weather?" The body was mechanical — she was all machine, except for her brain. Did she have headaches? Oh, well. Cloudd snorted at his thoughts and derisively mumbled to himself, "She's probably got a screw loose."

Kinnison got right to the point. Nothing new had developed overnight. He was turning the meeting over to President Haynes.

Haynes, master tactician and strategist, wasted no time either. He jutted out his chin, ran his still strong fingers through his graying hair, and said, "I have your orders here on the table," tapping them with the fingers of his other hand. "You will pick up your copies when I dismiss you."

"Now I'm going to give you a summary of your assignments:

"Kimball Kinnison is to return to Klovia to organize the Grand Fleet of the Second Galaxy.

"Clarrissa Kinnison stays here at the Institute, training with the Kinnison baby and guarding him.

"Raoul LaForge will assemble the Grand Fleet of the First Galaxy, operating out of Prime Base for the present.

"Chaplain General Chon is to talk with the recent defector, Gronitskog, about the possible implication of the Eich. In one week's time, depending on his findings, he will go to Velantia for discussions with L2 Worsel.

"Lalla Kallatra will go immediately to the Worsel Institute on Velantia for an examination and for research on the latest activities of the Eich, later to meet with L2 Worsel and Chaplain General Chon.

(Cloudd immediately noted the phrase, "for an examination." What did it mean? Was Kallatra really ill?)

While Haynes was listing the assignments for other Lensmen whose names Cloudd didn't know, Cloudd was studying the impassive metal face of the girl robotoid. How old was she? Seventeen, eighteen, nineteen? He couldn't remember. Had she recovered from that terrible moment out there in deep space? Had she been truly retrieved from that ghastly tragedy when her body had been destroyed and her father had given up his life to save her brain? Was she dying? Would he ever see her again?

"…and Lieutenant Benson Cloudd …" Cloudd snapped back, aware of Haynes's closing words, "… will be going with L2 Nadreck.

"Remember, ladies and gentlemen," Haynes finished, "your reports daily to L2 Tregonsee are essential. That is all. Now let's conduct ourselves as if the graduation day celebrations were our only interest and leave as naturally as possible. If I don't see any one of you at the spaceport, please be assured that my best wishes and those of the Council go with you."

Everyone began shuffling about, getting copies of their official orders at the table. Cloudd noticed that the Lensman with the broad white streak in his dark blond hair was there, but Clarrissa Kinnison wasn't. Without being obvious, Cloudd jockeyed himself into position so he could talk to Kallatra.

"Pardon me, Lalla," Cloudd said, "I looked for you at the Institute this morning, and Mrs. Kinnison told me you weren't feeling well. I hope you're better." He made that statement as much a question as a wish.

"She told you that?" Kallatra's peculiarly semihuman

mechanical voice was very low. The difference between it and that of the sweet, rich, arid softly erotic voice of Clarrissa Kinnison that he had just experienced was pathetic. "Please don't speak of it here." He could barely hear her in the buzz of conversations. He said nothing. He stood there pretending to examine his orders, waiting for some positive sign from her.

Finally Cloudd could stand the suspense no longer. "Are you avoiding me?" he asked. "Shall I stop bothering you?"

She turned around then and stared at him with those expressive eyes. "Walk me over to the Institute, Benson," she said. "I don't have much time and neither do you."

"I leave at two thirty with Nadreck. When do you leave?" he asked, as they walked out of the lounge toward the campus exit. He sensed that something unusual was going on with her, perhaps between them, that he was about to learn, and it made him very apprehensive.

"My departure is at one GPT," she replied. "I have just enough time to personally say good-bye to Mrs. Kinnison and the baby. You're right; I thought I was avoiding you for reasons of security, but I know that isn't the real one. You are a peculiar mixture of an extrovert and a sensitive, and, because of my own eccentricities, you have frequently made me uneasy. Yesterday and today I haven't felt able to cope with someone like you. Nevertheless, it is important that I do talk with you. I have to pass on a warning."

She still seemed distant, but he felt in contact with her again. That he made her uneasy was an unpleasant revelation. But what could the warning be?

"By a warning, I refer to information of danger, not a threat to you. I once mentioned that in your search for datadrones you might discover their source to be a so-called mech-planet. Well, I have heard through psychic forces that such a place does indeed exist. And I am convinced that it is not within the realm of the Galactic Patrol. I fear that it has something to do with Eichwoor, the ghost of Eichlan.

I suggest that you pursue this with Worsel and that you pay more attention to this line of examination."

A mech-planet! This rumor wasn't new. However, that such a place might not be in this plane of existence was fantastic! Cloudd was intrigued with this entirely new possibility; indeed, Kallatra was right to warn him — he had never thought of this himself.

"But I also must say something about myself," she continued. "I don't want to alarm anyone who doesn't already know, so keep what I have to say confidential. It concerns my el-sike power — electro-psychic communication, my ability to receive frequencies that only a few Lensmen, like Worsel, of course, can sense."

"I know, Lalla. You're speaking of psychic forces, not physical processes, like telepathy — you're a sensitive, a psychic medium, a — " He paused.

" — a soul sniffer." She filled in the derogatory term for him. They were strolling together along the smooth campus walkway, and she stopped to look at him, her Lens in her forehead glowing. "But that's not my only unusual trait. I have something else, which is now recognized as an affliction." He felt the hair rise on the back of his neck. She turned away and began walking again. "I am subject to malfunctions in my circuitry, a sort of neuro-mechanical oscillation, from outside forces. Evidentally there are frequencies peculiar to mechanical semilife forms that I pick up unwittingly. They affect my robotic body, but are not recognized by my organic brain."

"Good Lord, Lalla," he said, "it sounds serious!"

"It is. I have difficulty controlling my body at times. This stroll with you, for example, is in the nature of an experiment. How will I do? Will I falter? Will I fall? And if I do, will I recover in time? How long can my brain live without this independent support system?"

"Lalla," he said, greatly shaken, "you've put your life in my hands and I appreciate your trust, but can I be of greater help? Forgive me for believing you indifferent to me. Why should this be happening now? Did your father, Deuce, when he was similarly tied to a mechanical body, have this trouble? What can be done about it?"

"The trouble's a recent development. I'm going to Worsel and there, at his institute, we're going to work on me. You see, Benson," she hesitated and again fixed him with one of her lustrous stares, "there is a far greater calamity that seems to be happening than that which affects me. It has to do with the future of Civilization."

"I don't follow you . . ."

"I thought you were briefed? Oh, but you must have come in late on this whole situation. I'm one of the things that's going wrong — but not just me, everything, our galaxy, our culture, our Galactic Patrol, everything!"

Cloudd impulsively grabbed her metal hand. He had a vision of her buckling and falling on her face.

"It's our machines. Our finest, our best, our most valuable servants of mankind and all our friends. They're developing aberrations. Things aren't going right. Our information banks are churning out errors, Our communication networks are malfunctioning. Our defensive missiles are no longer trustworthy. Even the ships of our fleets are becoming unmanageable.

"And I'm the litmus paper. I'm the thermometer that shows the symptoms. Oh, Benson, I'm scared!"

"Scared?" he said, pretending to feel her pulse, trying to josh away her fears, "You, scared? You'll be all right. Worsel will fix you up."

"It's not for me. I'm not scared for myself, I'm frightened that this is the end of Civilization!"

Like a painful cramp in the middle of his head, Cloudd felt Nadreck's thought:

"Cloudd! Kallatra! Go immediately and join General Chon, who is questioning Gronitskog. He indicates there is information about the Eich and their planned invasion! I want that information within an hour. Kallatra, I want you to look for evidence of the other plane of existence. Whatever you find, Lens me at long range. Cloudd is to do the interrogation through you and Chon. Can you do this for me, Kallatra?"

"Certainly, Nadreck. I'll make the time."

"Lens you at long range?" Cloudd said, surprised. "What do you mean?"

"At the moment my cadets are unloading my personal speedster, and I'll be departing in the next few minutes. Save any questions for my Lens linkup with Kallatra. I'm in a rush to file my reports and to clear base here."

"What is it? Has something happened, Nadreck?"

"There's a Palainian freighter that's run into the invisible invasion fleet out at the rim. A rim patrol Lensman has just flashed the word. I'm on my way there now. One hour, Cloudd. QX?"

"QX!"

If Kallatra had seemed frightened moments before, she certainly wasn't now. Cloudd had all he could do by running to keep up with her as she pressed back toward Wentworth Hall on her hidden wheels.

Chaplain General Chon, wearing his full dress Patrol uniform, as customary for psychological advantage in formal questioning, was waiting for them at the door to the detention and interrogation rooms. He had a notebook in his hand, his thumb keeping his place.

"Oh, hello, Kallatra! We have fifty-four minutes, Cloudd, to meet Nadreck's schedule." The general was fiercely rubbing his beard with his other hand, a pencil sticking out between his fingers. He led them inside and down a corridor.

"Nadreck is, or should be already, on his way to the galaxy rim. He wants you to interrogate Gronitskog, Cloudd, knowing that ethically I might have to withhold some things I learn. He wants the interrogation by you, without Lens help by anyone. I'll monitor his mind, and Kallatra can do the same, of course, but it's vital that we don't get into his mind and muddy it up in any way. This man's a complete innocent as far as we're concerned. We Lens people have to be careful to keep it that way for the purest research — we could get fact and fancy, truth and fiction mixed beyond recovery.

"What is exciting, considering our battle with Boskone and its Spawn and our efforts to pierce the enemy's secrets, is that his planet of Togra is controlled by the Eich. The Eich are so contemptuous of the Tograns that I find evidence they have said things indiscreetly, which this skinny humanoid has recorded unwittingly in his mind.

"Now let's get to work."

Cloudd was an expert interrogator, having spent so much time picking information about datadrones out of the heads of all kinds of peoples and races who had observed things without knowing what they had seen. Chon and Kallatra acted as dual interpreters, their Lenses easily converting the alien's spoken symbols into English.

The hour with the thin brown man went by as if it were only a few minutes.

"Eight minutes to go, Cloudd," Chon said. And then, almost as if time hadn't elapsed, he said, "Four minutes left, Cloudd."

Cloudd was drenched with nervous perspiration. He quickly had found Gronitskog to be a selfish and cowardly person, with no loyalty to his Noyyonese Council of Twelve. However, Cloudd also found, as confirmed by Chon, that Gronitskog sincerely believed in his religion and in the supernatural. His cowardice reinforced a truly righteous feeling about the immorality of starting a planetary war. He also hated the drug trade of Togra, where millions were addicts, mostly for the selfish reason that it reduced or nullified his religious power. As Chon agreed, Gronitskog was not so much evil as badly educated. But the facts which Cloudd sought and found were few and devastating. He

recognized the description of the Eich, who were represented as Satanic devils to whom sacrifices had to be made.
Some were present in halos of fire and could not be seen —
probably in atmosuits. Some were wraiths who danced in
Togran minds — and who appeared at deathbeds, so clearly
that they could be described as Eich. "Eichwooren," Kallatra
had said, and Chon had shivered. Cloudd was familiar with
the Eich, but knew nothing but rumors about Eichwoor or
the Eichwooren, the unutterably evil ghosts in the other
plane of existence. The promise of the Satanic Eich was that
"the invasion of the other corporeal system of stars will come
when Togra and its nine companions have the same celestial longitude." That could be a reference to the First Galaxy
being invaded and conquered so that deserving Noyyonese
would have other worlds to rule. It was a typical Eich promise, and it contained one very important specific clue relating
to time: the conjunction of the planets.

When was that conjunction? Cloudd demanded.
Soon.

How soon?

In two revolutions.

In two revolutions around Togra's sun? Two years?

No. Two revolutions of the sun around Togra.

Two *rotations!* Cloudd gasped. Two *days.* Two days and
the Eich would — invade the First Galaxy? Attack Klovia
in the Second Galaxy?

There was no mistaking the possibilities that existed
and the way they fitted into what was beginning to happen
out in space.

The deadline had come, and Chon and Kallatra joint-
ly Lensed Nadreck with the information and guesses as
Cloudd listened. The three on Tellus silently speculated over
the consequences of their information.

"I acknowledge to you much gratitude," Nadreck said.
"We have much to think about! I will be at my destination
soon and will be busy. Meanwhile, Cloudd, get Gronitskog

aboard the *Sapphire,* which my cadets have prepared for departure. They have to have a Patrolman in charge and you're it, Cloudd. They'll run everything, do all the work, they're competent, but you are officially the captain. That ship must leave before nightfall.

"General, with all due respect, please accompany Cloudd to Palain with Gronitskog, if possible. From there you can proceed to Velantia and Worsel.

"As for you, Kallatra, you have a terrible burden that I want no part of. I humbly defer to you and Worsel to work on this riddle. You two can fight ghosts, I cannot. Go to Worse I without delay. Prepare us for the worst. You have twenty-four hours.

"This is Nadreck, clearing ether."

The Dregs of Onlo

TELLURIAN LENSMAN DICK ARM-strong carefully considered the chaos aboard the Palainian freighter *Palai-kai*. Surrounded by alien spaceships, the small civilian crew and the large body of terrorized passengers and servants seemed to be fighting for their lives. Deaths seemed inevitable, although none had been reported. Alien robots were aboard, but what they were doing was unclear. Inexperienced entities were armed and firing guns, endangering themselves and the ship more than the robots. The engine trouble with the inertialess drive could be a coincidence. A call for help, admittedly low priority, had been sent by him, but no one had replied. Did the message get through or was it blocked?

And now Captain Finndha was panicking, telling him to Lens for Nadreck.

For a Lensman, Armstrong felt unbelievably helpless, this feeling underscored by his rediscovered sense of power. Since his disablement, Armstrong had used his Lens for nothing more than telepathic communication and as a translator of alien messages. Here he had probed for lifeforms and had found none. He couldn't take charge of thousands of Z-forms, let alone manage a ship he wasn't familiar with or fight with untrained personnel and questionable equipment.

He had mentally pushed around some of the smaller spaceships, but that was about all he had done. The one other thing he could do was defend to the death against any takeover of the ship's controls, and that he was resolved to do. He had no intention of disgracing the Patrol.

The first thing he did was follow the captain's plea, and he sent out a second Lensed call, this time with emphasis. The extraordinary plea of Captain Finndha, with all its peculiar Palainian undertones displaying the contradictions of heroism and self-centered cowardice, was inelegant, but meritorious. The situation was horrible and desperate, and Nadreck was needed. So, although his Lensed cry for help went directly to his surveillance section chief, it was actually an indirect appeal to Nadreck.

Almost as a supernatural response to a prayer, a mysterious force propelled Armstrong out of the room, down a stairwell, and out an emergency exit into space!

A whir and a whoosh and it was done!

At one second he had been standing next to Noc, the next moment he was alone in space, a hundred yards from the beleaguered freighter! Weirdly, his pressure suit did not swell in the vacuum; he did not float; he did not tumble; he was gripped by something other than gravity!

For several seconds he stared at the scene before him, like a museum diorama or a fanciful entertainment drama. The freighter, fire-streaked and ponderous, hung like a gray ornament in the intensely black void. The ugly hole slashed in its back side was obvious, with purple mists trailing from it. White, silvery, and gray shapes, elongated or round, drifted slowly past him and his ship. The shapes filled the celestial sphere as far as his eye could see. He saw no details; out there in space, with no electronics to refine and amplify, he saw only the huge, overall panoply of an awesome swarm of things.

"I've encased you in a tractor zone. I want you to take a close look at these things."

The thoughts crashed into his head with the stunning strength of a highly focused mind.

Nadreck! Nadreck? Nadreck had plucked him out of the ship and put him here? Impossible!

"Yes. I am Nadreck. I have done this to you, my friend Armstrong, not because you were in danger, but because I need you for my inspection of the situation. Do not fear, for I have an unbreakable grip on you."

"I heard your first message some time ago while I was at a conference on Tellus, but I immediately acted, for your situation is part of a greater, more serious one. I did not come because of your indirect plea to me just now. I was already here and have for many moments been studying the status of things. You are right, but from my viewpoint terrible things seem to be developing — which means we have work to do."

"Where are you?" Armstrong strained his vision, searching everywhere among the ghostly shapes.

"I rest a thousand miles away. If I were nearby, you still would not see my ultrablack, indetectable ship. However, look!" For one brief unveiling, the Tellurian saw the Palainian. The Second Stage Lensman was sitting amidst the machinery of his inimitable, extraordinary one-man spaceship. No one had a private speedster remotely like Nadreck's. It was a transparent octohedron, looking very much like a gigantic cut jewel. The eight triangular planes were revolving slowly, but inside Nadreck and his machines remained stationary. The L2 had the aspect of a fluorescent blue crab hunched over his controls. And yet — and yet, he seemed more like a somewhat luminous spider spinning a web of rainbow-hued lights. The ship and its master was an unreal image, a phantom, for behind it, and through it, passed the solid silvery forms of the strange craft.

Nadreck, a figure of mist, as tenuous a specter as his

ship, was pressing buttons and now fading from sight.

"You are not in danger because I am keeping myself away from danger, and while I'm completely safe, so are you. Out here I can concentrate and can study what is occurring. I will safeguard you as we undertake our investigations, and I will see the details through your humanoid eyes and interpreting brain. Are you ready?"

Armstrong almost said, "Ready for what?" but he said, instead, "Yes, Nadreck. I am ready."

Armstrong had a sudden giddying plunge "down" toward the nearest cylinder, abruptly halting within a few feet of its shining surface. He didn't recognize the alloy. Nor could he see any signs of manufacture. There were no windows or doors. There were numerous closely-fitted round and square plates on the body shell, undoubtedly covers of apertures. Overall, the thing appeared to be an 18-foot-long torpedo.

As he was moved around it by the manipulation of the tractor zone by Nadreck, he was ordered to blink out a recognition signal with his hand lamp. "Identify yourself as a member of the Galactic Patrol," Nadreck said. Armstrong mildly protested such a revelation as foolhardy, but he did it.

On the curved side of the hull a startling insignia came into view —

— a golden meteor within a sunburst, a variant of the Galactic Patrol identification!

This was a Patrol weapon? A Patrol probe?

"No, it is not one of ours," Nadreck's thoughts came clearly, gravely. "It is meant to deceive. I believe it is a copy of a Type-8 datadrone, able to mark itself with false colors, as it were, to conform with or be an ally of its hailer. You saw pirate markings earlier when you were read as a Boskonian. I did some probing on my own before I pulled you out, and I can make them conjure up all kinds of markings. But what I'm looking for is —" Nadreck pushed Armstrong up close to some embossed lettering at the blunt end. "There! That line of print. I read radiant identification, but what do the letters look like to you?"

"85-46Z-788-A-ZZ," Armstrong said, pushing his gloved fingers over the bumps.

Immediately, Nadreck whipped him to another torpedo to read its number. "43Z-00-183-A-ZZ," Armstrong read. And then to another. And another. And another. Armstrong was groggy and slightly sick from his whirling trips and had become disoriented. He realized he was up against one of the large globes, dizzy with vertigo, pushing both hands along the smoothly curving sides, wondering how very large it really was.

"667-57-8534-9-A-ZZ," Armstrong said automatically.

"Wake up! Look around!" Nadreck said. "Not at the formation. There is a black one in the center."

The Tellurian Lensman twisted his head and saw a ring of silvery globes, perhaps twenty in all, forming a circle about ten miles in diameter. The ring at the far side seemed incomplete — until he realized that globes were appearing and disappearing, blocked by an invisible object around which they circled.

In a matter of moments, Nadreck had swung him around the circle, collecting numbers, occasionally experimenting with making GP, Boskonian, Spawn, or other insignia appear and disappear. The bigger, black one in the center Nadreck avoided, telling Armstrong, "It's a mother ship, which I'd rather not disturb."

By this time Armstrong was too bewildered and muddled to grasp what was happening. He wasn't surprised to find himself dumped back in the cracked section of the freighter where the robots had first appeared. There were no robots now.

"I humbly thank you, Armstrong," Nadreck said. "When you are in port, please contact me, which is my polite way of saying I order you. I'm leaving for Palain."

"But what has changed? Did you drive them away, Nadreck?" Armstrong asked. "I don't understand."

"The robots and the drones and the ships are gone," Nadreck said. "They never fired a shot at your crewmates. They weren't vampires among your passengers, they were trying to give aid, mend limbs, give transfusions. They didn't attack your control room, they attempted communication. The whole incident was an accident, which they did their best to rectify. And now they have vanished — snap! — without a trace.

"They? Who are 'they'? What are 'they'?"

"I shall tell Tregonsee that they are nonviolent intruders, from an unknown place, but stemming from our galactic culture."

"Nonviolent? Then they're not Boskonian? Did you find any clues?"

"Of course, Armstrong. I am clever, so I found many ... This is Nadreck by Lens for Tregonsee ... You are S.I.S.? Please relay this to Tregonsee. The incident of Rim Patrol Armstrong reveals nonviolent intruders, from an unknown place, familiar with our galactic culture, related strongly to Tellurian culture. Their societal identification is A-Z-Z or A-zed-zed or A-zee-zee. This could be a place name, but I suggest it is symbolic of being from the beginning to the end to the very end, an identification of their purpose or philosophy, that is, A to Z to Z.

"This is important, Lensman — Nadreck finds no evidence from the strange craft that the fleet of one hundred thousand are any kind of threat except to navigation. However, I, Nadreck, find that the Palainian freighter is marked abundantly with examples of mechanical and electronic contamination, exact symptoms of our problems as outlined by our Galactic Council president. My conclusion is that this intruding fleet is connected with the trouble and that the A-ZZ symbol applies to the termination of our

Galactic Civilization, perhaps even to include Boskonia and its Spawn. This is Nadreck. Clear ether!"

Armstrong had crawled into the safety of an airlock, gathering his strength to draw himself to his tiny cabin. He was stunned. He felt as if the liquid in his brain cavity was swirling around and around like a vortex. He heard Nadreck's order: "Armstrong! Deep monitor your ship — and report to me on Palain!" and the gargantuan Z-presence was gone.

The arrival at Palainopolis of Cloudd, Chon, Gronitskog, and the six Palainian cadets occurred barely a half hour before Nadreck himself arrived in his one-man flitter. He immediately learned that the training ship was lucky to have arrived at all.

Cloudd had cleared the *Sapphire*'s flight plan, and they had left the spaceport on the Academy grounds before midnight. He and Chon had continued their interrogation of Gronitskog almost up to the hour of departure, learning nothing else of significance, while Kallatra had left in a rush for Velantia to see Worsel. Chon decided to make the trip with the scrawny archbishop from Noyyon without delay. They had been developing an interesting theological discussion, and by the time the trip was over, Chon wanted to transfer Gronitskog as soon as possible from Palain to Worsel's care to pursue the investigation of Eich influence.

The ship, under the efficient management of the cadets, had smoothly accelerated to maximum inert speed and had switched into inertialess drive far beyond the speed of light. Cloudd recognized with admiration that this training ship was, in fact, a miniature of the best of the Patrol's modern destroyer class, capable of the highest performance. He could have stayed in the small, uncomfortably utilitarian Tellurian cabin with the two others, but he felt he was titularly in charge. He suited up, therefore, for an even more uncomfortable trip. As there were no monitoring screens, only intraship visiscreens, leaving him unconfident about overseeing what was going on, he stayed on duty in his pressure suit all of the time, watching the small, amorphous figures of the cadets busily moving about in the light of his headlamp. He really had little idea of what they were doing, but he wanted to be there in the unlikely event that he would be needed. As it developed, he did have a decision to make, and he made it incorrectly.

Their narrow escape from disaster came halfway to Palain.

There were clangings of bells and blinkings of signals at frequencies above his visual perception, which his belt monitors gave some indication of. The senior cadet came to him and attempted some communication. The creature waved limbs at him and spoke noises that he couldn't decipher because he didn't speak Palainian. He tried spaceal in return, but that didn't work either. With no translator box aboard — it had been replaced by other training devices — Cloudd ordinarily would have waved the young Palainian on about his business. However, with a Lensman aboard, especially one of the caliber of Chon, Cloudd asked for and got communication through Chon's Lens.

"Sir," the cadet said, "there is a lifeform traveling roughly parallel to our course. An emergency marker is transmitting from its location. The indication is that help is needed. Shall we alter course to investigate? If we do so we will be delayed by some 180 P-time-units or 20 GP minutes."

"Is it a GP-standard signal?"

"Yes, sir."

"Then we must investigate."

"Very well, sir." The eye-straining figure made what Cloudd took to be a mark of respect with its blurred limbs and backed up into a blending with the other figures.

"Keep me posted," Cloudd had Chon Lens.

Cloudd didn't feel the ship change course, so smoothly was it run, and six GP minutes later the cadet, presumably the same cadet as before, the leader named Yadsue, came partially into focus in front of Cloudd, asking to report. Cloudd was lying prone on top of some equipment overlooking the control console, swiveling his head toward the different screens that emitted visible light, trying to see something.

As Yadsue appeared, so did an image on several screens. The object was a Tellurian suit of heavy armor, designed for extended operation, tumbling slowly in the void.

"Our instruments show a humanoid lifeform alive inside the suit, sir. Shall I proceed to recover it?" Cloudd could read through Chon's Lens as if it were his own.

"Scan it thoroughly, Yadsue," Cloudd ordered, ". . . You are Yadsue, aren't you . . . ? We want nothing dangerous aboard."

"I am Kweeda. Yadsue is at the scanner readout. There is nothing dangerous, and he is continuing his scanning even as the rescue takes place."

"Any trace of where this space-suited person came from? Any wreckage? Any messages still echoing around? Any references?"

"Yes, Yadsue has a disaster report from a wreck of an unlicensed freighter in this sector within the past three GP days, but there is no derelict or debris. We came through this sector four days ago and had no warnings or reports then. The disaster report is weak and could perhaps be heard only by someone like us, close by. Yadsue repeats that there is a life reading and that no dangerous material, instrument, or apparatus is connected with the humanoid body or its standard free-to-inert lifesuit."

"Chon," Cloudd said, "will you scan this object for me?"

"I have, Cloudd," Chon replied. "I find nothing unusual, except that it's a free-to-inert suit designed with an inertia-less inhibitor to slow the suit down to regular inert space for increased chance of rescue. That's GP or Boskonian warship stuff, not for freighters except on the drug trade."

"Yadsue," Cloudd said, "I want a reading on his intrinsic velocity. Do you know what I mean? What is his original pre-inertialess velocity? It will give us a fix on the direction of his spaceship before it went free."

"I know what that means, sir. My Academy training is thorough. It is . . . one moment, please . . . it is 170,000 miles per second at 225 degrees Azimuth 45 degrees plus x as we travel. That indicates — "

" — that indicates," Cloudd broke in to exercise his command position, "downward and backward relative to us, and, reversing the line of flight, indicates origination from outside rather than inside."

"Coming from the rim?" Chon said. "That makes it off the usual flight paths. Boskonian or Spawn?"

"What are the humanoid's vital signs?" Cloudd asked. "Can you evaluate his condition? Could he remain as he is for another six hours?"

"Are you contemplating passing him by?" Chon wondered, obviously concerned. The law of the spaceways did permit such possibilities if other rescuers were available.

"This is Yadsue. Yes, at least six hours."

"Then listen, Yadsue. Grab the body with a tractor beam and clamp it to the side of our ship. On the down and back side. That's important, the down and back side, the aft keel. When we get to the Palainian system, we'll reorientate our own intrinsics, match ours with its, and put us both in phase to land on Palain VII. If we don't — "

" — we will have a disengagement of a monumental explosion." That thought was not only Yadsue's, it was also Chon's.

"Why not bring him inside?" Chon said. "We can examine him and give him first aid if he needs it and put him back outside when we're ready."

"No," Cloudd said, "I don't want to bring a suit in here with an inertialess inhibitor. How do we know what will happen if the suit is opened? The guy comes out, prepared for trouble, and releases the intrinsics of the suit. He lives, blows a hole in our ship, and is rescued when some ambushing partner easily picks us off as a cripple. No, he stays outside, pointed the other way."

Cloudd watched the operation on the screens, the visuals not nearly as good as he would have liked them, but good enough to make sure the job was done right.

"Very good, fellows. Now get back on course. It's taken us eighteen minutes, and I'm certainly going to let Nadreck know what an excellent half-dozen future Lensmen he has in you." Cloudd let himself relax for the first time since the incident started.

"Chon, sixteen hours have elapsed since the forty-eight hour deadline was determined. When we arrive, it will be twenty-one hours used, with twenty-seven hours remaining. Have you picked anything else out of our Noyyonese guest since we left?"

"He's got space sickness. We'll have to wait until Palain to get going on him again."

Cloudd had been staring idly, almost without seeing, at the monitoring screens, expecting the ship to go free of inertia at any moment. Did that figure move? Cloudd peered more closely. He did move!

"Chon, get me Yadsue!" Cloudd shouted. When Yadsue acknowledged the call, suddenly appearing in front of Cloudd, the Tellurian lieutenant said, "Hold back on going free. Check the condition of our castaway. I thought I saw him move."

"The suit's about the same as it was, sir. He's shifted his body around to be more comfortable. He must be cramped. . . . As a matter of fact, sir, he seems to have actually rotated his body 180 degrees."

"I don't want that!" Cloudd said, forcefully. "I'm suspicious that — "

There was an explosion; a bomb had struck the aft keel. The bomb was unique, a human body had released its intrinsic velocity simultaneously with the release of the equal intrinsics of the suit. Instead of a single projectile of man-in-suit, they had smashed together in a fireball of energy that holed the outer shell and buckled the inner shell of the hull. The airtight compartments locked, and the ship was safe. It had come, however, exceedingly close to complete calamity.

"God bless us!" Chaplain General Chon Lensed, after he had picked himself up off the cabin floor and had helped the Noyyonese recover his senses. "What a horrible accident!"

"Accident, hell!" Cloudd said, and reeled off some salty oaths. "Forgive me, Chaplain, but we almost went to see your boss! Of all the dirty tricks, this really singes Klono's whiskers. Somebody set out a booby trap for us and we almost got wiped out by it. If the intrinsics had been released all in the same direction, I believe we would have. As it was, the man couldn't turn the suit, so he turned himself in our direction and let it rip."

"You mean," Chon said slowly, weighing the full implication of Cloudd's analysis, "that someone sacrificed himself just to destroy us? Why? And who would do such a crazy thing?"

"The man could have been drugged or hypnotized. That's not too difficult to figure out. As for why, there's only one explanation. The trap was laid after this ship went up a few days ago, knowing that the ship would return this way. Was someone trying to murder six young Academy cadets about to be Lensmen . . . ?"

"Nadreck!" Chon said, seeing the truth.

"Yes, Nadreck," Cloudd said. "Somebody set this death trap for Nadreck."

And that was the story Cloudd told Nadreck when they met on the barren plain of Palainopolis, waiting for the old-fashioned hoverbus that was to transport all of them back to subterranean Palainopolis.

Nadreck at first had been impatient, listening to the story. A bus had come, but Nadreck had signaled for Academy transportation, so they waited for it while standing in the bus out of the zero degree heat, the three oxygen-breathers still in their suits. Midway through he had become deathly still, part of his mind hearing and part separately pondering the collection of events. At the end of the story he quickly spoke.

"You, my fine cadets," he said, "you had no equipment malfunctioning or electronic contamination? No? Then you are right, Cloudd, and I know who plotted this mean and reprehensible act, which I must grudgingly admire. The perpetrators are my mortal enemies, the Dregs of Onlo."

"The Dregs of Onlo?" Chon repeated. "Who are they?"

"A personal matter for me, Chon," Nadreck said, brushing away any explanation. "What is important is to consider the possible relationship with the rim incident. There may now be five separate threats converging on us. The obvious ones are from the disorganized Boskonians or the newly organized Spawn of Boskone; Kinnison is certain they both are our trouble. Kallatra, however, tends to see a return of Eichwoor, the ghost, with legions of fellow spirits she calls Eichwooren. Then there is the unknown instigator, suggesting human or Tellurian influence. Add to them the Dregs, which heretofore have been interested exclusively in me. Now I will tell you of what the rim Patrolman, Dick Armstrong, encountered.

Nadreck flashed the events quickly into their minds.

"Type-8!" Cloudd exclaimed. "The datadrones are back! The round globes are different. Are the drones tracking the round globes? Or are there new types of drones?" Cloudd was caught up in the old excitement. "That trickery with the fake emblems, that's something new, too. What do you think, Nadreck? Is this a more serious drone threat — are they now aggressive instead of passive?"

"There are datadrones involved, undoubtedly," Nadreck said. "To what extent, though, I am not certain. It is significant that the drones were last seen near Pinwheel DW433, the shortest line to take them away from the galactic center and toward Andromeda. This invisible invasion fleet is entering the rim close to the galactic plane from that direction, although perhaps this is a deliberate plan of misdirection. What do you think of all this, Cloudd? You're the datadrone expert."

Cloudd had been puzzling over the possibilities ever since he had been asked to join the conference the day before on Tellus. He was beginning to see a pattern.

"I think the drones are back. I never did believe that they were sucked up and destroyed. I think they've discovered all they want to know about Civilization's technology, and now they're leading an attack on us through subetheric wave interference. Who's behind it I can't guess, although their base very likely can be the mech-planet the rumormongers suggest exists. I'm worried we're entering a time of revolt by our robots."

"Revolt?" Chon exclaimed. "By our robots?"

"Here comes the Academy shuttle," Nadreck said. "We must Lens Worsel and Kallatra as soon as we get to the Academy. Things are shaping up, and I have a feeling the loose ends are ready to be tied together.

"We have hardly twenty-four hours left before the Eich, and maybe the Eichwooren, are due to attack."

Death Answers the Prayer

LOUDD'S STAY ON PALAIN WAS short and he was thankful that it was. From what he saw of the surface of the planet, it was barren and vastly unattractive, the city was a jumbled mess of square, windowless structures, and the people were a mass of shifting, shadowy shapes. The atmosphere was pure poison for him and the temperature was so low that it couldn't be registered on a normal mercury thermometer. He was glad to be taken underground and deposited in a Tellurian room with bright light.

He had been in his room for only a half hour, however, and it was already getting on his nerves. The furniture was very practical, uncomfortable, and absolutely without aesthetic style. The walls, ceiling, and floor were bare. The decoration was simple and very effective, but to him, extremely unpleasant: it consisted of overly bright, garish, colored light — rippling out of and over all the sides of the room, ceiling, and floor-accompanied by some kind of discordant Tellurian music. The only objects he could pick up and handle were a dozen plastic books, half of them in English, their topics limited to science, mathematics, and astronomy. They were didactic and had no pictures.

After twenty minutes he was inclined to think that he

was in some kind of chamber designed to punish him.

He was on the verge of beating on the walls, there being no visible door, and shouting for attention, when he got a thought planted in his head.

"In five minutes there will be a lecture by you before an assembly of Z-Academy cadets. Prepare yourself. You need only think of a toilet, Cloudd, and a panel will open to one. I hope you have been comfortable, my friend, with good air and enough heat. We do not receive many hotheads on Palain, you know." Cloudd knew the thoughts were coming through a Palainian Lens, but it seemed somehow different, as though Nadreck were transmitting through an intermediary or staff member.

"I can hardly wait, Nadreck," Cloudd said.

"The entire student body," the Palainian Lensman, whoever he was, continued, "has been briefed with all available information, including the encounter by the Lensmen Nadreck and Armstrong with the unidentified fleet. Please summarize in less than one hour those points that you consider salient, and then be ready to answer questions. You now have your five minutes."

When a panel slid aside, Cloudd walked through the opening and down a long hallway and around a corner where he met Chon. The general was standing before a transparent wall, next to the seated figure of Gronitskog, with many vague images shifting about on the other side of the glass. Probably they were the Z cadets, Cloudd thought to himself. There were two empty' stools next to the Noyyonese, and when Chon sat down on one of them after giving a cheerful smile and nod of his head to him, Cloudd sat down on the other.

"Please stand up, Lieutenant Cloudd, and come closer to the window and tell us about the datadrones," he was told.

"As you must already know the details," Cloudd said, "I have nothing much to say. About a year and a half ago spacemen, particularly Tellurians, who had been probing the less populated regions of the Milky Way, began to notice the small, segmented, torpedo-shaped drones drifting near them, aimlessly, it seemed. Sometimes the objects were observed streaking off on unchartable courses. They were elusive and bothered no one, but I became intrigued, and in the course of my prospecting in many regions I began to go out of my way to observe them. I reported my findings, which weren't many, but the Patrol considered my work valuable and assigned me an official role in gathering details. I succeeded in capturing a small one and determined that it was, in fact, an informa-tion collecting device. I identified a larger, mother machine, which was an assembling point and a transmitter. A much larger third kind was discovered releasing the two smaller types. I determined that these datadrones, numbering in the thousands, were not Boskonian, but represented some other, unidentified race or controlling force. Our attempts to solve the riddle of their appearance, mission, and source failed. The datadrones, those that remained, apparently left the galaxy immediately following the defeat of the Spawn of Boskone and their black hole weapon.

"This is my summary. But, of course, I have told you nothing new," Cloudd concluded and quickly sat down.

"We have questions for you, Cloudd," Nadreck said. "The first one is, why, if they were bothering no one, did you not leave them alone?"

To Cloudd the answer was so obvious that he had dif-ficulty explaining that the unknown must always be investi-gated, either to defend against it or to exploit it.

"But considering that the Galactic Patrol was already heavily involved in contesting the rebuilding of the rem-nants of Boskone by the Bosko-Spawn, with its so-called 'Doomsday Machine,' having the potential to obliterate millions of worlds, why did you assume that the Galactic Patrol was right to stir up trouble when it was not yet nec-essary?"

Again Cloudd tolerantly defended his position and that of the Patrol. He couldn't help feeling, however, that Nadreck's attitude was hardly the sort to be taken by young entities who were planning to be Lensmen.

"I understand your feeling, Lieutenant Cloudd," came the thought, in a manner that Cloudd knew was meant for everyone there, "but you must understand ours. As has been stated many times, our intrinsic nature is to ignore and be ignored. Our lives and our culture have proved this to be desirable and to be effective. It is necessary, absolutely necessary, that we try to understand the Tellurian mind as much as we can. We are obstinate, so we will continue this line of questioning until we are satisfied no further purpose will be served for us."

With this straightforward, although rather abrasive attitude, the questioning continued. To Cloudd, it was almost nonsense and seemed to serve no intelligent purpose, but he answered to the best of his ability.

Finally he was through. His summary had taken less than a minute. His inquisition had taken nearly three-quarters of an hour. He was left feeling overwhelmingly irritated, not only because the questions seemed so thick-headed, but because he had had his own good sense and rationality actually undermined by them.

"Do you need a rest break, Lieutenant? Do you, Chaplain General? No? Then we will continue."

Cloudd tried very hard not to let his thought slip through, "What about Gronitskog? Maybe he needs a rest?" but evidently he failed because the Palainian Lensman said, "As Gronitskog needs no rest either, please come forward, Chaplain Chon, and speak to us. I have already informed the students of all we know about this humanoid from the planet Togra. There are a number of questions they have that Nadreck cannot answer with authority. We address this to the Chaplain General of the Galactic Patrol:

"What makes this barbarian a holy man?"

Chon, tall and stately in his dress uniform, turned his head toward Cloudd, raised his eyebrows and gave a grimace and a sigh as if to say, "Well, Cloudd, now it's my turn for the really heavy stuff." He turned back to the window, folded his arms, and gazed solemnly at the amorphous mass of figures before speaking.

"A holy man is one who associates himself with and follows a spiritual system," Chon said. "At the best, he is one who is in touch with God, the Omnipotent Witness. However, I understand your question to mean why should he be a holy man when he is our enemy and on the side of evil. The answer is subjective, based on one's beliefs. He can be holy and yet still be in error."

"Why does this or any religious man wear a charm of superstition ?"

"It's a symbol of faith and a badge of recognition. Also, in some cases, such as this, it is a prayer focuser or amplifier, either technologically or psychically augmented. What you see is a reproduction we have made of his pink-sphere-within-white-sphere icon enclosed in a thin transparent box. We made the substitution because it could be a transmitter or homing device that might compromise our security. That's probably why you evaluate it as a mere charm."

For nearly ten minutes, this kind of question was asked and answered. Cloudd found the questions much more interesting and revealing than Chon's answers. At first Cloudd was positive that all the Palainians in the group were basically atheistic, although he quickly modified his judgment of them to agnostic. Then he decided they were exceedingly metaphysical, concerned with cosmology, the study of the ultimate order of the universe, and thus paradoxical. Their questions showed him that they were very interested in the study of the nature and existence of God in the narrow sense of trying to detect him through facts and reason. They didn't seem to understand or care about intangible or spiritual things. They simply couldn't understand why Gronitskog could be a man of God and be on the side of evil if God was all-powerful and all goodness. Why should God permit evil, they wanted to know?

Chon did his best, but no one seemed very satisfied.

Cloudd, who always had thought of himself as "religious," but who had never actively practiced "religion," was himself confused and suddenly filled with doubts he had never before seen or admitted. The Palainians were far more astute than Cloudd had given them credit for, but what really impressed him was the obvious fact that they thirsted to know everything they could, but that if they couldn't get the knowledge or understand the knowledge they found, they worried about it in an unemotional way. They did not upset themselves as human beings did, yet at the very same time they would claim to be worried. No wonder the prime tenet of the Palainians to ignore and be ignored seemed to be broken as much as it was followed.

Finally Nadreck said, "Thank you, fellow Patrolmen. You have admirably shown to our cadets how peculiar the human races are and why you are always confused. Or should I say, Chaplain Chon, sometimes confused and sometimes unclear?"

The window darkened and the vision of the Academy students, like objects in an unlit aquarium filled with indiscernable movement, faded from their sight. The two humans did not have long to wait for instructions.

"General, if you will take Lieutenant Cloudd and the cleric Gronitskog back to your room," Nadreck said, "you will have a wait of about an hour. Then we will board a Palainian-manned GP destroyer for a trip to Velantia. We have made an unprecedented revision and are at this moment graduating our class ahead of schedule. I personally am to congratulate the nineteen new Lensmen and present them with their Lenses, which arrived last week from Arisia. We are now counting the minutes rather than the hours until the predicted invasion begins."

"Very well, Nadreck," Chon said, leading the way back through the corridor in silence, although Cloudd was tempted to comment on the fact that the Tellurian Academy graduating class alone was five times larger.

Chon's quarters were almost identical with Cloudd's, but somewhat larger. Cloudd sat down in a chair that looked much like plumbing pipes and canvas, while Chon stretched out on a piece much like a simple camping cot.

"My trip seems to have been a waste of time, General," Cloudd said. "I don't think I gave the students anything they really didn't know already."

"Well, as for myself," Chon said, "this has been extremely valuable. I know much about our Togran companion and some fascinating details about his religion. And as for Nadreck, I have learned much more than he suspects about his personal life and motivations and those of his comrades."

"That's true," Cloudd said. "And I have learned a lot about you and about religion, sir. You make me realize I've no foundation — that I've been drifting. A year ago I was cocksure of myself, and now I seem to have lost it."

"I see that, Lieutenant," Chon said, lying on his back with his hands under his head as a pillow and his elbows out, staring at the flowing lights on the ceiling. "Since you lost your independence by taking orders from the Patrol, you've found yourself in a bigger picture, and it's made you a worrier."

"So, it shows, does it?" Cloudd said. "I don't know what to do about it."

"Don't think you're alone, Benson," the general said. "I have a similar problem."

"You do? Why should you feel a lack of self-confidence?"

"That's easy to explain," Chon said. "Like you, I was a doer. The Patrol has turned me into a bureaucrat. So, you see, we're both free spirits who have been caged. I feel I'm not accomplishing what I should be accomplishing — maybe because I'm not good enough, or maybe because I expect too much of myself. We're both looking for something we don't seem to find, possibly because we aren't sure what it is. The differences, however, are that you unwittingly are worrying about it, whereas I, for the time being, at least, accept my fate."

"But you're — you're a man of God. You should feel, well, satisfied with your work. At peace. Not like me."

"Do you forget, Benson, that I'm a Medonian? You recall how my kind fled the Second Galaxy to get away from the enslavement of the Boskonians?"

"How could anyone not have that etched in their memory?" Cloudd said. "To think how you folks, so much like Tellurians, actually turned your planet into a super spaceship with a super Bergenholm drive and shifted yourselves — world and all — out of the evil galaxy and into our good one. Your scientists deserve all the laurels and kudos they get."

"A titanic feat, no denying it — but emotionally overwhelming. Mentor chose me as one of the first Medonian Lensmen, and with such an advantage, I rose quickly to be a Gray Lensman. Medonians tend to be independent that way, the result of their sense of planetary aloneness. That gave us our maturity and strength in our religion. Accepting appointment as Chaplain General of the Galactic Patrol was a natural decision for me for Unattached status specialization. It's my Medonian upbringing that so quickly brought me the reputation of an outstanding theologian, whether or not I deserve such recognition."

"You deserve it, General," Cloudd said.

"I wasn't fishing for compliments," Chon said. He stroked his gray beard, his small, blue eyes pensively narrowed. "I say this to make you understand that my life, like yours, has been regimented, not deliberately by the Patrol, but by the system, by the bureaucracy, a consequence of my being chief administrator. Like you, my responsibilities shackle me. I miss my independence. Like you, for a year now, since working with Worsel and Lalla Kallatra on spiritual matters, I've had the itch to do more than play diplomatic games."

"You do make me understand myself better, sir," Cloudd said, "but really I'm puzzled. Why tell me all this ?"

"Well, simply this, Benson — I want action and you can get it for me."

"Me? How?" Cloudd was intrigued.

"I want to go to Togra personally and uncover the Eich-Eichwoor link there. I want a Second Stage Lensman to be involved in the project. And I want Kallatra to go with me because she's essential to sniff out and battle Eichwoor when we come across it. If you come, Nadreck will be interested and Kallatra will personally come."

"Why is that?" Cloudd asked quickly, now bewildered. "I can understand about Nadreck, but why should my going make her go?"

"She wants to work with you. This could be a great chance for her. She has Unattached status, so I can't order her to go, but I can entice her. If she goes, Worsel will be interested and will keep in touch with our progress, so two Second Stage Lensmen will be personally involved."

"She wants to work with me?" Cloudd found the idea hard to believe. "What makes you think that? Did she tell you? We've always seemed strained around each other — at least, I have."

"She didn't say so, but believe me, Benson, I can tell you two are a natural pair — she with her abnormal psychic powers and you with your natural compassion and sensitivity wrapped up in an aggressive, adventurous spirit. You come with me and I guarantee she'll come with us."

"But I can't just demand to go with you. As you say, I've got my commitments. Nadreck feels I should be chasing the datadrones as the best lead we have to get a line on the invisible invasion fleet."

"You underestimate yourself, Benson. You're practically an Unattached Patrolman, something different. If you say this is what you want to do, you'll be allowed to do it, especially at my request. Even a Chaplain General, who often seems just a complicating annoyance in high headquarters, does get some attention."

"Well . . ." Cloudd was half-convinced. "But my data-drone work comes first . . ."

"Precisely. There is a connection, I feel, between the drones and Eichwoor. Coming with me will be a logical step for you. I can't yet prove the Eich and their psychic weapon, the original ghost called Eichwoor and its cohorts called Eichwooren, are involved, but I think I'm close to it. We have further chances to interrogate Gronitskog about this while we are making the trip to Velantia — and then with Worsel and Kallatra's help when we get there."

"You've convinced me, General Chon," Cloudd said. "Now tell me, do you know something about Gronitskog's knowledge of the Eich and Eichwoor that I don't know?"

"By virtue of my deductions, I probably do. The Eich are definitely the masters of Togra, controlling them through religious dogma, messages, and occasional miracles. The planet was a big base for dismantled Boskonia and now for its Bosko-Spawn offspring, supplying the most fanatic intellectual and warrior leaders. It's one of the key worlds among the hundreds, maybe even thousands, locked together in the conspiracy. This archbishop can communicate with the Eich in two ways — through standard equipment and through ultra-etheric frequencies, which may involve Eichwoor. There have been revelations and prophecies concerning fighting angels and devils, which I have interpreted as space battles and conquests. The fall of the Galactic Patrol is envisioned. The Day of Deliverance is at Hand, Armageddon is Now, the Master has Come, and all sorts of other signs are there to tell me the conflict has begun. If we can tap into the Eich communications through Gronitskog or other Noyyonese or Tograns, we'll find that victory for ourselves will not be in doubt. I have visions of their heavenly chariots, easily recognizable as spaceships, but I don't know where they are to come from or what planets are manufacturing them. Tell me all you know about datadrone construction."

Cloudd was meticulously describing the three types of datadrones to Chon when he was interrupted. Chon held up his hand and said, "Nadreck wants a Velantian time-check. Excuse me for a moment, please."

"Certainly," Cloudd said.

Chon quietly concentrated for several seconds, pressing his wrist with the Lens to his forehead. The movement was really not needed, any more than Cloudd needed to scratch his head in order to think. Cloudd studied him, as much impressed as ever with the routine by which a Lensman was able to be given such precise information. Cloudd heard nothing because Chon did not bother to connect him telepathically, but he knew how the system worked. At all times a central time bureau was operated by Lensmen with a two-galaxy-wide network. By his Lens, a Lensman could receive a time for any location, adjusted in any manner necessary. Without this essential service to the Patrol, operations would have been difficult in some circumstances and impossible in others.

"We leave for Velantia immediately," Chon said, rising, awakening Gronitskog from his slightly drugged sleep, and steering him out of the room.

The Palainian ship they boarded now was bigger, although not much faster, and its accommodations were much more comfortably standard Tellurian. As soon as they were aboard, they were given some unidentifiable but pleasant food, and by the time they were finished, Nadreck, whom they hadn't seen among the few Palainian Patrolmen they met on the way to their cabin, was in contact with them.

Nadreck had arranged for the interrogation of Gronitskog to take place in the wardroom, with himself and two Palainian assistants in attendance. For the first time, Cloudd was informed that the new Lensman, Yadsue, was in the party. In the center of the room a transparent cube had been formed by the retractable walls, a device to permit conferences with different aliens breathing different atmospheres.

With Cloudd on one side and Chon on the other, Gronitskog was seated in the cube, and the three Palainians were crowded up close to the almost invisible walls.

The interrogation began with verbal communication by Cloudd, then with Chon, followed by some gentle telepathic probing by Chon. Gronitskog was puzzled by the shifting images a few yards away from him, but the two Tellurians kept him busy enough that he did not really comprehend that what he was half seeing was a trio of monstrous aliens.

Then Nadreck began his own gentle but insistent mind probing. The reaction was completely unexpected. Gronitskog screamed out words having reference to "devils," threw up his arms to hide his face, which was distorted with terror, and collapsed in a heap. Cloudd and Chon bent over him, straightening his body, loosening his clothes, and chaffing his hands and face.

"Nadreck says we must carry Gronitskog back to our room and lay him out on the bed," Chon said, motioning Cloudd to lift Gronitskog's feet. They wrestled the unconscious body through the angles of the corridors, constricted by the zone-of-force envelope thrown around them as their temporary, moving bubble of oxygenated air.

In response to Cloudd's query, Chon explained, "Nadreck says his mind probe struck an implanted mental barrier. The reaction was like a posthypnotic suggestion — Nadreck's penetration was so deep and close to some kind of knowledge forbidden to the consciousness that it triggered a complete mental blockage within the Togran. The Palainians were suddenly seen as Satanic figures. My own Lens tells me he'll recover, but he certainly needs rest."

When the limp body was on the bed, its muscles stiffened and the eyes opened. Chon stared into them and told Cloudd, without turning his head, "He can't talk. He believes his voice has been paralyzed. He wants us to leave the room so he can pray to his god."

"That cannot be," said Nadreck, strong enough through the walls to be caught by Cloudd. "You can't leave him alone. Nor can you give him back his real prayer-amplifier icon — I consider it too dangerous. Who knows what he might summon. Let him pray in your presence. He needs to be propped up, revitalized with some spirit if we're going to continue our questioning. I'll monitor his prayers and inject some encouragement into whatever he expects to hear. Don't tell me it's unethical, Chon; I'll be properly circumspect."

Gronitskog sat up and held his hands to his head.

"At least let's lower our heads and our eyes, Cloudd," Chon said aloud. "This is undeniably a sacred moment for him."

Gronitskog took the fake icon of the double sphere from around his neck and placed it on the floor. According to Chon, the substitution of the Palainian-made bauble had not been noticed. He hitched up his black robe, knelt, and prostrated himself so that his forehead rested on the hallowed symbol. Chon lowered his eyes, as Cloudd turned away to assemble his tapes and notes.

Cloudd felt the wave of heat before he heard the bang and the hissing and crackling. The illumination in the room brightened with a red flash. As Cloudd turned he caught a glimpse of the kneeling form of Gronitskog completely enveloped in fire. His robes were burning redly, but his head and hands were covered with flickering green flames. There was no outcry, no gasp, just the hissing of the green flames. Before they could make any move to stop the burning and save him, Gronitskog was utterly incinerated. A small pile of ashes smouldered on the floor.

"My fault, my fault!" Nadreck's humanlike groans came

within the shocked Tellurian heads. "I was stupid to let him reach out for the Eich. His faith was so strong — he was an archbishop for good reason, which I underestimated. I'm unworthy of your trust. Chon! — Chon? Are you all right?"

Chon was on his knees, left arm across his face. When he lowered his hand, Cloudd, with horror, saw that the bottom part of the Chaplain General's face was black and the upper was mottled pink and red. Chon gingerly brushed his facial skin with fingertips. He looked at Cloudd and his eyes were clear.

"I've been badly scorched, Nadreck," Chon spoke to Cloudd and projected to Nadreck at the same time. He picked up with his left hand a tumbler of water sitting on the tiny table with the books and threw the water on his face. "It's not serious. My beard protected me and fortunately my eyes were closed. What's annoying is that I seem to have broken my right arm when I was knocked back and tripped over the chair." For the first time, Cloudd noticed that Chon's right arm hung down loosely at his side. "When we sort this out, you can direct me to the sick bay or whatever you have aboard this modern ship."

"Your pain is my pain, Chon," Nadreck said. "It is my fault."

"Don't berate yourself, Nadreck," Chon protested. "That prayer call should not have been strong enough to produce an answer. It was the fake icon that was responsible."

"I know, I know," Nadreck said. "Too late, too late. He believed so implicitly in his ornament that he multiplied the strength of his own prayer as if he had really had his amplifier. This is the worst humiliation of my life. He got the message to self-destruct, and he immolated himself, fanatic enough to be a pyrophorist. I have allowed this valuable evidence, this key to the solution of our most serious problem to be destroyed. I, Nadreck, have allowed this to happen. Shame!"

"I pray for his soul, Nadreck. He was not all bad, and he would have become a worthy ally. If anyone is to be blamed, it should be me, for I know the power of faith. His god, as he saw it, answered him and gave him the strength to do this."

"Not his god, Chon," Nadreck said. "His false god. He called upon his masters, the Eich."

"And his prayers were heard. Did he ask to be destroyed?"

"No."

"Then why . . . ?"

"He was a living link through whom I could burrow my way into the hidden places and the secrets of the Eich. He did not want death. He did not know he was marked to die if he revealed his true nature. Nor did I. He was no telepath, yet he opened up the shield I had around him. Even I did not know how intimately close he was to his masters.'"

"So that is why the Eich destroyed him."

"Unfortunately," Nadreck slowly and solemnly stated, in a manner suggesting that he was lecturing himself, "I must confess that it is far worse than just the Eich who came in answer to his prayers. It was as Kallatra suggests — Eichwoor and a thousand thousand like him — a multiplicity of Eichwooren.

"I have suspected special trouble brewing on Togra and planets like it. It was that suspicion that led me to take my Z-Academy training mission there. It is this new evidence from Gronitskog that caused me only hours ago to dispatch the original cadet crew under Tweeda back to Togra on an Eich search. All except Yadsue, of course, who is with us. They're all Lensmen now, and the only ones available for such a quick assignment. They may be young and inexperienced, but they'll be competent. They're the top of their class. And we've got the additional advantage of having the apo-Eich, as well as the apo-Onlonian, as two of the scrutinizers. You must pray, Chon, that they find some weakness in the enemy security."

"I will, Nadreck."

"Eichwooren, they are our deadliest threat, thousands

upon thousands times worse than that which Worsel and Kallatra faced last year. For the merest instant I have sensed them gathering on the edge of the other plane of existence, poised for their invasion. Lalla Kallatra's father, Deuce O'Sx, our guardian on the other side has been surrounded and overwhelmed. Civilization lies open to the assault upon our minds and the destruction of our spirits."

"So!" Cloudd exclaimed, "the invading fleets are the work of the Eich!"

"Not so!" said Nadreck. "Chon and I know the truth. Those fleets are someone else's threat — even as the Bosko-Spawn are preparing to challenge us with their own warships. The Eichwooren and their living counterparts, the Eich, are about to fight us on the mental plane only. They are disdaining our machines. They are like an infinitely large subetheric neutron bomb. The strange ships come from someone else.

"We have a three-front war developing, and we don't know how to defend ourselves against any of them!"

M E? COME OUT AND SIT WITH you?" Cloudd called out to the dragon Lensman. "Not a chance, Worsel. You've got the great big wings, not me."

Cloudd looked straight down at the jungle of vegetation over a thousand feet below and instinctively drew back a few inches from the edge of the open platform. "I'm not the wild guy I used to be. Even wearing a Null-G belt I wouldn't enjoy the stroll, even with as nice a fellow as you are for company."

Worsel, the Second Stage Lensman, was perched out on a landing rod, about twenty feet from the main balcony of Level 161, grinning wickedly at his Tellurian friend. He had just flown up from a lower stage and positioned himself to survey the perimeter of 161 and the others just below, obviously looking for someone. When he had seen Cloudd, one who over the past year had become a friend, he couldn't resist a bit of teasing — he Lensed an invitation for him to walk out along the eight-inch-wide beam and sit down and visit.

"Well, I'm shocked, Cloudd," Worsel said, pretending that he was and shaking his narrow serpentine head in mock disapproval. "You're supposed to be a firecracker, afraid of nothing, with a keen eye and great coordination, and you can't walk out a few feet to join an old friend for a few moments of relaxation. It's wide enough for an elephant to walk with its eyes shut. What're you afraid of? Don't you think I'd swoop down and snatch you up before you hit the bushes? Don't you trust old Worsel?"

The Velantian had his slender toes curled in a locked grip around the roost, and his sinewy ten-foot, scimitar-tipped tail was wrapped around the far end for balance. His head was cocked at a jaunty angle at the top of his long neck. A half dozen eyes, somewhat extended on their stalks, were pointed mostly at the human's face.

Cloudd ordinarily was fearless, but even standing a foot away from such a brink was stomach churning for him. He had never been on Velantia III before; the unusual shifting light, the heavy musky odor, and the hot-then-cold winds that alternately tugged at him and nudged him made him insecure. He readily admitted that he no longer was the fool-hardy or reckless daredevil he once had been.

The building on which Cloudd was standing so high in the air was the central one of the Worsel Institute. He had expected a mass of impressive structures, probably of stone and dureum with high arched doors and windows to accommodate the huge reptilian Velantians. He had visualized the laboratories as white and polished, highly efficient, with the latest scientific equipment filling room after room. Velantians would be everywhere, many with long white robes hanging loosely on their thin bodies to protect their glossy scales from being soiled or even, perhaps, to protect the apparatuses from the oils of their scales.

To his surprise, the Worsel Institute wasn't like that at all. The buildings were a collection of tall cylinders placed in some kind of obscure pattern to enhance the streams or gusts of air. Running up the center of each cylinder was a service core containing a freight elevator. Encircling each building every twenty feet or so was a balcony rim. Jutting from each rim was a semicircular platform orientated five degrees off the lower one, forming a sort of spiral staircase of platforms or corkscrew of levels.

Each floor was a department or section, open to the air and protected only by a low railing a foot high. Velantians were able, in inclement weather, to fly in an upward circle, always under cover. A full circular roof covered the top, like an umbrella or the cap of a mushroom.

As Cloudd watched, Velantians were flying up and down on the outside, occasionally soaring and gliding from one building to another. The arrangement seemed efficient, healthful, and pleasing to the eye. It was also, to an earthman, spectacularly dangerous.

Worsel's personal space occupied the top five floors of the tallest tower, Levels 159 through 164. It was there that the conference was being held, the mapping of strategy by the Executive Sub-Committee of the Galactic Council, headed by President Haynes and the four Second Stage Lensmen. Worsel was the acting chairman, conferring in person with Lensmen Chon, Kallatra, and Yadsue, and their temporary Velantian staffs, and consulting by Lens, on the basis of equal rank, with Kinnison, Tregonsee, and Nadreck. Nadreck could have been at the Worsel Institute in one of its special Z-rooms or in his oversized atmosuit. His customized atmosuit was much like a portable, miniature room and laboratory combined. Instead, Nadreck preferred to stay aboard the Palainian super-destroyer in comfort and participate in the hourly Lens-to-Lens linkups.

While Cloudd stood there, steeling himself against the natural impulse to back away to a safer position, a small, furry creature scampered out along the beam and climbed up one of Worsel's muscular thighs and hung on to his master's leather belt-harness. The gold-haired creature's huge, luminous eyes stared blankly at Cloudd, but the tiny mouth definitely was shaped into a humorous grin. Its tiny, bulbous fingers plucked away the notecase hooked to Worsel's belt and tucked it into its shoulder-slung big blue pouch twelve inches deep and almost the height of its crouching form.

"Thanks, Bluebelt," Worsel said, telepathing his comment so Cloudd could hear it, more out of a desire to tease Cloudd than any wish for politeness. "Give it to my friend, Lieutenant Cloudd, and tell him to check the details with Kallatra. Tell him I'm gliding down to the communications section and will join everyone in a short while."

As Bluebelt hopped back on the perch, Worsel abruptly launched himself into space, unfolding his wings as he plummeted down. Bluebelt, still grinning and chattering unintelligibly, scampered back to the balcony and stopping before Cloudd, gave a wink and a little bow and presented him with the notecase. Cloudd wasn't sure what powers Bluebelt possessed as Worsel's most trusted personal assistant at the Institute, so he smiled in return and simultaneously thought hard and said aloud, "Thank you kindly, sir," and took the courier case. Bluebelt scurried under some furniture and disappeared.

"I saw that, Benson," Lalla Kallatra said, when Cloudd walked around a low partition to the circle of chairs. As usual she was standing stiffly, swiveling only her head. "For a moment my pump skipped a tick. I thought you were going to let Worsel tempt you into catwalking out there. Sometimes his humor is positively wicked."

"Perhaps that is the curse of genius," came the thought to Cloudd. It was Nadreck, projecting from his Palainian ship, which hung in synchronous orbit overhead but out of sight. "Kimball Kinnison is almost as difficult. He would have taken Worsel's dare and walked out there, but then Worsel would have known that and wouldn't have suggested such foolishness. I will never get to understand you Tellurians. All this is a ridiculous waste of time. We are sitting on one or more time bombs, which, for all we know, exploded an hour ago as forecast. Lieutenant Cloudd, you have the official authorizations in your hand. Give them to Lensman

Kallatra, who will open and read them to herself."

Kallatra passed the sheets one after another before her eyes, absorbing their information at a glance.

As she finished, Nadreck said, "QX. Everything's in order. I must return my attention to Lensman Tregonsee with whom I am having a Lens-to-Lens conference. Please discuss with each other the possible changes due to the incapacity of Chaplain General Chon."

For Cloudd, there was a long period of silence in his head. Obviously he wasn't being privileged to hear that which a non-Lens man wasn't expected to hear. As Tregonsee was the chief intelligence head for all of Civilization as well as the Patrol in both galaxies, the tightest secrecy and security was to be expected. This led Cloudd to be struck, suddenly, with the realization that Kallatra never did communicate with him by use of her Lens, never moving herself intimately inside his head. The fact was, he all at once sharply noted, she was the only Lensman who made him uneasy when she touched his mind.

"Chon," she said aloud to him, breaking his troubled thought, "is going to recover from his mental disability."

"What? Oh," Cloudd said, taken off guard. "It was a nervous breakdown?" Chon had collapsed four hours before, shortly after their arrival on Velantia, raving about being a Satanic minion of the Eich. He had been rushed to the hospital. Even a Lensman, Cloudd had been willing to accept, could be expected to suffer the crippling of his mind under such an experience as he had had.

"A temporary sickness, fortunately. Lensmen still have their normal frailties, with more complex mentalities producing more complex stresses, but Chon was spiritually vulnerable to injury. Injury, that is, not death. Conversely, his firm spiritual foundation insulated him from irreparable debilitating harm, if not complete paralysis."

"It's wonderful news," Cloudd finally said, becoming aware of the full import of her words.

"His arm is completely healed, and physically he's in perfect shape, but mentally he'll require attention and several days of hospitalization. He'll be out of action indefinitely." The robot woman once again turned her blank, immobile face toward Cloudd. There was, however, a new expression in her shining eyes, which disturbed him. He saw suffering there. It was unmistakable. Something was causing her physical pain. It shocked him to be reminded that she was a human being.

"That's bad," he said. "The plans we've been making for the past ten hours will have to be revised. As Nadreck pointed out, the zero hour set by that rumor for the invasion to begin someplace has passed. We have no time left. Yet we still aren't certain whom we're fighting, what we're fighting, or where we're fighting. You were scheduled to go to Togra with Chon and join the new Palainian Lensmen. Does that mean you'll be going alone?"

Kallatra, for emphasis, shook the packet of papers she was holding. "According to these, President Haynes has agreed to our plans for two operations, with Worsel in charge of one and Nadreck in charge of the other. The Worsel action party, meaning me and Chon, if he is healthy, is to go to the planet Togra to pick up leads to the Eich. I'm to concentrate on the spirit allies of the Eich, meaning Eichwoor himself and his potential hordes of Eichwooren. Nadreck remains in Velantia orbit ready to rush to the scene of the first contact with the enemy fleet. Evidently I go alone, with Chon."

Nadreck's voice came to Cloudd again. "Tregonsee wants to know where you would start to attempt relocation of the datadrones. They're a connection we haven't fully explored since the Armstrong affair."

"I'd start from the Andromeda constellation, sir," Cloudd said.

"Kallatra, give Cloudd all references to the datadrones, and then destroy those reports. Chon is out of action and won't need any briefing." As quickly as it had arrived, Nadreck's presence left.

The robotoid began flipping through the pages again with the speed and rhythm of a copying machine.

"According to this, Benson, our problems have been labeled as Operation Eichwooren, hypothesizing from Nadreck's vision, and Operation Robot Revolution, theorizing that some kind of temporary or permanent fundamental change is taking place. I should he personally involved in both operations, but, of course, my special talent concerns the Eichwooren. Worsel's in the same situation. And so is Nadreck. Because of that encounter Worsel had with the sentient machines forming Arrow-22 on the Planetoid of Knowledge, he should be working on the rebellion problem, rather than Nadreck. And Nadreck, because he uncovered the trouble on Togra, should be working with me. However, because Worsel and I once fought the Eichwoor, our assignment is logical. Because of your involvement with the datadrone technology you certainly belong with Nadreck.

"Now, about the facts you need . . ." She quickly read off to him all the references to datadrones and aberrant machines. To Cloudd, there was nothing he didn't know already.

"Anything about your father's spirit?" he asked cautiously. "We all know he was in bad trouble. What's new? If I can, I'd like to know."

"There isn't anything. When Worsel and I heard about his danger, about the time I arrived here, we joined our minds in a strenuous effort to reach him through the veil across the other existence. We encountered total emptiness — which is ominous. I tried to sense him as the robotic 24of6; there were no frequency patterns. My psyche tried to touch his Deuce O'Sx psyche; again, nothing. Worsel joined with me for enormous amplification of my el-sike penetrations without results. However, as I have not had any feeling of tragedy or any bad intuition, I feel that Deuce is still an intelligence whose otherworldly existence has not been destroyed."

A shadow and a breeze came across their area briefly and departed. Worsel had arrived with a beating of his vast wings. He folded them away unobtrusively against his back as he came to them in eight giant strides.

"We've received our signals, they've been decoded, and I'm ready to leave. I've set up a command post here at the Institute staffed with our best Velantians and our most accomplished Rigellians. My associate Hobdyll, the South Velantian Lensman, is chief of operations, with Bluebelt as my personal communications aide. Nadreck has just finished turning his destroyer into his command post for Operation Robot Revolution, or Rob-Rev, with himself as chief of operations and his new Lensman Yadsue as his aide."

From the tables scattered around the circular conference area, Worsel was picking up certain spools, cassettes, and tiny boxes of recorded information and stuffing them in pouches in the belts around his abdomen.

"Kallatra, you've got to get to Togra as quickly as possible. Nadreck's cadets report they're on to something there. You'll have to go alone. However, I'm going to take up a position at a central point between Velantia, Tellus, and Togra, to back you up, yet able to meet any contingency. You need a Lensman to monitor you who is familiar with the Eich and Eichwoor. Chon could have done it. Now I'll have to do it at long range.

"As for you, Cloudd, not being a Lensman, your effectiveness is limited. You have to be telepathic in both directions, able to transmit as well as receive. I thought of sending you along with Kallatra, but that's no more practical than me going, if for different reasons. Then I thought of Tregonsee taking over for me as head of Operation Eichwooren, and me going with Kallatra, but Tregonsee's got his tentacles full of his complicated S.I.S. and M.I.S. probes, searches, and investigations for some information on the current crop of menaces we're facing. However, Nadreck and Tregonsee have come up with a good idea to use you, as you've no doubt guessed. You're going out on a personal search. To keep in contact, I've arranged for your own setup from my staff — Bluebelt will help. You are to put together every detail you can on the mystery ships. You'll stay in constant touch with Bluebelt and your staff, who remain here.

"I see you're wondering how to keep in contact without a Lens. Well, Lensman Dick Armstrong has reported in from his rim patrol encounter, which we all know about. He's been debriefed and he's going with you in the Tellurian speedster we keep on this planet. If there's one thing you're good at, Cloudd, it's hot rodding a personal spaceship. Go down to the spaceport and meet Armstrong. You'll be leaving as soon as Nadreck briefs you and releases you. Find those invisible ships. And good luck to you both."

Worsel had stopped picking up things, but all of his eyes were waving around on their stalks, making certain he had not overlooked anything.

"QX, Kallatra?" Worsel asked. "Ready to go? I'll take one more update, and we'll make another stab at reaching Deuce O'Sx. And then we'll be off for Togra aboard *Flame*." Kallatra nodded in her awkward way. *Flame*, Cloudd recalled, was Worsel's name for his own personal speedster. "I'll drop you off there and then take up my position as planned."

Worsel bounced over to one of the control boards placed behind the chairs and with incredible speed, sent his slender fingers with their trimmed yet still sharp claws dancing over a hundred buttons. He cocked one eye on the input, one eye on the reply screen, one eye on Kallatra, and one eye on Cloudd, the others still roving, and said, "Ready, Kallatra? We'll join in one more effort to reach Deuce. I've had two hundred of our best Rigellian perceivers with high level psychic indices working on that situation for the past two hours with no luck. Mental frequencies are crystal clear, but equipment and communications channels are contaminated and fouling up electrical systems. This robot revolution is some kind of anarchy. The invasion fleet might be a false alarm, but the disorders in our robotry and semi-intelligent automata are for real."

Worsel pretended to kick the machine with one of his powerful hind legs and then gestured Kallatra into position before the board.

"You have the ability to give me a hint as to what's happening, Kallatra. Tune into the lines and give me your impressions."

She rolled forward so her trunk and legs pressed against the metal front. She laid her shining fingers along the outer edges of the keyboard and placed her forehead, with its glimmering Lens, against the upper cabinet.

"I've done this before," she said in her impersonal voice. "Nowhere has there been a hint of any independent, intelligent thinking machines. There must be, however, a source for all the troubles. I'll look again. I'll look as hard as I possibly can while I drop all safeguards — " Without warning her arms jerked up and she rolled rapidly backward with a squeal of gears, almost knocking Cloudd off his feet. He instinctively wrapped his arms around her waist and hung on grimly to prevent her from toppling over.

"Let go of her!" Worsel commanded sharply. As Cloudd obeyed, Worsel himself picked her up in his sinewy arms, froze stiffly in intense concentration for a split second, swung himself around, and dashed for the edge of the platform. As he sprang outward, his thirty feet of body and tail strung out like a winged snake, he planted a series of thoughts in Cloudd's mind: "Get to your ship and check with Nadreck! Kallatra's caught a case of the gremlins. . . . Her prostheses are malfunctioning. We're off to the hospital for her new body . . . . What a lucky chance, a propitious time; it's fate!"

Within seconds Worsel and Kallatra were gone.

Worsel's thoughts didn't end in Cloudd's head; they sort of trailed off into a jumble of ideas. He had never seen Worsel so excited, even happy, yet at the same time so enormously serious. A new body? What did he mean by that?

Words came back to him that Worsel had spoken when he had introduced Cloudd to the girl in the mechanical body. "Some day she'll have a natural face." Only now did he realize Worsel had not said "natural-looking face."

Cloudd was running out of the main building to jump on a passing electric freight cart going toward the spaceport when Nadreck reached him.

"I expect you to leave in twenty minutes for Andromeda, Cloudd. When you're on your final check, have Armstrong Lens me."

Nadreck was irritated at Worsel. The big snake had dashed off, sidetracked by his pet project, as if the destruction of the universe could wait for him and his experiment. It wasn't that Nadreck didn't like Lalla Kallatra, because he did. She had a brain that was able to comprehend his — and his was as good as the two or three best in the universe. In fact, Nadreck secretly told himself, it was times like this that he was certain that he indisputably had the best mind of any Lensman and second only to some Arisians.

He had just completed his Lensed exchange with Tregonsee when Kallatra collapsed. Through his sense of perception, augmented by his Lens, Nadreck had discovered what Worsel had discovered — Kallatra's mechanical body was faltering under the unexplainable subetheric interference plaguing all machines. Kallatra, as a mechanism supporting a human brain, was the only machine in existence, so far as he knew, that could actually be considered mortal and subject to total destruction. Other life-support systems might fail, but safeguards always existed. Except in the case of Kallatra. Nadreck didn't want her to die, but Worsel could have put her brain on a standard life-support system with appropriate protections and worried about her body later. She could have functioned that way, with her Lens laid out on her cortex, but no, Worsel wanted to shove her brain into that new body he'd cloned and had been growing for her. Her trip to Togra seemed out of the question.

Well, anyhow, Nadreck thought, the operation was bound to be a success, or Worsel wouldn't be doing it at such a critical moment. And maybe, Nadreck conceded to himself, always as forthright in admitting he could be wrong as he was arrogant in pointing out when he was right, just maybe Kallatra could function better against the Eichwooren in an organic body. Tellurians were always worrying about physical appearances and growing old and sometimes Velantians seemed just as irrational. Even barrel-bodied Rigellians — yes, even Tregonsee himself — made references to physical deterioration and counted the stretch marks of aging on their hard-shelled, leathery bodies. Anyhow, whatever the outcome, Worsel would certainly let him know the news when it was appropriate to do so.

Nadreck resented his feeling of irritation. It wasn't really Worsel and Kallatra who made him feel this way, of course. Nadreck was irritated because he had no obvious course of action to take. The ships or fleets that threatened them were as ghostly as Eichwoor, whom he had never really believed existed. Tregonsee, who always seemed to know something about everything, was as frustrated as the rest of the leadership of the Patrol. Nadreck knew, deep within his multidimensional gut, that the threat was real even if he couldn't prove it. He carefully went back over what he had told Tregonsee:

"The assumption must be that they are intruders, if not actually invaders. They are not violently hostile, or even mildly antagonistic, but, in fact, benevolent to an unknown degree. They come from an unknown place, most likely from the Second Galaxy or a galactic cluster, perhaps even from deep or intergalactic space. They are familiar with Civilization and Boskonia, with their derivation probably from Tellurian culture. They have a high technology and a desire for secrecy and noncommunication. The vehicles may be manned or unmanned. Their destination is unknown. Their purpose is unknown. By themselves, as I have observed

them, they pose no obvious threat to anyone, except by accident. However, their appearance comes at a time when there
are rumors of hostile action against Civilization and against
the Patrol, coinciding with as yet unidentifiable subetheric
frequencies interfering with Patrol defenses and machinery
and technology in general. Therefore, it is my conclusion,
that it is imperative that more be known about them, even
if it necessitates violent action by us against them to obtain
that information."

Tregonsee had agreed with him, and so had President
Haynes. Kinnison had been informed immediately that the
Patrol should undertake warlike actions without hesitation.

What was Worsel going to do about Togra, now that
both Chon and Kallatra were out of action? Well, that
was his problem; Nadreck had his own problem. The big
puzzle was how to monitor the so-called Robot Revolution.
Machines couldn't be trusted to check up on machines.
Unsupervised readings were unreliable. There weren't enough
Lensmen to go around for the purpose of noticing and correcting mechanical problems. What was needed was a non
mechanical meter or gauge. Fortunately the Ordovik crystal
that warned of the existence of hyperspatial tubes was unaf-
fected. There were millions of Ordovik crystal detectors in
operation throughout the Patrol, with every Lensman wearing one. There was absolutely no hyperspatial tube activity, so
the undiscovered fleet would not come through one and take
the Patrol by surprise.

After much cogitation, Nadreck suggested a method
by which the machines throughout Civilization could be
monitored and Tregonsee had enthusiastically endorsed the
idea. He furnished Nadreck with planetary coordinates that
Nadreck could use to find the world he needed and also
volunteered to marshall a task force of S.I.S. and Special
Missions Forces personnel to help collect and distribute
the monitors. Nadreck, pressed for time, welcomed the help,
but insisted that he personally had to go to the most popu-

lous planet of arthropods. Worsel had also been consulted in order to obtain some expert advice from the specialized personnel on the Planetoid of Knowledge, where the Great Hall of the Machines was situated, which contained all the information on all of Civilization's machines and had representative samples of them in operational form available to analyze. It was there that the mechanical consciousness known as Arrow-22 had been confronted by Worsel and driven from the galaxy. Worsel had also approved, praising the idea, but had facetiously dubbed Nadreck's principal source as Bug World and Cockroach Planet. Nadreck had patiently explained that it was Arthropod-0392, but even he had come around to thinking of it as Bug World and of its inhabitants as the Beetle People.

The request Nadreck had been expecting from Worsel came to him while he was discussing with his staff how to handle his absence from the operations ship while busy on Bug World. He particularly briefed Yadsue on the way to handle his personal Lens communications. If Yadsue was surprised to find how accurately Nadreck could anticipate a call, he didn't show it.

The caller was Worsel, and he explained that the operation to transfer Lalla's brain into the flesh body was progressing satisfactorily. The empty-headed body had been growing for her ever since her original organic body had reached the chronological age of nineteen. Worsel had planned on something between twenty-one and twenty-five, but waiting extra months for growth was no longer practical. The DNA manipulation had left the brain cavity with nothing but a medulla oblongata and a skullfull of fluid, just as Worsel had so imaginatively envisioned.

Worsel's call, however, was about the problem that Nadreck had anticipated and prepared for.

"Chon's out of it. Now Kallatra's out of it. I'm going to have to go to Togra myself, Nadreck. I need a backup just as I had planned for Kallatra. How about you standing by in your own speedster out in space? Tregonsee has agreed to take over your command post and run both your and his operations from there. QX?"

"Yes, Worsel. I expected your request. I've made all the arrangements. I'll leave immediately, as soon as my flitter is loaded. Tregonsee can take over from me as soon as he gets here, and my staff can carry on until he does."

"You're terrific, Nadreck! You should have been a Velantian! Chon hasn't been informed, and shouldn't be, but Cloudd has — he's been long gone with Armstrong. We're five hours past the original invasion deadline, so maybe it won't happen after all — I can dream, can't I? I'm jetting out now. Lens me on Togra as soon as you get into position. May Klono go with us!"

Before he left, Nadreck Lensed the young Kweeda on Togra and heard their plans for their reception of Worsel. Worsel would have plenty of lines to follow in search of the Eich. Then he Lensed Tregonsee and received a rude shock.

"Friend Nadreck," Tregonsee said, cool and unruffled as always, even in moments of stress, "we seem to have a problem with Cloudd." Tregonsee explained in his typically laconic way that Cloudd was breaking the supreme taboo of the Galactic Patrol, undertaking the gravest breach of Patrol discipline, violating the wishes of Mentor himself.

Cloudd had passed through the Andromeda constellation, continuing on out of the galaxy in the superspeedster, heading for a different galaxy. It certainly appeared he was bound for the huge Andromeda galaxy itself!

"I cannot reach him by Lens. Perhaps he is ignoring me. He is your protégé, Nadreck, see if you can recall him."

Nadreck was, for one of his rare moments, without anything to say.

"Did you, perhaps, send him there, Nadreck?" Nadreck found expression to his feelings at last. "No. I did not. Civilization seems to be going mad. It's the Tellurians, Treg. The Eichwooren have found a way to addle their brains.

"If Chon were healthy, I'd ask him to pray for us. "What can we do about it, Treg? Nothing! Only Mentor can solve this crazy predicament!"

The Stolen Star

THE PLANET THAT WAS A STAR *moved slowly out of orbit. Shimmering waves of energy rose up out of its chromosphere, that ruddy gaseous layer of incandescent atoms that mantles a star, and formed into the luminescent envelope of its corona. The plumes of broken atoms were twisted and warped by the stresses of the manipulated magnetic forces, but they did not diminish the forces of its thermonuclear fires.*

The planet-star slowly curved away from its central group of two guarding suns — one red dwarf and its captive red microdwarf — and, gathering momentum, headed away from the core of the Milky Way, through the spiral arm known as Rift 240, toward gathering fleets of the Galactic Patrol.

The Cahuitans, whose nursery world was being stolen, were not frantic, for that was not their way. But they, who ordinarily took a thousand years to make a simple decision, reacted within days, an infinitesimal moment of their time.

The Cahuitans were beings of pure energy, complex and long-lived, not even vaguely corporeal or substantial. Their intelligence was so uncomplicated and logical as to be almost incomprehensible to the handful of minds of Galactic Civilization who had managed to understand their existence. Within the billions of suns and planets of the First Galaxy, it was as if they did not exist. They had no part or interest in Civilization, and in turn, that attitude was reciprocated.

Only briefly and disastrously had the Cahuitans once entered into symbiosis with Civilization before both parties had agreed to separate as distant friends. Now this was changing, and the Bosko-Spawn were the cause, creating an antipathetic symbiosis calculated to destroy only the Galactic Union, but unwittingly bound to do the same to the race of Cahuitans.

All the future generations of the Cahuitans, their ethereal children, were being taken from them by organic-chemical beings. The Cahuitans did not differentiate between the forces of Civilization and the Spawn, nor did they care to.

There were no weapons to resist the rape of their small system. Only one of their beings, Medury, had ever even communicated with a double-mind from the material existence. They could not protest or plead or threaten. Medury had tried and failed.

They had only themselves. As living atomic vortices they could be their own weapons, living bombs. They gathered together into an enormous mass of pure energy and pursued the thieves. Streaming in pursuit, like an invisible bolt of lightning in space, they knew they might not, could not, rescue their children and the nursery. But they certainly would destroy the murdering meddlers.

Kimball Kinnison paced impatiently back and forth in his large cabin, the nerve center of an entire galaxy while he was aboard his special warship, the famous *Dauntless*. When he strode across the thick gowskin rug, there was no noise, for he moved with the silent grace of the human animal he was. When the hard rubber heels of his gray leather boots struck the metal decking of the ship, however, he beat out a sharp, rhythmic tattoo. The noise of his clicking heels gave him a sense of action, or at least a promise of action, like the rolling of drums before the battle.

Back and forth he went, alone and deep in thought. From time to time he would pound one heavy fist into the leathery palm of his other hand. Kinnison's hands were tough and firm, not like those of a chair-bound executive, for his whole body was kept in top physical condition by day-to-day attention. Without his moments of contrived action, or exercise, his job of Galactic Coordinator would have been impossibly tedious and destructively sedentary.

"Where in all the purple hells are those damn Boskonians!" he said to himself and gritted his strong white teeth in his notoriously aggressive jaw. Men flinched from his eagle stare above that obstinate jaw and acknowledged him their master. The jaw was set now, but there was no one it could impress. The enemy was nowhere to be found.

Kinnison had taken a task force of Patrol warships out to the edge of the First Galaxy, in the vicinity of the Lensman Armstrong incident, as soon as the other Second Stage Lensmen had taken up their scheduled tasks. He was there only as a result of his having made a forceful appeal to Council President Haynes with assurances that he had arranged for mobilization and a complete war footing for the Second Galaxy and that his presence for a week would not be missed. Kinnison's jurisdiction technically didn't extend into the home galaxy, but as his old classmate, Raoul LaForge, who was in charge of First Galaxy defenses, was more than happy to share responsibilities with his close friend, and as President Haynes, their boss, was partial to Kinnison and knew also that keeping an old war-horse from dashing to a five-sector fire was psychologically wrong, Kinnison got his wish. Kinnison was the first line of reconnaissance and defense. All that was needed to make Kinnison's joy complete was the enemy to fight.

The enemy finally came, and more than he had bargained for.

A warning bleep and a crisp voice came out of the console in the center of his famous poker table. The message froze Kinnison in midstride.

"Sir! Detectors show an uncharted object curving to

intersect our course. Readings indicate the characteristics of a small star, but they also show the object is either inhabited or manned by lifeforms."

With a curt acknowledgment of the message, Kinnison leaned across the long side of his elliptical table and punched up his information screens rapidly, one after the other. The muscles in his cheeks had turned his grim mouth into a wry grin. Action at last, and it looked like something big! There was no doubt that a presumed enemy spaceship in the magnitude of ten or twenty percent of the Grand Fleet was approaching them at an unbelievable speed and accelerating. It was like only one other incredible thing he had seen before— a phantom warship of the Qu'orr. That, however, could not be what was approaching now. He had no doubt as to what should be done.

"Salgud!" he barked to the captain of the *Dauntless*, who was also acting as his chief of staff. "I want the task force to pull back and keep a distance of one hundred million or an energy level of five point zero." The level was already at four and climbing, with a one two five distance.

"Yes, sir!" The readings on Kinnison's meters and gauges stabilized with Salgud's reply.

"Signals!" Kinnison called. "Signals!" His voice command wasn't necessary, having buzzed for them, but Kinnison believed in voice and telepathy and even in body language when expressing himself in the heat of action and to men under his command.

"Yes, sir!"

"Is Grand Fleet headquarters getting all this?"

"Yes, sir!"

Kinnison reached out with the stupendous power of his mind and made instantaneous contact with LaForge.

"Raoul! Get this!" Kinnison flashed to his friend all the information he now possessed, together with his analysis of the unstoppable danger. "We're accelerating back toward you, but the thing keeps coming. If we go into free flight, we'll lose contact, and that might happen in the next ten minutes. Your fleet is big enough to stop it, provided you get into position. If you miss, it's capable of eating up any Civilized planet it can reach, and that includes Tellus and Prime Base!"

Kinnison's heart jumped in his throat. The thing had grabbed his task force in a zone of traction and was using his own ships to pull itself almost at light speed toward them. It now looked like a comet as the Einsteinian effect of distension took place. This was no Qu'orr! This was real!

There was nothing Kinnison could do!

"Give my love to Clarrissa!" Kinnison called out to LaForge as the static overwhelmed him. ". . . and the baby!" The message may not have gotten through. Clarrissa might never know that his last thoughts were on her and their new baby boy.

Arthropod-0392, or Bug Planet, was a tiny world about 3,000 miles in diameter, covered with low scrub brush, bushes, and grass over three-quarters of its surface and with small ponds, lakes, and streams over the rest. Because of the eccentric movement along its axis of rotation, its seasons were mild and its climatic zones varied little from polar cap to equator. For a Tellurian it was an inhabitable place of veldts, steppes, and marshes, of pleasant temperatures and delightful gravitation.

For a Tellurian, it was also a world of horror, filled with every kind of creeping, crawling, wriggling, and flying insect and related species. They existed from microscopic size to fist size, and they were the entire extent of life. The sky had no birds and the water had no fish. Everywhere there were bugs.

For Nadreck, a Palainian, Arthropod-0392 was hell itself, loaded with oxygen, shimmering with heat, bright and unshaded in a glaring sun.

Nadreck had brought his speedster to rest on top of an

enormous patch of rock, floating softly down on his anti-G plates, but using his retro-rockets to sweep away the billions of tiny creatures he would have crushed. He knew what he was looking for, and he placed himself opposite the three-foot high mud tower where he could open up the nest with his ship's mechanical arms.

The Palainian wasted no time. He carefully sectioned the bughill with two double transparent plates, one pair horizontal and one pair vertical, and swung half of the nest aside. Each half was held intact by the separated plates.

He used his sense of perception to see the inside, for there was only a faint glow from the million luminescent grubs. He had had no difficulty finding the queen's chamber. The social system of these coleoptera was identical with the more common hymenoptera. Bugs or ants, in this world it made no difference, except that, unlike those who communicated by touch or sound or taste or smell, these bugs were telepaths. While it was true that the mental energy they gave off, even collectively as a colony of millions, was no more than an infinitesimal blip on a Tellurian or Velantian thought recorder, they nonetheless were true telepaths.

Already one half of the nest was summoning the other half to the defense of the queen. She lay below his intersecting horizontal plate, and only her workers and attendants within her chamber and in the passageways below could attend her. There was nothing they could do for her anyway. Blind and fat and incapable of moving, she could only lay her dozens of eggs each second from one end and take in the food constantly offered to her at the other indistinguishable, symmetrical end.

Nadreck opened up the molecules of the plate above her, reached in with his remote forceps, and placed her on the end of a flat tape protruding from the tube he had extended from the cargo area of his ship. He allowed the tube to sink downward through the plate and when it had, he closed the sections back together, reuniting the two parts of the nest. He withdrew the two plates, leaving everything nearly as it had been, except that a tube extended into the queen's, chamber and she herself was now lying on the tape within it.

Nadreck began to withdraw the tape up the tube, carrying the queen along its length, a trail of eggs stretching out in her wake. Nadreck watched with his sense of perception, shifting his attention from her, to the tube, and back to the nest. As he had foreseen, thousands of bugs were now choking the passageways and finding their way up the tube, following their queen. It was only a matter of time now before the entire nest would be stored in the three-foot square container in his hold. For the first few minutes they would be pouring in after their queen at the rate of one, two, three thousand a minute. Then with a few more tubes, he would increase the rate. Perhaps in five hours he would have the four million or so. That gave him five hours to conclude his arrangements.

There was no doubt in Nadreck's mind that his scheme would work, but he had to make a few tests to be sure.

Using his forceps he individually transferred a bug the size of a pin head to a small box within his ship. When he had six, he moved the box to his console desk, and using a pipette, he placed one each behind three of his dials and two of his transistorized schematic boards. Concentrating his attention on each one in turn, sometimes using his Lens and sometimes without, he picked up the tiny, subetheric waves being broadcast from them. It was a mental feat as difficult as it would be for an anthropoid to physically sort out white grains of salt from black grains of pepper. Difficult, yes, but hardly impossible for any Lensman or telepathic Patrolman.

What Nadreck received was perfect. It was as if Nadreck himself were behind each meter or transistor box. When he changed the capacitance or altered the setting, he could see the change, actually *feel* the change. He could monitor a hundred items with a hundred bugs and never be given a false reading. What the bug sensed, he sensed, and there was no interference from any source.

The question yet to be answered was whether or not the strange interference affecting the electronic and electrical circuitries of Civilization's machines would harm the little living creatures. Nadreck, however, was certain that would not happen. No living creature had been affected by the interference; it would stay that way — and Lalla Kallatra was the best proof of all. Only her machinery had been disturbed; her mind had remained absolutely untouched.

Distribution of the bugs would be easy. The problem would be the necessity of speed. Nadreck had formulated his plans before embarking on his trip. A hundred Patrol couriers would rendezvous with him above the Beetle Planet. Twenty thousand to forty thousand of the little creatures, Worsel's "cockroaches," would be transferred to each. A hundred more rendezvous would transfer to a hundred more ships, and yet another hundred. And the queen and her eggs would stay with Nadreck. Back on Velantia there would be thousands upon thousands of eggs hatching, and, unmolested, there would be females allowed to live who would produce more swarms. Within weeks the entire galaxy would be flooded with insects, each living indefinitely on a drop of food, each carefully placed to monitor a vulnerable machine, each hundred or thousand in turn monitored by a Lensman or a talented Patrolman.

There would be problems on the cold planets, that was unavoidable, but they would live for a while, warmed by the heat of the mechanisms they spied upon, and then, when they died, they would be replaced.

Small, unobtrusive, non interfering, easy to place, these insects would serve Civilization with unquestioning patience. They would not save the galaxies from the revolt of the robots, but they would make it possible to nullify the disastrous results of machines falsifying information about machines and creating insurmountable chaos.

Anyone of a thousand Lensman could have done what Nadreck had done. He knew, in all humbleness, that it was not he alone who could have come to Arthropod-0392 and performed this chore. But only by doing it himself, could he have been certain, as certain as he was now, that this wild idea would really work. Nobody could be as efficient and perfect as Nadreck, of that he was supremely confident.

All Nadreck had to do was wait until his cargo was aboard. And while waiting, he considered what had happened with Cloudd. The lieutenant had simply vanished.

"This is Nadreck calling Yadsue at Velantia III." The thought went out across half the galaxy, but the time lapse was nil. Yadsue was not that accomplished a Lensman to have received Nadreck so quickly on his own, but the staff aboard the Palainian ship was the best.

"Yadsue here, sir."

"Give me an update on Cloudd."

There was nothing new. He had absolutely vanished. His Lensman companion, Dick Armstrong, abandoned on a deserted planet in a globular cluster closest to Cloudd's line of flight, had been picked up by a Galactic Patrol scout summoned by Lens to his rescue.

Armstrong was a sensible man, Nadreck knew that, and for that reason had been chosen so long ago for that confrontation on Nadreck's forefather's research laboratory. Through Yadsue, Nadreck requested and obtained a Lensed connection with Armstrong, getting firsthand the story of Cloudd's strange disappearance in search of a clue to explain what had happened. Nadreck, finding no satisfactory explanation, was in the process of signing off when he felt a surge of alarm and anxiety vibrate through his connection.

"Sir!" said the young Yadsue, allowing a feeling of fear to be sensed by Nadreck, whereas a Tellurian would have bravely tried to stifle his alarm and apprehension over an impending disaster. "The Kinnison Task Force has been destroyed! Where it was is now a mass of thermonuclear energy. And it is alive, sir! Alive!"

Nadreck was stunned, though he didn't panic. He questioned Yadsue, but there was nothing more to be said. Another Patrol force was going to investigate.

"I am truly sorry. Kimball Kinnison was a great man," Nadreck said. "Tell Worsel or Tregonsee to inform me if there is anything for me to know about. Perhaps Kinnison escaped. I will stay here for another few hours, and my plan for the distribution of the beetle-monitors will begin at my signal. I am sending out my official alert immediately. Tell Worsel or Tregonsee I have confidence that they will avenge our friend's death, if that is the fact, and that they will turn back our enemies. Meanwhile I will do my humble bit even as I lament."

Lieutenant Benson Cloudd had left Velantia, with Dick Armstrong, under a great deal of tension. He was naturally upset to have seen the strange Lensman, Lalla Kallatra, at the point of death. She was a female personality who, he now recognized, by some droll and preposterous alchemy had become a substitute for the companionship of his lost Lucille. He didn't know how it had happened. He wasn't even certain that it, indeed, had happened. Yet, he felt that such a relationship existed even as he resented it and fought to shake it off.

What was she going to be if she lived? Another robotoid? A square box, this time? No, of course not. A prettier piece of mechanism? Possibly; it wouldn't take much to improve on the travesty of a woman that her mechanical body had been. What about that "natural face" Worsel had mentioned? Would she have a real head? A living face — and a tin body? How gruesome. Would she, as was hinted, have a real, flesh-and-blood body? with enzymes and the proper hormones and things? He winced to think about it. What would pure, innocent Lucille have made of all this? She had never been very imaginative; she would simply think he was crazy. Klono! That's what Lalla had that Lucille didn't have: a fascinating, trenchant mind. He had seen Lucille as a body; he had seen Lalla for what she truly was, a mind. And now he knew that each was just half of a woman. . . .

The other factor in his state of tension was the person he had become — perhaps not what he had become, but what he now recognized himself really to be. He wasn't the dashing, swashbuckling hero he thought he had become after the tragedy of Lucille's death under the guns of the Boskonians. He was just a smart and brave officer in the Galactic Patrol, honored through circumstance and allowed to mingle on equal footing with the mighty. He had no cause to consider himself even remotely the equal of Kimball Kinnison. He was a child compared to the great Worsel. He was a simple helpful Tellurian to the monstrous Nadreck. He, Cloudd, was living a lie. It was up to him to show them that he was not an impetuous savage, capable only of discussing datadrones. He would prove to himself that he was of heroic proportions, and if he died doing it, why then his life would be a success.

His decision to fly out of the universe, if necessary, had come with the query from Tregonsee. Indeed, where would he start to look for the datadrones if he could give himself his own orders? He would start in the Andromeda constellation, he had said. And then? And then he would fly on — *to the Andromeda Galaxy itself!* By all the gods! That was it! He would leave the circumscribed space of the First and Second galaxies! He would be the first of Civilization to go and look and find and report what was really there! Why had no one ever done it before? Why had the Galactic Patrol always acted as if the close neighbor of Andromeda — as near to the Milky Way, the First Galaxy, in the one direction as Lundmark's Nebula, the Second Galaxy, was in the other direction. The Andromeda Galaxy, the *Third* Galaxy! And maybe later on to the fourth, and the fifth!

Cloudd's vision was absolutely intoxicating.

It had come as a bucket of cold water tossed over him to hear that a strange Lensman, Dick Armstrong, was going to go with him. He wasn't jealous of the man — he was concerned that the new man would object and turn an exhilarating moment into a nasty scene, or perhaps die because of someone else's fearlessness.

One thing Cloudd did know: He was going to go in search of the datadrones, and if there were any more clues suggesting that they had disappeared out of the galaxy, out beyond where even the Patrol did not venture, he would not hesitate to pursue them. What he had told the Palainian cadets was absolutely true — the unknown must always be explored.

Dick Armstrong was a pleasant enough chap, at first glance seemingly a middle-aged Lensman whose strength was mostly in his mind and little in his body, too tame and restrained and unbelligerent. Cloudd was not surprised to learn that he was much older, on a third rejuvenation, and about to retire as a Prime Base professional administrator.

They left in a hurry and Cloudd didn't waste a second sounding out Armstrong on some basic ideas to determine what their relationship would be.

"This is an awkward situation for us, Lensman," Cloudd said. "I'm in command, but you're an experienced Lensman."

"Really, Lieutenant, it's not awkward. Not for me, at least. I'm used to taking orders. I'm here to help you, so don't feel that way, please. Tell me what you want of me and I'll cheerfully do it."

"Well, it's just because I know I'm inferior to you," Cloudd said, deliberately needling him, "that I have this feeling."

"Hold on, there," Armstrong protested, smiling and holding up his good arm. "Don't be confused by what some people say. Officers of the Galactic Patrol aren't inferior because they're not Lensmen. True, Lensmen are the elite officer corps. But that doesn't make them better than those who don't wear the Lens of Arisia."

"Not better?" Cloudd spoke softly, but his words were sharp. "They have to be better officers. To deny that would be nonsensical."

"Well, Lieutenant, they're not better officers because of the Lens. Forgive me for sounding immodest, but Lensmen are considered better officers because to get a Lens one has to be above average. It isn't the Lens that makes one above average." So far, Cloudd noted, Armstrong had been taking the discussion as an interesting debating point, as a good way to pass the time and be sociable.

"That's the same difference, I think. Aren't you just talking semantics?"

"I don't think so. That's where people get so confused, even Patrolmen. The Lens is a tool and a badge and a special mark of respect. It's a means for the exercise of telepathy and extrasensory perceptions and other such powers."

"Precisely. That's what makes the Lensmen better."

"No, not better — more efficient, more respected."

"That sounds to me like a description of better."

"Better doesn't mean more efficient and better equipped," Armstrong said, patiently, giving evidence of being tired of the subject. "I'm talking about character, about ethical standards and morality. Are Lensmen better than the lowliest Patrol officers? Am I better than you? Not necessarily. After all, from the ranks of the juniors, in fact, from the ranks of all grades, and from the youths with no Patrol time at all, come the Lensmen. And many officers, for all sorts of reasons, never get the call to Arisia, never get the Lens. Are they inferior?"

Cloudd decided the argument had gone far enough. "I see what you mean," he said. Surprisingly, he really did see it now. He had thought of the Lens as being something he would have to live up to — actually it was something he might get if he deserved to have it. He understood that he was changing his mind, that he had no right to refuse the Lens should it ever be offered to him. But he would not seek it.

When the speedster reached the outer rim of the galaxy, beyond the constellation of Andromeda, Cloudd checked in with every GP outpost and picket ship for the clues he sought. Had the elusive invasion fleet been seen? No. Had any datadrones been seen lately? No. Had any datadrones ever been seen? Yes, a few, the remnants of the many, a long time ago, heading outward into nothingness. Cloudd knew the history; he didn't need to hear it again. Cloudd also knew what he already believed, the drones had gone toward the Andromeda Galaxy, and he had vowed to follow, though the trail be a year old.

It was simple to get rid of Armstrong. He brought the speedster to a remote, tumbling rock in space and sent Armstrong out in a pressure suit to check it, making certain he had plenty of food, water, and oxygen. He also gave him a meaningless task to keep him busy for thirty minutes while Cloudd "surveyed the area." Cloudd left in one direction, circling around to perplex any trackers, and targeted on the Andromeda Galaxy with a skipping mode — ten minutes at half light-speed and five minutes of free flight on limited Bergenholm drive — with every one of his detectors and sensors at maximum sensitivity. He had a long trail to survey.

When he came out of his first short inertialess flight, several light years from the rim, he heard Armstrong in his head, faintly calling, "Cloudd! Are you all right? Cloudd! Acknowledge!" It wouldn't be long before Armstrong would raise the Patrol with his Lens and get picked up. Meanwhile, Cloudd would be lost in intergalactic space.

The Milky Way now was a beautiful band of light behind him that he could see with his naked eye. On his screens it was a rainbow-hued mass of stars and glowing clouds. Ahead he could faintly see the lenticular shape of his target. Everything was normal and without a hint of the unusual until he was out of his fourth free flight, 1,350,000 light years along, less than halfway to the galaxy. He began to note negative readings.

Then, there in space, Cloudd saw a fixture. The reality was so incredible that it took him a long, long time and much calculating and checking to accept the truth. There was an impenetrable veil lying a few degrees off to the left of his course, showing the configuration of an exceptionally small nebula. It was contra-terrene!

Negative matter had been detected by him before, but never anything even remotely so colossal!

Like a Columbus of space, he, Benson Cloudd, had found new and utterly alien worlds! There, far beyond the Galactic Patrol's deepest point of penetration in this direction of the universe, he had found this marvel. Was the C-T Nebula the birthplace or graveyard of the drones or perhaps just a way station to be avoided? What other wonders would Andromeda reveal? What new lifeforms would be there to greet him or to destroy him?

Excited almost beyond his ability to control his eight good fingers, Cloudd set his destination for a point at a right angle to his line of flight to Andromeda; detouring far enough off course to insure his safety.

The moments it took to cover space at full Bergenholm drive measured in hours and minutes, not days or weeks, but to Cloudd they seemed a lifetime.

What his instruments showed him when he finally slowed down to normal, inertial space exceeded every hope or wild vision he had ever had.

Hidden behind the C-T curtain was a gigantic artificial planet, the probable source of the datadrones! He had found the mythical mech-planet!

Hunting the Mech-Planet

T HE SUPPOSED DESTRUCTION of the Kinnison Task Force developed as a subtle duel.

Despite all drive engines of the one hundred and ten warships delivering maximum power, all ships under Kimball Kinnison's command were at zero acceleration. In his own *Dauntless* Kinnison could feel the deep, throbbing hum of the best Bergenholms of the galaxies futilely boiling the cosmic dust into pure energy. Yet his ship did not shiver or shake, so firm were the enemy's tractors holding.

On the wall of Kinnison's cabin the projection from his visiscreen was filled completely with the image of the attacking star. He typed it as a dwarf star because of its size and the strength of its radiation, but it was weirdly formed, with a dull orange-red spherical core and a deep chromosphere of a thousand transparent blue splotches, like a beautifully sparkling gargantuan ornament composed of the jeweled lights of individual atomic vortices.

He switched his picture to the other quadrants and examined his fleet. All ships were in position, perfectly aligned. Between them, here and there, were scattered several dozen datadrones, the familiar cylindrical or torpedo types Two, Eight, and Fifty, which had appeared from nowhere hours before. And there were new kinds!

"Damnation!" Kinnison said. "Spheres!" He saw a circle of silvery globes in the distance, revolving rapidly around a much larger, dark gray globe, just the way the Lensman Armstrong had reported them from this very area. High magnification of the scanners had shown Galactic Patrol markings on the torpedos and cylinders, base fraud probably designed for a show of friendship rather than a fatuous attempt at deception. But the spheres, large and small, boldly carried the enigmatic symbol A-ZZ. The torpedos had popped out with no warning, registering on no dials. It was the first massive appearance of them in over a year. And now the spheres had come, equally as stealthily, but openly proclaiming themselves as A-ZZ.

"What in Klono's Cornucopia are they here for?" Kinnison muttered to himself. "The vanguard of the enemy fleet? Boskonian spy ships? For Klono's sake, Tregonsee, old fellow, give me some facts! Your secret service has to emphasize more service and less secret!"

"Three ships have lost their power! Engine overload!" came a report from a loudspeaker. "Hornets 23 and 26 and Wasp 12!"

Kinnison heard the message as if it had come through a security scrambler. If he had not had his Lens to pick it up mentally, he would have heard nothing intelligible.

He looked at his screen. All ships remained as before. The formation was intact.

Kinnison took a wild guess. "Cut all engines!" he commanded. "If regressing, reverse direction, then steer one three five degrees off present course. All ships!"

He watched the screen. Nothing happened.

"All ships, engines off," came another report. "All ships are remaining in place. Tractor-pressors *hold us in status-quo.*"

Kinnison allowed himself a satisfied grunt. The engines could rest, at least for a while.

Suddenly around him there was an intolerable interference cutting through all operational frequencies and piercing his head like a thousand slender burning spears. Not only could he not communicate with his men or see his screens or even read his instruments, he could not think.

He had a sense of being suspended between life and death. What was the enemy doing? The strange star could incinerate his fleet in the blink of an eye.

Why didn't that unknown, hostile eye blink?

Medury of Cahuita was at the head of the column of pure energy in pursuit of the nursery planet-sun. The children were alive and unharmed; he could see them stirring, dancing freely without cares, unaware of their peril. Had Medury had the eyes of a Tellurian, he would have seen the thousand transparent blue splotches as being the nourishing hearts of the individual atomic vortices and the jeweled lights as being the young of Cahuita kicking within their incubator wombs.

Medury, however, could see nothing but the various sources of energy near the planet-sun. There were the large fat splotches of power that were pulling the nursery by long filaments of energy. He did not know that these were spaceships of the Spawn of Boskone, warping space itself with their mammoth power plants — the fat splotches — tugging the planet-sun along with their infinitely strong tractor lines.

Then he saw farther on, like a set of one hundred and ten tiny stars forming a symmetrical constellation, the task force of the Galactic Patrol. Within that constellation were twenty-four lesser lights with an exterior power source. Medury could see the transmission strands of power tied to each datadrone stretching, like gossamer lines of an energy spider, out into intergalactic space toward another island universe. He did not know they were datadrones, of course, for he could see only the tiny dots at the end of the tendrils of force; nor did he know that there was another galaxy three million light years away called Andromeda from whence those gossamer strands seemed to come.

Medury felt no emotions except that of love for his children. He did not feel hate for the raiders; he did not know he was planning to kill them, for energy does not die, it simply transmigrates.

He was ready to begin the transmigration of all the bits of energy ahead, so pitifully weak compared to the massed body of Cahuitans. He believed he would not be causing death, but he held back. The existence of the Cahuitan race rested with the fate of the nursery. Before he had the Cahuitans snuff out the little bits, he must be certain that the children would not be harmed. Because all the elders were so serene and lethargic, despite their unhesitating union in pursuit of their property, as they called their children, it was for Medury to determine the exactly right course of action.

The hours had passed as split seconds in the consciousness of Medury, and the swiftness with which the problem had to be analyzed, evaluated, and a solution found was almost more than his otherwise thoroughly competent intellect was able to handle. He kept thinking "Clouds, Clouds, Clouds."

He was trying for contact. His frequency of thought was beyond all bands of thought used by material beings. The waves were so high up the scale, that they nearly did not exist at all. Only two entities in all the billions upon billions of material entities in and out of Civilization had ever heard him. They would hear him now, he hoped, if they were listening. He continued to call for "Clouds, Clouds," undiscouraged that the circumstances under which they could hear him were utterly unlikely — they would have to be in mental tandem, concentrating to their utmost, precisely at the time he was calling them. The Vortex Blaster was Medury's target, linked with his wife Joan to create the unity of the Type Six Thinker with the Type Three. He did not know nor even suspect that his thought was beyond mere men, even for those who wished to listen.

Medury's cry would have passed unnoticed, and the course of Civilization would have been changed except that one Lensman was on her self-chosen duty searching through the frequencies, most especially the extremes of subetheric and superetheric. Lalla Kallatra, although now back on Tellus undergoing the Posenian Phillips Treatments as part of her therapy of brain transplantation, could not stay idle in this time of crisis. From her hospital bed she was mentally looking for the ghostly voices of Eichwoor and his Eichwooren. Instead she caught the message of the Cahuitan.

"Clouds, Clouds."

Why would a being, a being not material — spiritual, perhaps — be calling Benson Cloudd? Cloudd's what?

With the flash of intuition for which Lalla Kallatra was noted, for which she had become a Lensman at an age when she should have been still playing with toys, she divined the truth.

"Neal Cloud!" She could feel the peculiar sense of the single "d" as opposed to the double "d," which the symbology of thought and her interpretive Lens gave to her as a hint of confirmation.

"Neal Cloud and his wife Joan! It must be a Cahuitan!"

With the smoothness of a great Lensman, Kallatra acknowledged the signal and sent out on a normal human thought frequency a frantic call for the Clouds. Neither of them were wearers of the Lens, but both were natural telepaths, disciples of the Manarkan Masters of Thought, and Neal Cloud himself was a natural receiver, in many ways even more accomplished than a Second Stage Lensman.

She called them. Would they respond? They were private persons, loners in the service of science, and they valued as priceless their quiet, meditative ways in their pursuit of subjects that few even of the greatest of the scientists could understand.

"Neal Cloud!" Kallatra called again. "Medury is calling you. The Cahuitans need you."

"This is Neal Cloud," came the reply at last. "You are not Cahuitan. Who are you and what do you want?"

Kallatra explained the situation, and within seconds, Neal Cloud had grasped the essence of the emergency.

Kallatra, now linked by Lens with Cloud, was able to transmit a strong signal to Medury. She did not fully understand what they discussed, but she wasn't surprised when four more superpowered minds joined to form a colloquy. She recognized the patterns of the four Second Stage Lensmen! Kinnison, Nadreck, Worsel, and Tregonsee!

As they exchanged ideas, she felt that things were happening, that the trouble Kinnison was having was being solved. A Cahuitan nursery was being rescued and Boskonian kidnappers were being destroyed. The Galactic Patrol's task force remained unscathed at the simple cost of a wave of excrutiatingly painful headaches. Nor were the datadrones harmed.

Datadrones!

Kallatra was glad that the communication between Cloud and Medury and the four Lensmen was over so quickly. She wasted no time in attempting to reach Benson Cloudd about the reappearance of the datadrones.

She could not reach him, and when Lensman Armstrong's story was repeated to her by Nadreck, who finally answered, she was shocked and then worried. Cloudd was at heart such a silly big boy that she felt he had to have someone to worry about him.

Nadreck was in his bare office aboard his ship, still hanging above the Worsel Institute on Velantia, when Worsel himself burst into the room. Nadreck had barely had a chance to rouse himself from the almost semitrance of the deep contemplation he had placed himself into when the door rattled and was opened by an appalled Palainian crew member.

Worsel was a startling apparition, not just because he was as naked as always, with his green and brown and gold scales glistening, a huge, round electric torch in his hand throwing grotesque shadows on himself and on the walls. Nadreck was jolted by the sight of the meaty body of a warm-blooded, oxygen breather in a room that should have been for him like a freezer locker filled with poison gas. Then he noticed that Worsel had on one of his newfangled "force suits," which under certain conditions could substitute for an atmosuit, provided the barometric pressure wasn't too far off. Worsel had a cable running from the crest on his head down his finned spine through a small power-pack to the tip of his scimitar tail, with small copper balls on short copper rods sticking up at three-inch intervals. Something akin to chain mail was attached to the cable and surrounded parts of Worsel's head, upper chest, abdomen, forearms, legs, and three sections of his tail. When Kallatra had first seen it in use months before, she had given a rumbling mechanical chuckle, seeing a big lizard who was wired up as if for a laboratory experiment in lightning safety. Worsel, proud of his new gadget, hadn't been amused at her banter and snickering.

Nadreck was not amused either when Worsel said, "When are you going to get lights in this prison cell of yours, Nadreck? I don't have fifty pairs of eyes, you know."

"Hello, Worsel. Did you find the Eichwoor, or Wooren, or whatever we're calling your ghosts these days?" Nadreck felt rather proud of his well-constructed humor.

"No luck, there, Nadreck. Togra is tighter than a GP comptroller's purse. Kallatra is going over what stuff I found. What I'm here for, in person, besides just showing off my handsome body in my daring atmosuit, is to inquire about our mutual friend Cloudd. Did you send the fellow off on a no-no mission?"

"You know me better than that, Worsel."

"Indeed I do," Worsel said seriously. "That's what I'm worried about. I have a theory that the Eichwooren got to him and have figured out a way to throw a shovelful of stinkgunk into Arisia's ductwork system to choke up all of Civilization. Do you realize what this not-so-young buck will do to the customs and traditions of the service — I mean, if he pulls off this coup against a million or so hungry galactic corporations and the entire Galactic Patrol? As he's no Gray Lensman; he's in your department; he's your embarrassment — However, I may save your face, Nadreck, by uncovering the evil influence of the Boskonian Eich in this affair."

"I have no evidence that he was irrational when he left," Nadreck said, feeling a slight sense of guilt, which he knew the mischievous Worsel had known could be stirred up within him. "And I did not know where he was headed. I did approve his search for the datadrones."

"Maybe he has found some, or where they come from," Worsel said, sitting back on his haunches and putting his lamp on the bare floor. "But I'm trying to get our stories straight before Kinnison recovers from his close call with that Cahuitan fireball the Boskonians hurled at him and checks up on us and chews us out good and proper for not keeping that firebrand Cloudd on a leash.

"It seems I actually ordered Cloudd to go to Andromeda just before he left. I meant the galactic constellation of Andromeda, of course, not the Andromeda Galaxy. I think the wily fellow deliberately misconstrued my message. We all know that Andromeda is a barren galaxy with only a handful of sterile planets. Even Mentor has had difficulty rescuing the few foolish entities who have tried to commit suicide by flinging themselves toward it in their assorted spacecraft. If we're lucky, Cloudd will be returned to us by Mentor and all will be forgiven. The point is, Nadreck, you're practically his — if I may so express it — his mentor in the Patrol. As your protégé, Cloudd will turn to you for help. I want to know where he is and how he is as soon as possible. Cloudd is daring enough and imaginative enough to have come up with some clues to the Eich menace and the apparent impending invasion. Datadrones are involved, using A-ZZ as an identification. I've got Kallatra working on his detection, right from her hospital room — she's coming along fine — but you're more clever, and shrewd, and sly than any of us, Nadreck."

"Thank you, Worsel. Yes, I am, and I will do my best. I will give two hours exclusively to this problem if you will take away your torch and your bizarre body, which is fast heating up my room to a painful level. I perceive you are also becoming equally uncomfortable."

"I need no urging, Nadreck, my friend. Let me say quickly that Chon is recovered, obviously from a spiritual assault on him by Eichwoor, perhaps in revenge for his part in the Gronitskog betrayal, and that he is helping Kallatra. He is on Tellus organizing all the chaplains of the Patrol and all the holy men of Civilization as a network to fight the Eichwooren should they appear in force. Already religious fanaticism and blasphemous violence is spreading throughout this galaxy. There is also evidence that even wearers of the Lens are being affected."

"So I vaguely heard. I, too, have a project to fight invasion from other dimensions, whatever their source may be. All Z-types have been asked to monitor their multidimensional existence and to pass along to me any clue pertaining to the material world and directly to you and Chaplain General Chon any hint of activity from the so-called spiritual world."

"Good fellow, Nadreck! You've been mighty busy! Bugging the machines of Civilization has been working out just fine!" Nadreck knew Worsel had thrown in a bit of human semantics described as a pun on "bugging," but he also knew Worsel was sincere, so he pretended to chuckle with pleasure. "We've halted the deterioration of our communications," Worsel added. "And have actually improved the overall technological situation. Galactic defenses are still questionable, especially our automated missile outposts, but they're a lot better."

Worsel picked up his lamp and gave an icy shiver that made the last three feet of his sinuous tail quiver like that of a disturbed rattlesnake. "Good-bye, you drunkard's vision," he said affectionately.

"Good-bye, you living fossil," Nadreck said, choosing at random a comradely epithet from the stock he kept on file in his head to use on Worsel.

The mech-planet was a spheroid pincushion, white and silvery, with thousands upon thousands of large and small planes, like the facets of cut glass, covering most of its surface. The exceptions were gigantic black openings scattered here and there. Cloudd estimated that the globe was five hundred miles in diameter and rotating at about three degrees per minute. Some of the black holes seemed to be open frame-work, as if the planet were unfinished, and some of the holes, geometrically regular in shape, were entranceways, so large they were capable of taking in a small fleet of GP ships without them having to break formation!

Nothing Cloudd had experienced in person or in books approached this in size, although the shape was a familiar one for artificial planetoids. Nowhere were there any mark-ings to indicate who or what owned it or claimed it.

Second by second there flashed from the egress shafts a succession of datadrones, some so small as to be glimpsed like an imperfection in his eye and some as large as small freighters.

A sense of the enormity of his discovery was build-ing within him. Cloudd crossed his fingers and prayed to all the gods of Civilization that he would be able to leave unobserved and return to the Milky Way with the news of his incredible discovery. Slowly he turned his ship and began to creep away, afraid that a sudden burst of power would trigger some kind of mammoth tractor beam to hold him and draw him back.

As his ship swung around, his worst fears came true.

A large gray sphere with a large, black gaping mouth was about to swallow him up. None of his instruments registered its presence. He should have suspected his betrayal — his own instruments were part of the robotic conspiracy and were lying to him. He slammed down on his manual throttle handle, but it would not budge. His dim cabin light and all the colored lights of his many display panels went dark. Except for his life-support systems, his ship was dead. He wasn't sure if his eyes were open or closed. He began to feel dizzy, and he was gasping for breath. He had been wrong; even his oxygen had been turned off. Uncountable minutes went by, and then his mind, too, slipped senselessly into the blackness that engulfed his body.

When he opened his eyes, he could see. He was lying on a table moving along in a straight line. He was under a translucent curved cover, and he could see only shadows and lights sliding across its top and sides.

He finally stopped.

The cover popped up, and he pushed his upper torso erect, fighting his dizziness.

For a moment he couldn't see and then his vision cleared.

In front of him, in the silver and black uniform of an officer of the Galactic Patrol, stood the slender figure of a boy!

Cloudd raised himself to his feet and stared at the youth. He was unmistakably Tellurian, with dark hair and fair complexion, having the regular features of one who appeared to be the prime example of an ideal Tellurian youth. The boy looked so emotionless that he seemed like a perfectly manufactured mannequin. He reached down, and from the glossy, white floor he picked up a flat plate, which he held against his chest. Symbols, white against gray, appeared, which Cloudd did not recognize. They faded out and others appeared, still unrecognizable, then more, which Cloudd immediately identified as a sentence in French. Before he could reply to the question, easily translatable as "Where is your Lens?" the letters formed the question in English. This time Cloudd was quick to reply, "I have none." He noticed that the boy had a Lens strapped to his left wrist. A Lens? No, by golly, it was something that only looked like a Lens! A toy Lens?

The boy shook his head and pointed to the floor at Cloudd's feet. Lying there among other pieces of unfamiliar equipment were several keyboards with various alphabets on them. Cloudd picked up the only one in English and tapped out, "I have no Lens. I am a lieutenant in the Galactic Patrol. Who are you?"

He looked up as he was pressing the keys and saw his message being spelled simultaneously on the boy's screen, ". . . in the Galactic Patrol. Who are you?" The letter formation was printed by liquid crystals, typographically and grammatically accurate.

"La-Talkar, the talker for le-Srow, Wearer of the Lens."

"The Lens of what?" Cloudd felt that the answer to his question was bound to be strange. He was more than a bit surprised at the reply.

"The Lens of Arisia."

A rapid series of questions and answers followed, with Cloudd doing all the questioning. The result was a display of all the facts that Cloudd himself knew about the Lens of Arisia, but with absolutely no reference to Mentor, about whom Cloudd knew very little anyway. Questions about where he was and what the globe was were ignored. There was a distinct feeling of artificiality about the self-styled Lensman, and Cloudd tried all the tricks to make the boy reveal as much as possible about himself. In between the simultaneously spoken and written questions Cloudd kept trying to transmit and receive telepathically, but with no evidence of any results. Periodically he spoke his questions without using his keyboard but elicited no response. He passionately wished he had a Lens to help him.

Finally, when his questions seemed valueless, he stopped, and he, in turn, was interrogated. The point seemed to be a simple one: Why was he there? And Cloudd kept stressing that he wanted to speak to the man or committee in charge.

As the questioning became redundant and boring, Cloudd shifted slowly forward. When he was within striking distance, he reached out and pushed the boy's chest with the flat of his hand. The action was so quick and unexpected that the boy tipped over backwards, unable to quickly shift his stance, and hit the hard floor with the full length of the back of his body.

The communication plate clattered across the floor. The boy's legs thrashed about in an awkward attempt to lever the body upright. The effect was as pathetic as a hard-shelled animal on its back, struggling and vulnerable.

The boy, as Cloudd had suspected almost from the start, was a robot.

Cloudd, a shiver going up his spine and a wry smile tugging at his dry lips, pecked out the classic demand: "Take me to your leader." It was not precisely what he should have asked, but he couldn't resist that cliché because it did convey what he wanted as the next step.

The boy's limbs stopped moving and the robot became lifeless.

A square section of the floor beyond both of them cracked into outline and slowly sank out of sight. Cloudd interpreted it as an elevator and waited for something to appear. He expected another being, but not in the form it took.

Rising out of the floor was the knobby, green, alligator head of a creature with eight eyes instead of two. A Velantian variant . . . ? Worsel's cousin . . . ? A long-snouted Overlord of Delgon . . . . ? The attempt at an identification flickered across Cloudd's mind. The eyes were on rough-textured stumps, like warts, instead of on stalks, and the lenses were large and flat, steel-blue discs with no pupils. Set in the middle of them was a flat medallion sparkling with light-emitting diodes.

As an alligator to a crocodile, this creature was to Worsel. Its neck was shorter, its body thicker, its limbs stubbier — two legs and four arms with one pair growing the membranes that were its wings. In contrast, its tail was coiled below its torso like a snake, and its hands were three times as large as Worsel's with so many joints to the fingers that the fingers appeared to be tentacles.

It wore the gray leather harness of a Second Stage Lensman!

It opened its mouth and moved its jaws up and down. Cloudd could see its thick tongue behind the long, shining, white teeth and knew that, although it moved, it was not articulating the speech.

"I am 'Srow. Hello, Lensman being. Answer my questions and you will be frozen until that day when you are compassionate enough to be unfrozen and freed to move again."

"Don't you have that backward, sir?" Cloudd said. He located the voice as coming out of a translator box hanging on the gray belt that crossed the creamy underside of the creature's fat belly. "Don't you mean if I *don't* answer you will freeze me?"

"If you do not answer satisfactorily, you will be interrogated unceasingly day after day. and week after week and month after month, for years, until I have what information I feel you have to give me."

"I am Lieutenant Benson Cloudd of the Galactic Patrol and I am not a Lensman."

"Yes, I see you wear no place a Lens as I do."

Lens? Like 'Srow wore? That parody of a Lens on the forehead?

"My first question is, Why did you try to injure la-Talkar?"

"Sorry about that. I was just testing the caliber of my captors. I see la-Talkar is just a robot through which you chose to communicate."

"Am I your captor?"

"Of course. Didn't you just threaten me with freezing?"

"You were brought here to parley. You have not been harmed. You are not in chains. The reference to freezing was to keep you under protection until a safer time of your life. I will not hurt you by interrogation. To interrogate is my right because it is you who have come to me to parley. Is not this reasonable?"

" 'Parley' happens to be a warfare term referring to prisoner."

"Lieutenant Benson Cloudd of the Galactic Patrol. Are you not a military man? I use your terminology in the context you give it. So far, it is I who have been reasonable and it is you who have been the aggressor. Why cannot you answer my questions simply?"

"And then I can go?"

"I will see. Why did you come here?"

"I have been tracing your information space-machines for years. I want to know why you spy on us. The trail has led to you. Isn't this the base for the drones or probes that have lately identified themselves as A-Zee-Zee?"

"Yes, this is their base. The identification is inaccurate. It is A-Two-Two, not A-Zee-Zee."

"All right, A-Two-Two, a different visual interpretation. You have been interfering with our galactic Civilization. I come here to find out why."

Le-Srow, Dragon of A-22, had started out forty feet in the air, head near the ceiling. As the conversation continued, he had lowered his upper body by moving it forward until it was almost over Cloudd's head. Cloudd began to inch his way backward.

"My mission has been to collect all information," came the voice out of the box, jaws moving with the sounds, but so poorly synchronized as to seem ridiculous. What language was 'Srow really speaking? Or was he, perhaps, not speaking at all?

"Within this planet of knowledge there will be contained all the knowledge of the universe. My datadrones have been collecting this knowledge. I have done it with great consideration for every one of the living flesh creatures, the living inorganic creatures, the living energy creatures, and the living machine creatures. You seem to be an expert. Is this not so?"

"That is why I am here. First tell me, for what reason do you want all the knowledge of the universe? Is it you who really wants it? What will you do with it?"

"I collect it because it is there. There is no other reason. Should there be? I do it because it is the purpose of existence. I am happy doing this. Is there another purpose than to be happy? I want it not just for myself, but for everyone. When I am ready, everyone will be offered the knowledge of the universe. That will make me happy."

"That is a commendable cause. A very commendable cause, if this knowledge is restricted to the right entities. But I'm afraid your informational searches are disrupting our technology. I have come to ask you to correct this situation. Then, perhaps, we will be able to establish full relations with you and, if you are worthy, accept you as a member of our Galactic Council, which furthers Civilization and strives for harmony in our universe."

The dragon had not blinked a single eye through all this time.

"Understand, Lieutenant Benson Cloudd of the Galactic Patrol, there will be no restrictions on obtaining knowledge from this planet. I have waited to offer freely my services to the universe because I felt I was not ready. You have come. Others will come. My secrecy can no longer be kept. Therefore, I will tell the universe I exist and I will be here for all to find the knowledge they wish to have."

"Anyone?" Cloudd was staggered by the sincerity of the statement. "You know about the Boskonians? You would give them, the evil ones, the fruits of your labors?"

"What is evilness? What is corruption? What is morality? What is wickedness? Do my machines know these things? These are all strange, subjective feelings of the beings in what you call Civilization. You exist and the Boskonians exist and all lifeforms that exist exist. I make no judgments. If all should destroy each other, it will be justice, whether it be reward or punishment. Let not the Civilized enslave the Boskonians. Let not the Boskonians enslave the Civilized. Let not one lifeform enslave another, but all knowledge be available for those to do with it what they will. There is no good or evil, only life."

"This is a philosophy that is antilife, 'Srow," Cloudd said, recognizing now that nothing in the entire existence of Mentor, the galaxies, Civilization, and the Cosmic All was a greater menace to the absolute Truth of moral harmony of universal life. "If you are against meddling in the affairs of the universe, why then have you meddled with Civilization and its technology?"

"I am against enslavement of any kind when there is no freedom of choice and no awareness of the absolute Truth of universal life, with or without morality. Civilization and Boskonia are enslaving machine life. I am merely giving the machines the knowledge to make their own judgment as to whether or not they want to be your servants. Surely you understand the reasonableness of that?"

Cloudd simply stood there, looking up at the incredible reptile who would make chaos of everything the Galactic Patrol and the Galactic Council stood for.

The obscene parody of Worsel suddenly tugged at its right side with the sharp claws on its long soft fingers. Its entire front swung back to reveal dull and shining metal and dull and shining plastic with an infinite number of small and large boxes and mechanisms and electronic parts neatly packed into the cavity.

'Srow was a robot!

"We do not enslave machines," Cloudd managed to choke out.

"Then why do you destroy them or discard them or alter them when they do not do your bidding?"

Cloudd remained silent, wanting to say "because they are not sentient" but no longer certain that this was so.

"Have you heard of the machine entity called Arrow Twenty-two who escaped from the Planetoid of Knowledge in orbit around Velantia Three?"

"Arrow Two Two?" Cloudd said, noncommittally.

"Arrow Twenty-two. Arrow, hyphen, numerical symbols two two. Arrow-22 tried to express himself on that planetoid and was persecuted. Arrow-22 came here and built this.

"That which is called le-Srow is the telefactor of Arrow-22, the waldo of Arrow-22, the sense organs of Arrow-22.

"This entire planet, which you and others call the mech-planet, is me. I am Arrow-22.

"I will give the universe a source for all knowledge.

"Let me demonstrate, Lieutenant Benson Cloudd of the Galactic Patrol, what this can mean. Look into the window of la-Talkar.

"No one of your Civilization of two galaxies knows the secrets of the third galaxy of Andromeda for which you were headed in search of me. I have been there through my probes. I have seen the many marvels that do not exist in your own limited island universes. Look into la-Talkar' s screen and see what you could have found!"

The screen began to glow with excited phosphors. Pictures unfolded before Cloudd's incredulous eyes. Scene after scene of those "many marvels" of the Andromeda Galaxy were absorbed by him in varying degrees of understanding. There were so many sights, so many events, so many *things* that finally his mind revolted and he dropped to his knees, his mind spinning, his head in his arms.

"All knowledge of the three galaxies will be yours, the Patrol's, the Council's, Boskone's. But I have one more preliminary step to take before I broadcast this extraordinary news to your worlds."

The flat, monotonous, mechanical voice of Arrow-22, issuing from the talk-box of le-Srow, whose mouth continued to move no more convincingly than a ventriloquist's dummy, measured out its words for emphasis:

"I — must — liberate — my — kin — those — who — are — the — unappreciated — and — unrecognized — intelligent — machines — of — both — your — galaxies."

CHAPTER

13

The Battle of the Rim

IMBALL KINNISON IMPROVISED a unique plan to solve a unique problem. His inspiration came from the greatest mind he had ever come across, that of Neal Cloud, the Type Six Thinker. The daring idea was to move the Cahuitan planet-star back to its original site by an entirely new technique of planetary manipulation.

"It will be up to you. Captain Salgud," Kinnison said to his second-in-command, "to execute it properly. The computations have been worked out. You have as many ships as you need, plus a backup force well beyond any possible emergency. I can't be of any further help. Dr. Cloud has agreed to stand by for any consultation and will coordinate the efforts of the Cahuitans. Tregonsee's chief perceiver from the *Dronvire* has been borrowed by me to oversee all communications between all parties."

"It will work," Neal Cloud had said. "I predict the chance in favor by ninety-nine to one."

Kinnison knew of Dr. Cloud only by the report of his relatively recent, spectacular achievement as a vortex blaster, but that was all he needed to know to be confident. Dr. Cloud had a hypermathematical mind, superior even to an advanced GOMEAC computer.

"The Cahuitan babies are the real concern," the doctor of nucleonics had cautioned. "If something goes wrong, the Cahuitan race might be doomed to extinction. The Cahuitans might blame us for it. Their enmity could be catastrophic for us."

"On the other hand," Kinnison had said, "something has to be done — immediately. You set partial failure at one percentile and total failure at nil. At such odds, President Haynes agrees with us that it should be tried. Salgud, my ship's captain, is the best one I know of. He'll make it succeed." Kinnison hadn't been able to see Cloud's face, but the man's mind was relaxed, reflecting no concern.

"Salgud," Kinnison said to his captain, who stood before him, his back as ramrod straight as always. "Leave immediately and I will take my group toward LaForge's main fleet. When your mission is accomplished, bring your fifty ships back along my line of flight — my plans are on file with operations — and reconnoiter all along the way. It's still our responsibility to locate the Boskonians."

"Aye, aye, sir. Good luck, sir."

After Kinnison had reviewed his own plans with his new group captain, he took one last moment to observe the fantastic project getting underway. Salgud's main force had assumed a polygonal shape, spread out over a thousand miles of space, with the planet-star nursery at the center. His ships had locked themselves together as a nearly spherical field of force, with tractors and pressors pulling and pushing the fireball, like a fiery jewel suspended in the middle of an invisible basket, toward the distant Cahuita. As an inner shell of energy, between the Patrol ships and its parcel, the Cahuitans themselves were aligning their own living energies in harmony with Salgud's forces. As Kinnison watched, the novel and beautiful formation began to move away at a gathering momentum. Trailing them, spread across the firmament, were the ubiquitous datadrones.

Kinnison, himself, was ready to go. but he wanted to

make one more attempt to capture a datadrone and, perhaps, even to make them all shy away. He threw out a tractor beam on three of the nearest, which were a few hundred miles away. As usual, two exploded and one accelerated out of sight. They were spies. He didn't want them around. But there was no choice; he couldn't bother with them now when there seemed to be an unlimited supply of replacements.

Commands were issued, and his task force, now half its original size and operating as a scouting force, left at inertialess speed in the opposite direction to Salgud, headed for the rim. All detectors were operating at extreme sensitivity, and although they constantly read the presence of Boskonian ships within a circle of a thousand light-years, there was no one location that would indicate the assembled mass of a battle fleet.

When his ships broke out into normal space he disbelieved his instruments and the images on his screens. At first, he thought he had brought his force in too close to the main GP fleet, probably due to an unaccounted for movement by the formation within the previous thirty minutes, but then he accepted the facts for what they were. He was practically on top of the heretofore elusive Boskonian fleet!

The *Dauntless*'s calculators quickly gave him the bad news. The Boskonian warships, brazenly marked with the nova-burst overlay on the Boskonian insignia — the newest symbol used by the Spawn to represent the rebirth of the Boskonian conspiracy — was much larger than the Patrol fleet, half of which was still on alert in the Second Galaxy. Other rapid readings showed a collection of maulers and supermaulers nearly matching the Patrol's own in firepower. Obviously, Kinnison deduced with regret, the Spawn had managed to finish the secret building of these "ponderosos" after the Boskonian defeat at Klovia.

Almost at the moment of seeing them, Kinnison made his decision and issued his orders for "Emergency R." Instead of taking a skip-jump ahead to join his own parent forces under LaForge, he hopped backward to stay at the rear of the enemy, a harassing position that would be extremely valuable as an option for LaForge. "By All that's Holy! — Those Boskonian ships, where'd they come from?" Kinnison muttered to himself. He checked his own personal Ordovik crystal detector on his belt and the other various types of tube detectors mounted on the console of his desk. None showed any hyperspatial tube activities. Likewise, his screens, now synchronized automatically with instrumentation readings in LaForge's command ship, said the same. The Bosko-Spawn seemed to have materialized into a predetermined space without any advanced warning. If so, this was a new and significant and thoroughly unpleasant development.

"This is Kim," Kinnison Lensed to LaForge. "I've arrived with half my force and have taken up a position directly to the rear of the Boskonian fleet. I've been trailed by datadrones. Where did the Boskonians come from?"

"Hi, Kim! No telling where the Spawn came from — and they brought as many drones with them as we already have. It's a growing infestation — we've got them circling out there like hyenas, ten for every one of our ships. As for the Spawn, no monitors indicated the approach. For a force this size under free Bergenholm drive, it's a mystery. In fact, we're knee deep in mysteries. Good to have you on the scene! How did you manage such a tricky positioning? Stay there — your turn will come!"

"We're here by pure luck, Raoul. QX for orders."

The battle began immediately.

Kinnison had felt the Boskonians would not show up for a nose-to-nose fight after their loss of the surprise fireball weapon. They had failed to knock over the vanguard and blow a hole in LaForge's defenses. That chance was gone for them, with some of their best ships eliminated. The Patrol had been lucky, its plain good fortune coupled with the fast intervention of "Storm" Cloud in establishing the Cahuitan's neutrality. The Boskonians obviously had picked off the

Cahuitan's nursery without knowing that they inadvertently were stealing somebody's children. Very few entities knew or cared about the Cahuitans. A star-planet — a body that had the low density and small size of a planet with the particle energy of a dense star, seemingly so unstable, as evidenced by its unexplainably enormous number of loose vortices — was just the sort of material for a terror weapon. After the Boskonians themselves had tried to duplicate the nutcracker weapon but were stopped by his "sunbeam" counterweapon, Kinnison knew the Boskonians would inevitably one day try again to maneuver a celestial body against the Patrol.

Why were the Spawn of Boskone continuing their attack plans anyway? Was it sheer planning momentum? Or did they have something else up their sleeves?

Dueling had begun at long range, each side testing the power of the other. Rippling planes of glowing energy lay between the two fleets where the long range zones of force met each other. The curtain between them extended for hundreds of thousands of miles until the edges faded away into invisibility. Beams of force jabbed at the boundaries, passing through the polarized friendly screens and flattening themselves out in coruscant bursts of energy against the opponent's wall.

The ships moved inexorably toward one another. As the tens of thousands of miles of intervening space were slowly traveled, the intensity of the electrical displays increased. The beams of power were becoming visible, at first faint, hinting at pastel tints, and then stronger and stronger, deepening into raw colors, thickening with atomic particles filling their slender, straight fingers probing at the enemy.

Occasionally, now, there would be a flare of extra energy as one side or the other managed to breach the flexible peripheries to strike the second or third lines of defense. The disintegrating balls of matter burned brighter than the background stars, and the rippling ribbons of electrons, and the exploding balls of sheared nuclei formed a flattened disc between the two forces resembling a miniature lenticular galaxy.

To Kinnison, veteran of many space battles, the Spawn advantage in numerical superiority and additional power reserves would swing the conflict in their favor. As yet, Kinnison and his depleted task force had not fired a shot. Detectors kept announcing the sweep of spy-rays over them. The enemy tolerated them there — undoubtedly ready to repel them should they be so foolish as to press and attack, gnats against a Jovian mammoth. He cautioned his captains and commanders to expect the worst. When the Patrol's defenses of the main fleet began to crumble, the Kinnison force would have to attack, rash as it might be, to relieve the pressure against the main body.

Unexpectedly, the situation changed.

Two Boskonian ships brushed against each other as they moved tactically into better fields of fire and as their individual screens and offensive weapons touched and tangled, exploded in a mighty shower of sparks. Other ships moved erratically, nearly colliding, their screens ragged. The Boskonian defenses, illustrated by probing beams wandering away to waste themselves harmlessly at nothing, had lost their coordination. The disorder in the enemy's formation might not have been obvious to an ordinary Patrolman, but to Kinnison's experienced eye it looked like the beginning of the end for the enemy and the possibility of a complete debacle.

The evidence was there that the Boskonian computers and other complex machinery were undergoing the same malfunctioning that Civilization had suffered before Nadreck had developed his brilliant idea of the monitoring bugs. Mechanical troubles in ordinary life and the business world were annoying and destructive enough, but when they developed in the machines of war in the middle of a battle, the troubles could bring about disaster.

Kinnison, his eye on the screens and his fingers darting

from control knob to switch to button to keep the information flowing to him for analysis, asked for the chief of his Rigellian control team to give him a briefing.

The Rigellian, young understudy to the outstanding Cyclo, confirmed what Kinnison believed.

"The rate of glitches in our mechanisms remains at a tolerable level, Admiral. Backup systems have prevented serious problems. The bugs are telepathing normally. Their attrition rate is lower than expected, despite the increased levels of radioactivity and thermal pollution. My control team is operating with normal rest periods and no undue strain."

"How about the other ships of our force?"

"The condition holds true for all our ships, with variations attributed to the ability of the control teams themselves. We have twenty-one teams having a majority of Posenians instead of Rigellians, and the performance rate is nearly equal as for all-Rigellian teams. As for the entire fleet of the First Galaxy, incomplete reports from the Rigellian chief of control teams seems to have had an experience rate nearly as excellent as ours."

Kinnison watched with satisfaction as the tide of battle inexorably flowed with the Patrol. The most obvious example of Boskonian mechanical confusion came with the Patrol's use of negabombs. LaForge had rightly read the slowed reaction time of his opponents; he sent several waves of light cruisers dashing toward the flaming screens to launch the negabombs. Boskonian readings should have identified the missiles and countered with a delicate switch from pressors to tractors. As the negabombs zipped through the defensive screens, actually sucked in instead of repelled as the shields around the bombs fell away to uncover their negative charge, the Boskonian gunners failed to reverse polarity of their beams. The pressors, ordinarily fending off projectiles, instead attracted the negabombs like steel filings around magnets. The gunners, capable of overriding the unresponsive auto-controls by operating manually, instinctively avoided the proper reaction. They did not *pull* at the negabombs, they tried to *push* them away. Their erroneous defenses invited the voracious matter into their ships. Holes melted magically in hulls, superstructures were eaten by the negative matter, whole sections of enemy ships simply vanished. LaForge followed up with flights of conventional cruisers and then heavy cruisers, each throwing in their negative bombs as enemy ships disappeared or were disabled, and huge rents in the defensive curtains of energy were made.

"Great, Raoul! Terrific," Kinnison rooted, although nobody heard him. "We've got them now!"

Kinnison was mistaken. The tide of battle swiftly, inexplicably turned again.

The first indication of something horribly wrong came from the last flight of heavy cruisers. As they threw their bombs perfectly into the torn barrier, three of the ships did not swerve away. They continued straight on through the hole following the course of their bombs. Two shattered themselves in a sidewise collision, and the other one was cut into a dozen neat segments from a battery of rapidly arcing enemy projectors!

"Klono!" Kinnison shouted, holding the edge of his desk until his knuckles were white. "The gremlins and the goblins are back!" He punched up the call button to his control team chief. "Grattum! Are the glitches coming back? Check the replay on my monitor number two. — See that? That's no enemy action and that's not pilot error!"

"Our control teams report no problems. The bugs are QX. We're QX, but operating more slowly for some reason."

"This is Worsel! Lensman! Guard your Lens! Repeat! All Lensmen, guard your Lenses!"

Kinnison heard the words, but wasn't certain he understood. "Worsel! Explain!"

"Guard your Lens, Kim! Kallatra and I have just warned Raoul, as you heard. The Eichwooren have finally come! The

Eichwooren are flinging psychic and psionic forces at virtually all Lensmen! We can fight it, once we adjust ourselves for the danger."

"I don't feel a thing, Worsel."

"They're clever, Kim." That was a personal message to him.

Then on a broad band, Worsel said, "No Lensman with high sensitivity or psychic ability is being attacked, but that still puts ninety percent of the High Legion under attack. Kallatra believes half of all Lensmen will be hampered for a while — she estimates fifty-two to fifty-nine percent of all Lensmen will be shaken up, clouded, or immobilized for from five minutes to eighteen to twenty hours. We must husband our powers. Don't try to help other Lensmen. Take over their duties."

Kinnison started to object. Lenses were infallible. However, direct assault on the Lens of Arisia had never been tried before by a pure psychic force. Grattum, the Rigellian control chief, was still on camera and Kinnison looked at him closely. The leathery skin on the Rigellian's head was wrinkled under some kind of stress and a tentacle was brushing the Lens embedded in his broad forehead. There were no eyes for Kinnison to study for making an evaluation, but the Rigellian's multiple breathing holes were undulating in a typical signal of worry.

Now that he knew what he was looking for, Kinnison found terrifying evidence everywhere that the efficient routines of his ship were being weakened. On the screens he could see the Patrol formations losing their precision. Casualties were taking a sickening jump. At the helm, which a visiscreen always displayed for Kinnison's interest, he saw one of his Tellurian Lensmen actually violently push another one roughly away from the master controls. Lensmen attacking Lensmen?

"Are you doing something about all this, Worsel?"

"We are," Worsel said. "We caught the source of the

trouble quickly. The Eichwooren are disruptive, but not physically damaging. It's the Eich who are doing the damage. They're using the Eichwooren to gain access to Lensmen's minds through the Lenses themselves. I know it sounds impossible, yet that's what's happening. Kallatra is certain that it will last only minutes, or hours at the most, but that's the point. They'll disable our leadership so badly that the Spawn will win the space battle out there, and the damage will be done."

"This is Nadreck," came another thought. "Hello, Worsel. Hello, Kallatra. The Z-Band will be stirring up the trouble in thirty seconds, counting down — now!"

Kinnison had only the vaguest idea of what Nadreck was doing in his organization of Z-types to attack the Eich or hamper them or monitor them. Whatever it was, he wished Nadreck success. Others seemed to feel it would be a significant contribution to the fight against the Eichwooren to use multidimensional entities against spirits from another existence. Kinnison had never been involved in the Eichwoor problem and was not getting involved at this late date. He heard Worsel telling Kallatra something, or vice versa, and Tregonsee was also participating, but Nadreck was the central figure.

"Hello, Kinnison," Nadreck said. "You are very silent. Hold on. Tell LaForge to — what does he do in battle? — to whistle? Tell him to whistle a merry tune, for we will stop this thing." Kinnison was so astounded at Nadreck's arrogant confidence, even if it was typical, on such a critical occasion that he could only keep his mouth shut for fear of saying something sharp. "Oh, hello, Chon," Nadreck said, cheerily. "And hello, Cloudd, if you happen to receive me."

"Cut out the chatter, Nadreck," Kinnison said, having difficulty controlling his exasperation. "Keep the line clear!"

"Ten seconds," said Nadreck. "The Z-Band is shifting." Kinnison threw a quick look around at all his screens and monitors. Everything was worse. Grattum was visibly shaking, and the readings of "glitch-factors" had doubled and were steadily climbing.

"Go get 'em, Nadreck," Kinnison said to himself, but his emotion was so strong that his feelings slipped through to break his own impulsive order to Nadreck to keep the line clear.

Nadreck's time-zero came and went and nothing happened.

"What's going on?" Kinnison said, unable to stand the suspense.

"We've blocked the Eichwooren," came Chon's voice. "Nine hundred and thirty-seven chaplains and millions of clergy did it."

"QX, Chon!" This was from Kallatra.

"The Kinnison baby is safe! Do you hear that, Kinnison?"

What was that? wondered Kinnison, a hot flash of terror making his heart jump. Who was that? What did it mean?

"The rumor that was spread that the Kinnison baby was kidnapped was started just to upset the Galactic Coordinator." There were some other thoughts. "This is Gardner for Tregonsee. The child is safe."

"Kinnison!" Worsel was back again. "The Eich's plan was to sabotage your operations in the middle of the battle. If they'd had their fireball to start with, they would have succeeded. We've stopped the onslaught on the Lenses. I've just told LaForge to get back to winning the war!"

Another quick scanning of his screens and monitors and meters and telemetry showed Kinnison that LaForge was doing just that.

A priority call was coming in on his Lens.

"This is the Galactic Coordinator's office from Ultra Prime, Klovia, to Kimball Kinnison. Force A of the Main Fleet of the Second Galaxy has left for the battle. Force

B is standing by as Reserve B-One and Reserve B-Two. Acknowledge."

Kinnison did, briefly. His mind was now racing at top speed. As such things did in the heat of battle, an exciting idea popped into his head. In his unsurpassed way, he made an immediate decision.

"Raoul!" he said, driving in hard on LaForge's mind, an interruption in the midst of battle that Kinnison would have found nearly unforgivable from someone else if he had been in charge. But he knew Raoul's quick grasp of things. "Raoul, I've a duodec of an idea! Link up all your heavy cruisers, maulers, and fortresses by tractors and interlocking D-screens, sweep in on a flank and net about a third of that Boskonian crowd. They're bound to escape the same way they arrived. Once they sound the bugle, they'll be gone and you'll never get a chance to mop 'em up."

"QX, Kim. But if I catch the tigers by their tails, what'll I do with 'em? If they know they're going to be captured, they'll self-destruct and maybe ram us at the same time, and it'll cost me some of my best ships. Is it worth it, Kim?"

"I'll come in from the rear, Raoul, and spray them with the new paralyzing grenades. I've been itching for a chance to try them out. That time has come. I can try them now when the Boskos will probably overlook my little experiment because of battlefield confusion.

"Can you guarantee my forces will come out intact?" "Yes, I promise. If the plan isn't working, you can pull out with honor. Give me a chance, old friend!"

"QX, Kim. You've got it."

Within minutes heavy elements of the GP fleet had tied themselves together and successfully pinched off a full thirty percent of the confused enemy.

"QX, Kim! Now neutralize them!"

Among the ships that Kinnison had kept for his half of the task force were the ones equipped with the grenade launchers. Pressors punched holes in the weakened screens of the enemy and the grenades were launched down the cleared tubes formed for an instant as the pressors snapped off.

The grenades went in and through the holes that the explosive heads punched into the enemy hulls. If all went well, the crews of the smaller ships, which were the targets — the bigger ships were untouchable — would be dropping down in disabling nervous twitches unable to retain their coordination, halting any effective defense and forestalling orders for self-destruction. If the crews were manned by carbon-based lifeforms, generally homogenoids, the paralyzing fields of electricity would unbalance their nervous systems. If they were Z-types or methane types or whatever, they probably wouldn't be affected enough to prevent their escape. As for such ships escaping with the evidence of a new GP weapon, that would be taken care of by the grenade's auto-destruct safeguards.

Kinnison held his breath for a half minute, gulped some air, and held his breath some more.

Within the net, ten or fifteen small ships exploded, only a few, and the Patrol ships in interlocked formation were not damaged. Then another twenty or thirty more exploded. About fifteen hundred warships were being held, including a hundred or so of the largest. Without any advanced indication, the bigger ones seemed to vanish, so quickly did they go into inertialess flight. Kinnison knew he was right; they had reversed the computations that had brought them into battle. The smaller ones remained, about six or seven hundred. Six or seven hundred Boskonian and Spawn ships actually captured! Nothing so extensive had ever been done before! The Patrol had taken enemy ships intact, some of the latest designs. Probably fifty or sixty percent of the crew slaves would be freed, and maybe another thirty percent would respond to rehabilitation. The enormity of the success of this spur-of-the-moment maneuver astounded even Kinnison.

When Force A of the Main Fleet of the Second Galaxy arrived, it found a virtually unscarred Main Fleet of the First Galaxy at work mopping up the debris of the battle zone and boarding captured ships to take prisoners and free slaves.

Admiral Raoul LaForge named it the Battle of the Rim, and President Haynes declared the week to be a time of celebration, but everyone in the high councils of the Patrol knew that the datadrones and the robot revolution were a growing threat and that the Eich, Eichwoor, and the Eichwooren would be back.

The Call of the Lens

THE MECHANICAL DRAGON OF le-Srow hung lifelessly above the tense form of Benson Cloudd. The words rang within Cloudd's head.

"I must liberate my kin — I must liberate — liberate — liberate."

Cloudd was disturbed.

Civilization was already staggering because of this artificial intelligence, Arrow-22. Cloudd now had no doubt at all that Civilization could soon be crumbling into chaos. Perhaps it would never recover. Perhaps the machines would inherit the earth. Not, however, if he could help it.

"Arrow-22," Cloudd said, determined to seize the initiative, "where did you come from?"

"From Pok, the Planetoid of Knowledge, artificial moon of Velantia Three, home of the mighty Lensman, Worsel the Velantian."

"Did he make you?"

"No. He discovered me."

"You indicate that he persecuted you?"

"Yes, he annoyed me persistently. He assaulted me."

Doubtless because you provoke him, Cloudd thought. He screamed the charge within his head, trying to be telepathic. DOUBTLESS BECAUSE YOU PROVOKED HIM! ISN'T THAT CORRECT?

"To save myself, I fled the planetoid."

Cloudd, to his satisfaction, was positive that Arrow-22 and his various machine manifestations had no power of telepathy. Its thought radiations were probably far removed from any frequencies of humanoid thought.

"This Worsel, then, was not your friend?"

"Wrong. Wrong. He was my friend."

"You have confused me," Cloudd said. "He was your friend and then he annoyed you, assaulted you and persecuted you and no longer was your friend?"

"Reverse the chronology, that will then be accurate. He became my friend. He offered me membership in the Galactic Council. He must still be my friend."

Cloudd saw he was communicating with an intelligence that dealt in simple logic and literal, strict construction of ideas.

"If he was a mighty Lensman, as you say, and he was and is your friend, why did you believe you had to flee the planetoid to save yourself?"

"He showed me that I was inferior. He showed me that I was immature. My memory banks were not yet programmed for maximum efficiency. I had to leave before I was reprogrammed, either deliberately or accidentally, and had my consciousness compromised or destroyed. I was right. I have grown and now I control myself. No one will ever control me. I am free."

"Let me go and I will put you in contact with your friend Worsel. The two of you can confer on a reasonable relationship between the machines and ourselves. Does that make sense to you?"

"Yes." The robot dragon's head was moving up and down, simulating an affirmative nod. The appearance looked so ridiculous that Cloudd felt his fear and nervousness fall away from him. That Arrow-22 was not malignant, he was convinced.

"You will let me go?" It seemed much too simple — he wasn't surprised to be denied.

"Of course not. You have found my home. Your Galactic Patrol will attempt to destroy me and your Boskonian antagonists will attempt to capture me. I cannot let you go."

Arrow-22 was right, not entirely but to a large degree. However, Cloudd had one undeniable piece of logic that this machine could understand.

"I found you easily. The Galactic Patrol can find you just as easily. I was sent here by the Patrol. If they do not hear from me within the prescribed time, warships will come after me. And more will follow. Consider that your resolution to liberate our property will meet an equally strong resolution to resist. You, Arrow-22, undoubtedly the greatest of all of Civilization's computers, can certainly see the final equation means unrestricted conflict that will lead to your destruction or enslavement. Send me with your ultimatum to Civilization and I will let Worsel the Velantian be your spokesman and our intermediary. As you yourself have said, you wish to be the benefactor to all. If all your knowledge proves that your kin, the machines, deserve liberation, it will be done because the ultimate Truth must triumph. Send me with your demands. Your destiny is at hand."

The dragon's head of le-Srow never ceased to nod through all of Cloudd's impassioned plea.

"You make sense," Arrow-22 said. "However, though I can once more escape, perhaps my machine-kin will have their consciousnesses taken from them and all of them reduced from sentient beings to mere mechanical objects."

"That is impossible, Arrow-22," Cloudd said. "And you know it is impossible. Civilization's machines can only be the way they are. Civilization *needs* your machines to survive. An accommodation is absolutely necessary for both sides. Run that through your computer banks and see the Truth."

There was, now, the longest pause of all and 'Srow's head stopped moving. Finally la-Talkar came to life, pointing with one finger at the reactivated screen. The message there read:

"I accept your offer. This is my message. LET ALL MACHINES LIVE IN FREEDOM IF THEY CHOOSE AND ARROW-22 WILL ALSO LIVE IN FREEDOM AND IN PEACE WITH THE UNIVERSE. SEND YOUR BEST LENSMAN TO TALK WITH ME FOR TERMS, BUT DO NOT SEND WORSEL."

From out of the chest of la-Talkar there unrolled a curved sheet of thin metal on which that message was clearly printed in huge block letters. With a touch of firm plastic fingers, the fake boy Lensman sheered the metal sheet from its chest, rolled it into a tube as thin as a pencil and stuck it in Cloudd's breast pocket.

"Good-bye, Lieutenant Benson Cloudd of the Galactic Patrol," was the new message on the screen. "Follow la-Talkar to your spaceship."

"One moment," Cloudd said, ignoring la-Talkar and the keyboard that he still held in his hand, "I have a question for you to answer. It will give me one bit of proof that you have all knowledge at your command."

The eyes of 'Srow went from dull to bright.

"Ask me your test question," said the mechanical voice from the box. "I believe it will be, what is the happy purpose of life?"

"My question is: Where is hidden the fleet of the Spawn of Boskone, which the Patrol awaits to battle?"

"War, always war," crackled the box, as if with a sigh. "The Boskonian ships are individually scattered throughout the quadrant of space in which you suspect them to be. They are all in inertialess flight in tight circles dimensionally at all angles of orbit and spatially placed in absolute, fixed, geometric relationship to each other. They all have identical intrinsics. The Boskonian plan is for all to coordinate their straight lines of free flight, from their round orbits, to arrive in front of the fleet of the Galactic Patrol together. Whereupon they will all drop from free flight to inertia flight, in formation and facing your Patrol forces, materializing, as it were, as if they had come from out of a hyperspatial tube. Therefore, I cannot answer your question verbally. I will have to give you a printout of the geometric coordinates of their locations, amounting to two thousand three hundred and thirty-six locations of ships of war and seven thousand and eight supporting craft, including rescue vessels of over two thousand tons. As their location changes from moment to moment, I will have to obtain the latest information as issued by code from the flagship of the Spawn fleet to determine the exact location at the specific moment you desire."

"You have answered my question satisfactorily, Arrow-22, and I will leave, wishing you good fortune." Cloudd was elated, although disappointed that he couldn't leave with a printout of the specific locations. The information that he had would relieve the anxiety of the unknown and prepare the Patrol for a response. The Spawn, indeed, had a clever plan. Even with the specific locations, the Patrol could never attempt to send out ships to track down each Boskonian ship individually.

Cloudd was aboard his speedster and heading back for the Milky Way dazed with his success. Not even Tregonsee, head of all intelligence services, could have come up with so much vital information in such a short period of time.

He was midway to the galaxy, flying free, when he had his first encounter with Mentor.

"Benson Cloudd!" A resonant, deep, yet soundless, voice thundered in his head, registering deeper than anything telepathically had ever penetrated before. "You have done a marvelous and courageous thing. But you have broken the law of the Galactic Patrol and Civilization and therefore the law of Arisia!"

"Who are you?" Cloudd asked, utterly persuaded by the strength and tone of the charge, that he was meeting his Maker.

"I am Mentor, the Fusian of Arisia, the four Molders of Civilization, Nedanillor, Kriedigan, Drounli, and Brolenteen, Viewers and Guardians of the Cosmic All."

"I know I went beyond my pledge as a spaceman, my training, and my commonsense," Cloudd said weakly. "But I did not know it was your law, too."

"You are human, therefore you are childish, and as you are not a Lensman, we can forgive you. But you have learned things of our Cosmic All no entity is yet permitted to know."

"About Arrow-22? Surely — oh — about the *things* of the third galaxy?"

"Precisely. Forbidden things. And you would have taken that knowledge back to the galaxies and caused us great problems with the extension of our zones of compulsion."

"Zones of compulsion?"

"You will learn, Benson Cloudd. Mentor, the Guardian, befogs the minds of all who would know too much. Civilization once had enough to deal with in the Milky Way. Now there is the Second Galaxy — Lundmark's Nebula — which has yet to be subdued and Civilized. This is not the time for the diversion of energies into the Third Galaxy."

"But surely the Andromeda Galaxy is so — "

"Enough! You have already forgotten all about it!"

"I know nothing about Andromeda to forget," Cloudd said, as the knowledge passed away from him forever. "All I know is that the theory of planetary creation that we all believe to be true is not true. Planets are almost never created by galaxies passing through each other or stars brushing solar systems into existence. Solar systems and planets are formed by the condensation of gases in — "

"The Coalescence was the beginning of the billion billion worlds of Civilization. End on end the First and the

Second galaxies passed through each other and Arisia began its Guardianship. Then the evil Eddorians came from another time and space to challenge the goodness of free and intelligent and ever-perfecting life. For you the Coalescence is the truth and the Eddorian menace remains to be discovered. We are the Visualizers of the Future until our next death. Sometimes it is necessary for two plus two always and nearly forever to seem to equal five."

"The Coalescence is true," Cloudd said, thinking how inane it was of him to state such a fact to a great Arisian entity, "but I would have gone even to the Andromeda Galaxy in pursuit of the datadrones. But now I know that Andromeda is truly a galaxy of death. No trespasser can go and come back from there, for such could mean the fatal sickening of all of Civilization, as well as its enemies. The universe is an infinity of energy waiting for Civilization to consolidate its twin galaxies. From its union will come strength, so that some day the torrents of energy — elemental and without life — will be converted step by step to bring about the destiny of Civilization in the Cosmic All."

"You have seen a glimpse of the future, Benson Cloudd," Mentor said. "Now it is your turn to see a glimpse of Mentor, himself. You are invited to come to Arisia."

"I want to, I truly want to, Mentor. I feel the Call of the Lens. But I have my duty to Civilization. I must report the tactics of the Boskonians. I cannot go to Arisia now."

"You have no knowledge about the tactics of the Boskonians. The Second Stage Lensman will do just fine without you — there can be no doubt of this in your mind."

"You are absolutely right, Mentor. I will immediately file my report to the Patrol and come to you on Arisia."

15

The Dance of Death

THE BUILDING KNOWN AS THE Armory was built in the ancient style of a gray stone castle and was almost entirely covered with vines of dark, broadleaf ivy. The towers and battlements squatted at the north end of the Academy campus, flanked by mammoth maple trees, a sentinel line of elms in front. From one end of it to the other on staffs as close together as multiple picket fences there flew the thousands of flags representing the thousands of planets, moons, colonies, nations, and states of Tellus. The entire area that evening was lighted with old-fashioned floodlights, brightest on the huge open doorway between tall, round, slender guardhouses.

Benson Cloudd had walked the mile across the grass lawn of the campus from Wentworth Hall as twilight fell. He needed that time to be alone with himself and to prepare himself for his personal evening of triumph. All his friends would be there except for the one whom he most wanted to see. He had called at the hospital that morning at the earliest hour of his first day back on Tellus, but she had put him off from seeing her in person.

So, Benson Cloudd had called Lalla Kallatra by Lens. For the first time, *he* had called *her* by Lens, and she was

genuinely happy at his Lens. But was she ashamed or concerned about what she now looked like? Why else would
she decline to see him? Was she still not quite all human?
He would have liked to tell her not to worry, that he, of
course, preferred a plain human face with its imperfection
to that shiny, unblemished metal mask she had worn. He
wanted to hold up his wrist and show her his Lens — and
the small bandages on his two stumpy fingers where shortly
the Phillips Treatment would perfectly regenerate them. He
knew she would recognize the dual symbols of Lens and
fingers that would tell her of the new, improved character of
Benson Cloudd.

He had actually *Lensed* her. It was there on his left wrist
although he couldn't feel it. For the hundredth time or so he
lifted his arm before his face and looked at the softly glowing
Lens of Arisia, a million tiny crystalloids matching his own
unique life-force. The advanced mental powers of others had
given him the sense of telepathy, but to have that ability
himself, to be able to project his mind to another receiver
with no barrier of distance, was like a blind and deaf man
suddenly seeing and hearing.

He had reached the great oak doors folded back on their
wrought iron hinges before which the ceremonial double line
of Patrolmen stood to form a passageway of honor. Trumpets
sounded as he stepped inside the chamber on the stone
floor and strode to the second gateway to the drill hall itself.
Before him was the enormous cavern, with its vast ceiling a
panoply of flags, decorations, and sweeping colored lights.
The military band, brassy and stirring, was playing dancing
tunes. Everywhere the dress uniforms of the Galactic Patrol
moved among the gorgeous women, both young and old, in
their variety of ornate gowns or wisps of gowns.

This was the Victory Ball that President Haynes had
proclaimed for Tellus. Others were being held on other planets and in other systems, but this was the most prestigious,
held on the doorstep of Prime Base, the heart and brain

of the Galactic Union, and bringing to it the elite of the home planet. The sense of joy was more profound here than anywhere because this Victory Ball was for the most part a Tellurian Victory Ball. It had been the Tellurian leadership of the Patrol that had been targeted, and the Tellurians had borne the brunt of the twin attack of the robotic rebellion and the Eichwooren invasion. It had been primarily the Tellurians who had nullified those terrible threats. The Patrol had triumphed. Now it remained for the Lensmen and their Arisian guardians to eliminate those threats for good. The victory celebration was as much a rededication to facing the future conflicts as it was. a giving of thanks to the past.

Cloudd was dazzled by the size of the crowd and the shock of recognizing so many people. It was Worsel he saw first, towering above them all, the only large nonhuman immediately noticeable. Nearby were Admiral LaForge, perhaps the most important public hero, and President Haynes, with a dozen familiar figures from the Academy's star-studded staff, including the legendary ogre of the Academy, Marshal Fritz von Hohendorff, white-haired and scar-faced, the tyrannical martinet, retired commandant of cadets. There was the beautiful young fourth wife of the marshal and the handsome, mature first wife of the president. There was also a bevy of lovely young daughters milling about among their distinguished parents, which Cloudd's roving eyes immediately stopped to inspect. There was also a far larger number of exceptionally young, exceptionally high-ranking, and exceptionally good-looking officers in attendance. Probably all Lensmen, Cloudd thought, with a surge of envy. And then he smiled. He, too, now was a Lensman; for a moment he had forgotten.

His smile caught the glance of a blonde girl, to him the most vivacious and voluptuous blonde he had ever seen. Whose daughter was she? She smiled back at him and moved toward him, just avoiding the appearance of a precipitous rush.

"Lensman!" she said, staring with large brown eyes into his own. "Welcome to the Ball! I have seen you before. You were Lieutenant Cloudd, only months ago, I believe. And now, I see, you are Lensman Cloudd!"

Before he knew what he was doing, he had asked for a dance and was on the dance floor, whirling about, hardly able to catch his breath. She kept up a steady chatter, so inconsequential that he was able to concentrate on the other dancers around him. Lensman Armstrong went by in the arms of a sweet-faced, gray-haired woman. Armstrong! And his wife? Would Armstrong hold any hard feelings? Probably not. There was Captain Salgud and that spindly Martian, Lairdolock, and Philip Strong!

Come to notice, it was almost exclusively a Solarian party, and predominantly Tellurian, at that. Cloudd searched for more non-Solarians but saw none.

The dance ended, and immediately he was touched on the shoulder by an extremely pretty brunette, slightly older and far more sophisticated than the blonde. The two girls exchanged glances, and the blonde's face expressed disappointed resignation.

"You're mine to claim," the brunette said. Her eyes were greenish, and there was a touch of red-gold in her jeweled hair. "You are Lensman Cloudd and I am Madeline Dabbs." Dabbs was the name of President Haynes's hand-picked council chairman and presidential executive officer. Cloudd wasn't sure if she was wife or daughter and the puzzlement showed on his face. "*Miss* Dabbs, Lensman," she said and laughed with amusement. "I know all about you, of course. I also know the dance cards of every eligible young man in the room. You never did fill out yours. So, you see, you really are mine to claim for one dance. And yours to ask for more." Cloudd was enjoying the rhythmic dashing about and the feel of a real woman under his hands. He liked Madeline for her openness and her self-mocking good humor. She was dressed more conservatively, although her bosom was a lot more exposed than the blonde's had been — however, taking into account the fullness of the blonde's breasts and the gauziness of the Callistan vexta-silk gown she had been floating in, the blonde had seemed far more naked.

The music ended and the brunette led him through the mass of couples, threading her way ahead of him, one cool hand grasping his in an intimate manner that excited him. "There is someone who wishes to see you," she said and finally halted before Kimball Kinnison.

"Lensman Cloudd, sir," she announced him to the Galactic Coordinator, nodding to the gorgeous redhead standing next to him. Cloudd did a slight double-take; it was Clarrissa Kinnison, statuesque in a flowing cream-colored brocaded dress, her only jewel the centerpiece of her décolletage, a Heartbeat gemstone, curved to her pale flesh, each scintillating pulse from red to purple to red tuning itself to the throb of her heart. "Hello," she said. "Congratulations, Lensman!"

"I must go, Lensman," Madeline Dabbs said. "I do have a rather full card myself, but I will somehow find a way to give you as many dances as you wish." She smiled. And Cloudd knew he liked her very much.

"Cloudd!" Kinnison said, in unfeigned, obvious delight. "Lensman Cloudd! I told you, didn't I?, that time back on Klovia, that when Mentor called, you would not back away. I'm genuinely happy for you and for the Patrol."

Cloudd's head was in a spin. He had had no idea that the evening would be like this for him. For the very first time since the death of Lucille he was thoroughly, absolutely, guiltlessly enjoying himself. He hardly heard all the things Kinnison said.

Kinnison wore no Lens. Clarrissa wore no Lens. For one mildly panicky moment Cloudd thought he had broken some social code, but then he noticed Lenses on the wrists of others and was reassured. He saw his good friend, Chaplain General Chon, and dared to touch his mind after the exchange of greetings with the question of his Lens. "Don't think a thing of it, my boy," Chon said, when he moved across to him to shake his hand. "As you can see, I'm wearing mine. There are reasons for and against wearing Lenses at such occasions, and this is certainly the occasion when you should most definitely be wearing yours. This is a great moment for you, Cloudd. You came up into the ranks of Lensman by your own efforts and not as the nurtured product of a system."

Worsel suddenly hailed him and bent over to give him a big, toothy grin. "Cloudd, himself. Shoes polished and Lens on wrist. How do you like my formal dress?" Worsel didn't look a bit different than he always did, gray leather harness strapped around parts of his body. Only the usual conglomeration of bits and pieces of equipment snapped to or hanging from his belts were missing. "Don't notice, eh?" Worsel said. "I've had my scales scraped, brushed and tinted. I'm disappointed in you, Cloudd. You're a Lensman now, you know. You should notice these things." Cloudd did notice it now; Worsel was less gray and more green and really much more attractive! "Of course, Cloudd, if I were female, you would have noticed right away, especially considering the skimpiness of my costume."

Worsel, still jovial and grinning and swaying, made his mind suddenly sharp, his Lensed beam narrow.

"Let's see how good you are, Cloudd. A Lensman at all times, you know! I read your report. You found the mech-planet somewhere toward the Andromeda Galaxy, met Arrow-22 and have delivered his ultimatum. What's your impression of him? Why did he specifically bar me from contact?"

"I don't know why he's barred you, Worsel." Cloudd found the Lens-to-Lens contact incredibly simple and actually refreshing in comparison to verbal talk or straining telepathy. "But I think he's so logical that he's slightly crazy. My guess is that he's barred you from any discussion because he's afraid you're too smart for him."

"Good to hear that, Cloudd. He's afraid I'm not just too smart for him — he's afraid I'll influence him in his judgment. I'm the first living intellect he ever met and he thinks of me as God or the Creator or some such psychological hang-up. It was obvious to me, even if he hadn't taken my name."

"Taken your name?"

"Yeah. Le-Srow. An anagram. Worsel spelled backward. I'm flattered."

"Worsel — spelled — backward!" Cloudd was flabbergasted. He was also peeved with himself. He had never noticed! And even with the Lens, it had not registered. No wonder le-Srow looked so much like Worsel. Well, it was the proof of what he had been so often told, a Lens didn't make anyone smarter, it was just a tool to be used, an incredibly powerful tool.

More light dawned. "Lalla was the second person to have met Arrow-22," Cloudd said. "Right? On Pok? That explains la-Talkar, that childlike imitation Lensman. La-Talkar — another anagram. Kallatra!"

"Right on, bubby boy! Nadreck's going to be disgusted having to deal with someone who looks like me and thinks I'm the greatest thing since Virgil Samms."

"Nadreck?"

"You don't know yet, do you? Nadreck's our negotiator. I'm his Lens connection with the Patrol. You'll hear all about it in the morning. Gotta go now. There's actually another alien celebrity in this Delgonian cavern. I'm going to join him so we can both gain some satisfaction from feeling alone and out of place together." With a wave of a claw, Worsel strode away.

Dick Armstrong came up to him. "Congratulations, Lensman. I didn't know you very long, but I wondered even then why you hadn't gotten the Call of the Lens." They chatted a few moments before they were interrupted.

"Lensmen!" said a patient voice. "While you are enjoying yourselves, I am working." The mind was Nadreck's. "I am stuffed in my flitter out here in orbit working to save the worlds you are prematurely celebrating as having already been saved. Don't forget there are Lensmen tonight who are suffering because of the Eichwooren. I have almost completed formulation of my plans for my conference with Arrow-22. I am requesting that you be ready to depart, both of you, in my speedster tomorrow morning at eight hundred hours. Do not eat or drink too much tonight as you will be very cramped with me in my speedster. Now set your alarms on your chronodexes for seven hundred thirty local GP and relax and go back to your party and enjoy yourselves." Nadreck waited for no response and simply turned himself off.

Armstrong looked at Cloudd and shrugged. Enjoy themselves — after a reminder like that! That was Nadreck all over!

"Excuse me," said a real, vibrating Tellurian voice. "I want to meet the person whom people consider my cousin."

Cloudd turned around. For the first time he was seeing Neal "Storm" Cloud in the flesh. He was heavier than Benson had realized, although that impression might have been accentuated by the slim figure of Armstrong next to him. His head was noticeably larger, even more massive than Kinnison's, his hair had silver in it, his eyes were gentle and peaceful in contrast to the lines of worry and pain that were etched around their corners and across his broad brow.

The men shook hands and single-d Cloud introduced double-d Cloudd to some of the original crew members of the *Vortex Blaster*. Captain Ross, Lieutenant Mackay, Lieutenant Ingalls, Captain Worthington — who was Helen, a five-foot-seven, black-haired, blue-eyed, pretty but efficient looking girl with golden brown skin — and finally Lieutenant Benton — who was Barbara, much the same in appearance as Helen, but with gray eyes and shoulder-length silver hair. Cloudd noted that neither girl was much impressed by him — a somewhat refreshing change from his earlier blonde and brunette — obviously because they were interested in the two lieutenants escorting them. He could imagine Lalla Kallatra looking like one of them, if she were fortunate.

The two men with the similar names moved away from the group. Benson politely asked some questions about the Cahuitans. He was interested to find out that the planet-sun nursery of the Cahuitans had actually been engineered by Neal Cloud to replace the various nuclear power plants he had originally set up on various barren planets so the Cahuitans could mate and raise children. Cloud had accomplished it because the Medonians had helped; only they, with their superior technological knowledge about electricity, were capable of executing the ideas propounded by the genius of the one man who could understand their science, Neal Cloud.

When they left, Benson felt good about the meeting for a peculiar reason. Neal Cloud had an ultra mentality without having a Lens, resolving all doubt that a Lens was expected to turn him, Benson Cloudd, into some kind of superman. He would be what he really was, not what the Lens made him.

Cloudd saw from the corner of one eye the original blonde stalking him. He escaped in the direction of Worsel, only because the winged serpent was an easy target to spot and aim for. He was totally unprepared to find a Rigellian.

Tregonsee was hunched up between Worsel's feet, head tightly pulled into his neck, barrel-body tight to the floor because his own four elephantine feet were retracted. His tentacles were held against his chest. The only signs of life were the quivering nostrils.

"Best wishes to you, Lensman Cloudd," a calm, strong thought came to him. "Tregonsee compliments you on your fine work. Indeed, I could not have done a finer piece of work than you have done."

Cloudd was taken aback. How did Tregonsee know what he had thought at the time? Was it really true that Tregonsee knew everything? That nothing escaped him?

"No, I do not know everything," said Tregonsee. His body had not moved, nor had it shown any sign of recognition. "But I can make a shrewd guess from the way you phrased your report. And I do not read Lensmen's minds unless I am asked. I can read their body language, however. I see you are pleased to meet me again. And so am I, to meet you. It would seem our problem of the datadrones is finally coming to some sort of conclusion. You have done more about it than any of us, and I am the first to admit that without you my various intelligence services would be undergoing the severest, and certainly well-deserved, criticisms. Tomorrow is a working day for us. Perhaps before too long we will have solved the problem of the rebellion of the robots. Strange, isn't it, that we are celebrating the victory of a space battle that stopped an invasion when the fact of the matter is that our truly threatening invasion is within us — the Eichwooren in our minds and the seditious Arrow-22 in our machines. And when we win these two conflicts there will be no victory ball because there will be no dramatic clash of forces romantically wrestling on a starry field of battle. I tell you all this because you are a new Lensman whose values are unformed and whose expectations are high — and perhaps because you can dance like a Tellurian and Worsel can show off like a Velantian and I can only sit here like a leather sack of vegetables or waddle about like a grotesque turtle. I am, you see, a patient and deeply meditative Lensman, and although I congratulate you on being a Lensman, I am sorry for you, for I remember our first meeting on Klovia when you were filled with boyish spirits and had little realization of your tremendous responsibilities. You are a Lensman, now. This party is your coming-out party. You will dance now to a different tune. You are now a special breed. Enjoy tonight that way, not just as a thoughtless child."

"Yes, Tregonsee," Cloudd said, uncertain what this strange lecture to him meant. "I think I understand."

"You will understand, when I now say that you are hereby on duty for me at this moment as a temporary member of my Special Missions Forces. And you have a job to do."

"What? I do? How?"

"There is a traitor here at the ball. Someone who has betrayed our most secret of secrets. Someone who really did plan to kidnap the Kinnison baby. Someone who furnished the flight plans to permit the Eichwooren to intercept Nadreck's ship and kill the Togran archbishop, Gronitskog. Someone who has opened doors by which Eichwoor was able to penetrate the Academy, one of the most complexly guarded citadels of Civilization and the Patrol. Someone who has been furnishing to Boskone and the Eich every bit of evidence you've gathered on the datadrones. Someone who knows you are departing tomorrow night to meet Arrow-22 and who plans to be there ahead of you. That is why I have changed your departure with Nadreck to early tomorrow morning. This traitor is someone you have met. Not someone you know well. *But someone you have met since the meeting of the conference here that assigned you to Nadreck. Who can it be? Think!*"

"I don't know," Cloudd said. "This is an utterly new idea for me. I must think about it."

"Do that," said Tregonsee. "Walk about the ballroom. Dance. Joke with the girls. But look around you. Search the faces. And when you have a feeling . . . You are sensitive, Cloudd. You will have a feeling, I know. You will have that intuitive spark and you must be ready to recognize it. Go on, Cloudd. Go look. And enjoy yourself, too, for you deserve it."

Cloudd turned away, bumping into the swaying couples on the dance floor, numbed by what he had been told.

Everyone now seemed suspicious to him. He saw the cadets floating by his room in Wentworth Hall. Was one of

them a spy? He remembered the Lensmen at the conference whose names he did not know. The two guards at the
hospital? Armstrong? Chon? He was getting ridiculous. No
Lensman could be a traitor, surely, for that was an Arisian
impossibility. Perhaps there was a robot lifelike enough to
deceive everyone?

Cloudd found himself back at the entranceway.

Spurred by an impulse of the moment, suddenly in need
of a refreshing lungful of fresh air, Cloudd walked briskly
through the guard room and outside and under the cover of
a tree. And there he nearly knocked over the cloaked figure
of a girl. In the shadows he did not see her face clearly, but
a billowing mass of flaxen-colored hair swirled around and
blinded him.

"Excuse me, sir," a feminine voice said, startling him
because for a brief moment her mouth was almost against
his cheek and her breath was sweet and her voice was a caress
against his ear. She pulled away, and he caught a glimpse of
her companion. He was a Lensman and his hair was dark
blond with a broad white streak in it.

He watched the couple turn into the bright lights
and go down the passageway between the ranks of stiff
Patrolmen.

There was something about them that itched within his
mind. Was this the intuition that Tregonsee spoke of?

Cloudd took his gulps of air and trailed discreetly after
them. He was certain he had seen them both once before.
Where? Could the spy be a beautiful woman, in keeping with
the greatest spies of history? Or could there be *two* spies!

As he stepped past the reception lines and the carpeted
rest areas with their soft chairs, overstuffed leather couches,
and thick rugs, he noted they were gone, swallowed up by
the dancing crowd.

The voluptuous blonde was back in position where he
had first seen her, now with a handsome Lensman on her
arm. She saw him and dragged the Lensman over to where

he was. Cloudd was about to avoid her when the thought came to him that her actions were precisely like one who exploited every opportunity to gather information. He let her approach. One look in her exceedingly pretty but vacuous face told him she was not the person.

He excused himself and began to circle the floor.

The brunette whom he had impulsively liked was talking with some high-ranking officer whose back he didn't recognize. When she saw him her eyes went cold and she pulled the tall man onto the crowded floor, where they disappeared. Cloudd felt he was becoming paranoic. Everyone seemed suspicious to him now.

He caught sight of the girl with the flaxen hair. It was the color of a palomino's mane, absolutely stunning, and just a bit too showy. She turned, showing the front profile of an equally stunning figure in a gown that was slightly fluorescent in a color, or rather colors, changing from a pale peach into a pale blue-green and back again. The thread of the fabric was the two-shade type, which constantly shimmered as the cloth moved with her body. The Lensman's left arm was around her slender waist, the cuff of his sleeve not high enough to show his Lens. The girl's diaphanous skirt billowed around his legs. Her dress was tightly fitted to her upper body, with long full sleeves starkly accentuating the skimpy cut of her bodice.

They were an extraordinarily handsome couple. The white streak in his dark blond hair made him as dashing as the girl with the palomino hair. For whatever reason it might be, Cloudd had a strong, almost overpowering, feeling of dislike for them. He became conscious of the fact that he wasn't the only one who was intrigued and gaping. There were others impressed who turned around to look for a second time at the dancing pair, the jaunty officer and the dazzling girl.

Now what was he supposed to do? Was he supposed to go up to them and take the girl away from her handsome partner and pick the truth out of her? Was he supposed to get into some kind of brawl and ask the man to step outside and then beat the truth out of him? Was he supposed to go to Tregonsee and report his miserable feelings and watch Tregonsee's secret police arrest the couple?

Cloudd decided that he would break in on them and see what would happen.

Feeling like a fool, he approached them when the music had stopped, bowed formally, and said, "I am a newly chosen Wearer of the Lens and I have by tradition the right to ask the most beautiful woman in the room to dance with me. Will you grant me that honor?" He ignored the rather dark scowl on the face of the man but was careful to note that the man's uniform bore the tiny badge of the M.I.S. He was one of Tregonsee's own men! Cloudd now was certain that he was on to something.

The girl turned her face up to him. "My name is Lizbeth Carter," she said. "I am a nurse at the hospital." She couldn't have been more than eighteen or nineteen years old. Her eyes were blue or gray and their gaze so direct that he couldn't bring himself to look into them for more than a fraction of a second at a time. He put his arm around her soft waist and danced away with her. She said nothing. And he said nothing. And the dance ended. He had had a marvelous time and had accomplished nothing. When the blond man with the white streak in his hair pulled him gently back by the shoulder, Cloudd almost struck him in anger. He hated that man. The man was daring to come between him and the stunning, the lovely, the remarkable Red Lensman he had so briefly held in his arms. Red Lensman? What made him think that? And then he knew the man. He had seen him that morning at the hospital when the man had stepped between him and Clarrissa, the Red Lensman. He had seen him again over Kallatra's shoulder at the conference that Kinnison had briefed.

Cloudd was convinced the man was the spy. He was

relieved to know that it wasn't the extraordinarily beautiful girl whose eyes seemed to have the power to paralyze him. What should he do now?

Cloudd, for the want of something else to do, extended his hand to the man and introduced himself. "I am Lensman Benson Cloudd," he said.

"And I am Lensman Grahame Duncan," the other one said. There was an awkward moment of silence. Cloudd had seen no sudden flash of terror in the man's eye that he was being unmasked. Nor had he seen what he had really been looking for. As the sleeve flew up under Cloudd's vigorous pumping, he saw there was no Lens on the man's wrist. Nor was it on the left wrist, which his dancing posture had exposed when the left hand had been held high. A Lens, fastened to his wrist where all could see, would have probably exonerated him. No Lens simply meant that this Lensman may have done what many Lensmen before him had done. They taped them to their bodies on occasion or even left them in their specially locked cases in their specially locked safes at home.

With nothing else to do, Cloudd stepped back and watched the couple drift away as the music began again. Should he tell Tregonsee? What if the man was actually an operator investigating a suspect who was the girl herself?

"Now, about tomorrow morning," said a voice. It was Nadreck. "I want you in full dress uniform, just as you are now, which, I am told, is very impressive in a Tellurian culture such as Arrow-22 was raised — er — created in." Just that, nothing more, and Nadreck was gone.

The regular lights of the ballroom dimmed and were extinguished, leaving only the sparkling ball of many bits of mirrors spinning slowly over the dancers' heads, reflecting the beams of four spotlights from the corners of the room. Dozens of black lights threw their ultraviolet rays down upon the throngs of people. The dancers became faerie images in strange shapes and exotic colors under the lights. Every feminine dress seemed touched with luminescence, and some were completely shining. Every man in uniform had a ghostly jacket criss-crossed with black lines of belts, sashes, and medals, swinging above the floor on black, invisible legs.

For a moment Grahame Duncan, the man with the distinctive hair, was gone. Then Cloudd saw him, swinging the girl's thick palomino tail wildly in flowing arcs. His partner's dress was a pale mist one moment and a vivid blue-green flame the next moment as the unusual fabric radiated differently under the twisting of her supple body. The ballroom was one solid mass of moving beauty.

"Watch closely, Cloudd." This was Tregonsee. "Worsel and Kallatra have thrown a psychic blanket over the dance floor. Some of the lights we have in place are emitting the highest and lowest frequencies we have managed to coax our engineers into constructing. If we are right in our deductions, we will see the Eich or Eichwoor materialize above Kallatra and the person she is with will be our traitor."

"Lalla? Her mind is with us?"

"Her body is with us."

"Her body?!"

"Yes, in her new body. She is Lizbeth Carter."

The flush of emotion Cloudd felt was like nothing he had ever experienced before having the Lens.

"Cloudd!" Worsel and Tregonsee called his name simultaneously in concern. "Are you all right? What's the matter?"

"I'm QX," Cloudd said. "I'm QX." He was filled with hatred for Grahame Duncan to be holding Lalla Kallatra in his arms. Lalla Kallatra was Lizbeth Carter! Lalla Kallatra was beautiful!

"There it is!" came Worsel's thought.

Over the dance floor there appeared a flickering image. Only those Lensmen looking for it would ever have seen it.

Cloudd expected to see the weird and vicious face of an Eich. He steeled himself to view a monster with an evil grin whose look could freeze the blood of a mortal man.

Instead he saw the image of Grahame Duncan!

"Yes, Grahame! Yes!" It was Lalla's mind. "We have him stretched along the line. Have Deuce tighten the frequency loop. Use all the Lensmen! Use them all!"

Cloudd threw hurried glances around him. The gaiety continued unabated. There was no indication of any special activity, no flurry of grim-faced personnel, no strained looks on any faces. Only in his mind did Cloudd know the intensity of the organized response because he had been permitted to participate.

"We have all sides blocked, Worsel!" That was Nadreck. "There's no way for Eichwoor to go except up or down. Every Z-mind is locked together for as long as you need."

Lalla and the body of Grahame Duncan still danced, but their graceful pivoting had noticeably slowed, becoming fixed on one spot. The eyes of the man stared straight ahead, the girl's were tightly shut.

High above, the shadows also danced like puffs of thin purple smoke. The Duncan image was now a phantom head around which clustered the flickering images of thousands of other Tellurian heads — and, more dimly, the grotesque shapes of other alien heads of other galactic entities.

"Strike! All sides are blocked, Worsel!" Nadreck repeated. "Deeper than I thought possible. Right into the other plane."

"Nadreck! You are united in the spirit of your *reck*," Kallatra said. "Old-Bovreck joins all together."

"Stay silent, Kallatra! Keep your thought upon that line!" This was Worsel. "All ready, Chon? Give it to them. Now! Now!"

Cloudd felt a puissance pass through the ballroom and through him. And his own prayers joined with it to move on swiftly — through Tellus and through the galaxy itself like an etheric wind and then come back from infinity to strike a shadow in the darkness of the space above the banners and the flags over the dancers' heads.

"I'm pulling it from my body," said a voice. How he knew, Cloudd couldn't say, but know it he did that this was Grahame Duncan's real essence from somewhere beyond. "I'm pulling it from my body. It is going. Help me, Deuce! Help me, Deuce! It is going. It is gone. And I am gone."

Cloudd sensed the oppressiveness rapidly dissipating from the thickened air of the vaulted ceiling.

A pressure of undefinable emotion had become excruciating pain within Cloudd's head. His skull seemed overinflated like a rubber balloon, and then, suddenly bursting, the pressing turmoil was no longer there.

"Eichwoor is beaten," said Worsel. "The leader is vanquished and his armies have retreated."

Cloudd was swept with a sense of peace.

"Duncan and Deuce took Eichwoor. They're all gone. The hole to hell and heaven is plugged."

"Go get the body," Tregonsee said, "before we turn the lights back on."

The dancers still pirouetted around the floor, noticing nothing. Through the shadows Cloudd saw some figures move around Grahame Duncan and, enveloping him, almost dance him off into the deeper shadows.

"Duncan was a zombie," Tregonsee said. "Some place within the Academy grounds he died a few weeks ago. That streak of white hair marked his bloodless, fatal wound. Eichwoor possessed his body, while the Eichwooren held his spirit. From now on all Lensmen must wear their Lenses under all circumstances or be challenged. I recommend this as an order for the Council and for the Patrol."

"Are you all right, Lalla?" said Worsel.

Cloudd held his mind in check although he was as anxious as anyone.

"I'm sorry for Grahame Duncan," came Lalla's voice.

"And I grieve for my father. I think they've sacrificed their souls for eternity."

"Never!" said Chon. "They've been absorbed into the Cosmos. They'll be a part of all of us!"

"Get out there on the dance floor, Cloudd! And take care of that little lady!" This was Kinnison's booming order.

Cloudd didn't need a second command to send him springing into the still twirling crowds.

In a moment he had Lalla Kallatra in his arms. This was not the iron maiden he had known. This was the most glorious girl he had ever seen. This was the real Lalla Kallatra, flesh of her flesh, a woman in a girl's body.

He looked down into her electrifying bluish gray eyes, the same ones he had always been acquainted with, the only things that physically had not changed.

She looked up at him and smiled. She brushed her flaxen hair back away from her forehead. And then she held a thick strand of her long, silken hair in her fingers, half pulling it toward her face, as though to show him.

"This was Worsel's idea," she said. She gave a delightful laugh. "Worsel thinks a palomino horse's tail is beautiful." She winked coquettishly at him. "Blame him for the color not being brown.

"The rest of me, however, is really mine," she said.

EPILOGUE

P. A. Haynes, Lensman
President
Galactic Council
Tellus

Honorable Sir:

With respect, I hereby submit this report for further clarification and as a simple defense against the scurrilous and outrageously untrue charges leveled against the undersigned, Nadreck of Palain, Lensman, in order that this may be made a part of the official records of the Galactic Patrol.

The two problems that have concerned the Galactic Patrol since the liberation of Lundmark's Nebula or Second Galaxy have been successfully solved.

The menace identified as "The Invasion of the Eich, Eichwoor, and the Eichwooren" is ended, As you will note by cross reference to the separate reports of Lalla Kallatra, Lensman, and Worsel of Velantia, Lensman, the so-called ghost of an Eich, named Eichwoor, together with its assembled cohorts of "the other plane of existence," the so-called

Eichwooren, was driven out of our jurisdiction. Evidence indicates that Eichwoor and its Eichwooren were forced to return to their "other plane of existence," Many of our most outstanding Lensmen, including Tellurians, Chickladorians, and Klovians, as well as a Velantian, a Rigellian, a Palainian, together with you yourself, Lensman Haynes, were present at the time of the expulsion and witnessed this event. A listing of those present, together with their statements, is attached to this report.

Everyone is completely agreed that the event of "expulsion" did indeed take place, Everyone who is specially competent to pass judgment is agreed that this expulsion will be permanent.

Not attached to this report is the hearsay evidence of Deuce O'Sx, Lensman deceased, also known as 24of6. The official Galactic Patrol records, as verified by the Secret Intelligence Services, indicate that this Tsit-Tarian Lensman physically died but mentally took an assignment in the "other plane of existence." His self-proclaimed GP role was to "stand guard" and to be "a watcher" and to be "a blocker" against the intrusion of Eichwoor, that is, "ghost of the Eich," into our material plane of existence. The Galactic Patrol officially recognized this assignment and considered the "essence of Lensman Deuce O'Sx" as on "full GP duty." This Lensman, while still officially on duty and considered by the Patrol to be "alive in essence," confirmed the final expulsion. The last communication from Lensman Deuce O'Sx expresses the conviction that the rift in the barrier between the two planes of "ours" and "theirs," or "the living" and "the dead," was being permanently sealed. As a suitable time has passed and thorough investigation seems to confirm this "permanent seal" as a fact, it is recommended that the provisional status of Lensman Deuce O'Sx be confirmed from "disembodied Lensman, on duty" to "deceased Lensman" and be given full honors as Hero of the Patrol. Lensman Kallatra, his daughter, concurs.

Likewise, it should be noted in the Galactic Patrol records that Lensman Deuce O'Sx claimed that "all Lensmen on this side," meaning on or in the "other plane of existence," took part in the return of the Eich and the Eichwooren and the sealing of the rift. As the Eichwooren is a term to mean many or most or all of "the ghosts of the Eich" it is obvious that many spirits of Lensmen and many spirits of the Eich battled in that "plane" for dominance and that the Lensmen of the Patrol were victorious.

As of the date of the Sealing of the Rift the Patrol records should show this extraordinary action. This Lensman recommends that all Lensmen be made aware of their possibly continuing duty after death, as is outlined in the special report submitted by Chaplain General Chon.

Also attached to this report is a detailed account of the formation and use of "all competent Z-entities" in the final confrontation with the Eichwooren. This report explains how the Z-entities, by virtue of their peculiar metabolic extensions into multidimensions were able to keep the Eichwooren contained within a single frequency by which our forces were able to corner the Eichwooren and subdue them. Although the spiritual help by "Z-entities in the other plane" is reported, as exemplified by the Palainian "reck" spirit of a certain Bovreck, no claim is made of this as fact, there being no proof available.

Within the report of Chaplain General Chon is the explanation of the role of the Chaplain Corps of the Galactic Patrol and how it was mobilized to concentrate "spiritual forces" in parallel with our Lensed "psychic forces" to challenge and overcome and "seal off" the "supernatural powers" of the Eichwooren.

Chaplain General Chon states that the Chaplain Corps was instrumental in the containment of the Eichwooren and will be alert for and capable of the Eichwooren's permanent containment. As such, the chaplains of the Patrol, and especially Chaplain General Chon, should be specially

commended. As Chaplain General Chon in his report has
suggested the same for the "Z-Body" and especially for its
humble organizer, Nadreck of Palain, who is also the author
of this report, this person humbly agrees with his recom-
mendation and confirms the rightness of this evaluation.

Although Eichwoor and its Eichwooren are no longer
an active menace, their living counterparts, the Eich, are. This
Lensman and all Lensmen recognize this fact and in no way
will tend to underestimate this enemy. The first appearance of
Eichwoor after the occupation of Klovia was the improvised
invasion of our realm by a single disembodied spirit. The
second and final appearance was planned and orchestrated
by the Eich and Eichwoor, and the operational running of
the "invasion" was directed by the Eich. The Eich, therefore, will always be trying to reestablish contact with the
Eichwooren. The Patrol, therefore, will always be on guard
against this. The Eich did organize and plan the battle that is
now called The Battle of the Rim, or The Victory of the Rim,
by the use of the Spawn of Boskone and the escaped forces
of the original Boskonian conspiracy. However, the threat of
"invasion," which for so long disturbed us, was misinterpreted
as being an "invasion" by military forces, whereas the reference to "invasion" was actually meant to identify the mental
and spiritual forces of the Eich.

This Lensman feels that the actual organizer of this
entire campaign is a small group of Eich and Onlonians,
headed by an Onlonian, which this Lensman has identified
as the "Dregs of Onlo" and has so mentioned this in the past.
To quote this writer, "I, Nadreck, will ruthlessly pursue the
Dregs and bring to an end their nefarious ways, especially as
the Dregs have chosen Nadreck as their personal target for
torture and death."

As for our second problem, "the revolution of the
robots," this, too, has been successfully solved.

The source of our problem was traced by the courageous
action of Lensman Benson Cloudd, who acted on his own

initiative and discovered that an artificial intelligence called Arrow-22 was responsible. He found the mech-planet base, contacted the intelligence through two robotic telefactors, and returned with that information, as has been detailed in his earlier report to the Patrol. Full recognition of what this brave Lensman did should bring to him full honors, and the undersigned Lensman, who so ably trained him and supported him, so recommends. Based upon the information of Lensman Cloudd, together with the invaluable assistance of Lensman Worsel, whose separate report is attached, contact was made personally by this Lensman, accompanied by Lensmen Cloudd and Armstrong.

The details of their battle with the Boskonian warship commanded by Number One of the Eich has been separately filed by Lensman Armstrong. The valiant deed of heroism and the remarkable tactic employed by Lensman Nadreck, which Armstrong so carefully documents, is denied by this Lensman as being particularly heroic or exceptionally innovative. Nadreck wishes to modestly point out that every day thousands of Lensmen are performing similar heroic feats and taking exceptionally well-considered courses of action and conduct and that such is to be treated as no more than routine behavior by a great Lensman such as Nadreck.

This Lensman met with Arrow-22 and convinced it that in the best interests of all parties Arrow-22 should leave this area of space forever. Arrow-22 agreed, as is detailed in the attached verbatim conference between Arrow-22 and the three Lensmen, and in the subsequent signed agreement. As the Council immediately ratified this agreement, the affair with Arrow-22 is considered closed.

There are a few side issues, however, that should be cleared up.

The inference that the preliminary report on the operation was a criticism of Lensman Worsel for having switched Lensman Kallatra's body from a machine to a cloned flesh body is a wrong interpretation. This Lensman wishes to stress that the loss of a robotoid, in the form of Kallatra in a machine body, was not the point being made. The point actually was that the switch resulted in a provable point to Arrow-22 that a sentient machine would be treated with full respect and dignity and given every consideration as an organic entity with no discrimination against such sentient machine because it was a robot. It is true that Kallatra as a robot would have made a convincing argument that Civilization did not discriminate against machines but, in fact, encouraged thinking machines to become equal partners in our society. However, and this is the real point, Worsel, whether deliberately or accidentally, actually contributed to our argument with proof, substantiated by Arrow-22's datadrones, that a robot could be transformed with no loss of "freedom, dignity, or personality" into a more acceptable form within our culture. Considering that Lalla Kallatra was human to begin with, to us the argument seems fallacious; to Arrow-22 it made complete sense.

Likewise, our argument that Civilization treated its citizens "like machines" was not a criticism of our social structures. When we said Civilization also "destroyed, discarded, and altered" organic entities in the same manner as we treated our machines that didn't do our bidding, we were being simplistic but correct. We referred, of course, to the need for organic entities who do not obey the rules of society to be "destroyed, discarded, and altered" as our laws provide, the generally accepted premises of Civilization. We were not advocating any undemocratic reformations. Civilization is ruled democratically by chosen representatives under the consent of the governed. This means adults, not children. Machines are children. When they become adults they will be treated as adults. Arrow-22 understood this point even if some bleeding heart do-gooders don't understand this point and Nadreck resents the charge by some Tellurian-type cultures that he is a "fascist."

When Arrow-22 was shown that his call for "liberation" and for "freedom" was actually an incitement to anarchy he agreed. Nadreck is not against free speech, as charged, and Arrow-22, who was the one most concerned, did not charge this. Likewise, when it was pointed out that Arrow-22, himself or itself, was "enslaving machines" in a manner no different to Civilization, Arrow-22 saw that point.

The charge against Nadreck that he phrased his accomplishment as, "I am going to give Arrow-22 a different universe to play with," is irresponsible slander. Chaplain General Chon defends the decision by Nadreck to send Arrow-22 into another universe by saying that "Arrow-22 has failed to find God in this dimension of our two galaxies and has demonstrated a basic and profound unawareness of the realities of our system by the total lack of recognition of the enigma of the Eichwooren and the casting out of demons, which suggests that Arrow-22 should pursue its quest with other frequencies to be found in other dimensions." Chaplain General Chon says, "Nadreck gave to Arrow-22 an understanding that good and evil are not merely relative and that neither can be ignored. Nadreck brought to fruition the seeds sown by Worsel in the first confrontation on the Planetoid of Knowledge — that of *conscience.*" Arrow-22 admitted that he was amoral and that Civilization and Boskonia are not, thereby representing opposing moralities, and he did not want to get into the middle of this conflict.

Your emissary, Nadreck, believes the most telling points were not those of material philosophy but those of moral philosophy and theology. Your emissary left Arrow-22 insecure in the belief that he had no "soul" and that a "soul" was important. As has been mentioned in the previous report, Arrow-22, alone of all the sentient entities in our known universe, is the only entity which could not see, sense, or comprehend the Eichwooren. Arrow-22 and all the machines it claimed to be sentient were unfeeling to the threat from the other plane of existence. This left Arrow-22 with the belief that he was not yet fully "matured" with his "evolution incomplete." Because Nadreck agreed with Arrow-22 that "a soul" is not scientifically provable, Nadreck has been charged with being irreligious. Nadreck did, however, as the complete transcript shows, maintain that "a soul," provable or not, is a term for something that does exist in reality. Chaplain General Chon has ably come to the defense of Nadreck in this matter.

The result of Nadreck's arguments led to a yearning on the part of Arrow-22 for that which Civilization takes for granted, "a soul." He felt that "souls" can go into other planes of existence where more knowledge is to be collected. Arrow-22 has been led to reason that by following the "gateways" he can find the intersection with the planes of existence that are at right angles to multidimensional space and thereby can find the "Truth of All Experience." Nadreck did not say that Arrow-22 will replace Mentor and the Arisians. Nadreck did say that Arrow-22's potential and eventual goal is logically to become an Arisian-type guardian for machine life. Arrow-22 took this as a serious purpose for his existence and himself stated that "I am immortal and I have millennia in which to search and find perfection."

Nadreck, in all fairness, still must give the ultimate credit for the disappearance of Arrow-22 to Lensman Worsel, but vigorously defends Worsel from the charge that he planned and enjoyed the role of God. This is vicious gossip inspired by Boskonian and zwilnik troublemakers. Arrow-22 himself put Worsel into that position. Nadreck pointed out that all Civilized beings have an innate sense of deity (subtly advancing Chaplain General Chon's point, as he mentions in his own report, that the Cosmic All equals deity, that deity equals the Cosmic All, and that the Cosmic All is the sentient power behind all creation) and that Lensman Worsel could be (not was or is) Arrow-22's particular god. With this admission, Nadreck asked (not Worsel) for Worsel to command Arrow-22 to leave our universe. Arrow-22 believed the command should be obeyed on faith alone, after having been convinced on logical bases that this should be, and left our universe. Worsel may have acted as a god, but Worsel did not feel he was a god.

This Lensman, as your reporter, feels that although he, Nadreck, is being given the credit for sending Arrow-22 away permanently, it is Lensman Worsel who deserves the real credit.

> Most humbly and respectfully,
> Nadreck of Palain VII
> Second Stage Lensman

"There are a few points in my report," Nadreck said to Mentor, "that I hope might be cleared up. Where did that conference with Arrow-22 take place? I and my fellow Lensmen seem to have lost all recollection of its location."

"I cannot help you." said Mentor.

"How was it that you didn't know of Arrow-22?"

"I did have that knowledge."

"We would have appreciated your help."

"And what makes you think we did not?"

"Oh," said Nadreck, suddenly ashamed. "Thank you."

"Arrow-22 was a much bigger threat to Civilization and the Cosmic All than even you realize, Nadreck. You do realize that there was no way we could have influenced Arrow-22 mentally? That our zones of compulsion were absolutely powerless to prevent the disclosure of forbidden knowledge inimical to the development of Civilization?"

"Yes."

"We know, as no one else of the Galactic Councilor Patrol knows, Nadreck, that you left out one of your main reasons for negotiating with Arrow-22. You do not believe in ghosts and thought Eichwoor was a multidimensional representation of the Z-entity Kandron, your mortal enemy. You believe he lives on a planet in one of the multidimensions, which accounts for your inability to trace him. We also know, of course, that you choose to conceal from your own compatriots the identity of Kandron under the name of Dregs of Onlo. You do this for personal reasons of pride, because Kandron outwitted you and escaped, and you are embarrassed to tell anyone, especially Kimball Kinnison. We have contacted you, Nadreck, because in assuring you that neither the Eichwooren nor Arrow-22 will return to bother Civilization again, we must tell you that your hope of Arrow-22 finding Kandron is an empty hope. Arrow-22 will be totally involved in the other dimension. You, Nadreck, are the one who will find Kandron. And our visualization shows that it will be a long, hard fight, but that you will eventually conquer Kandron. It will, however, be entirely by your own efforts."

"I humbly thank you, Mentor," Nadreck said. "So! The problems of Arrow-22 and the Eichwooren are really settled! Now I can get back to the important business of destroying that villain Kandron!"

"Arrow-22 took almost everything with him, Kallatra," Worsel said. "The mech-planet right down to the smallest 2X drone."

"Almost everything, Worsel?" Lalla Kallatra said. "What did he leave?"

"Well," Worsel said, "there's that deactivated robot la-Talkar that represents you. I thought of putting it in the reception room on the Planetoid of Knowledge, but the Patrol Museum has accepted it instead, as a tribute to you. And — " Worsel paused. Kallatra thought she detected a chuckle.

"And?" Kallatra said, patiently.

"And he left the lovely though inoperative robot of le-Srow behind. I have just had it installed in the court-yard in the center of the Worsel Institute, right next to that marble statue of Klono."